I0723859

TAPPED BY THE ROCKSTAR

Mile High Rocked

Book 4

CHRISTINA HOVLAND

For rights information, please contact:
Prospect Agency
551 Valley Road, PMB 377
Upper Montclair, NJ 07043
(718) 788-3217

Holly Ingraham, Development Editor
Audrey Nelson, Copy Editor
Shasta Schafer, Final Proofreader

Cover Model Photography by:
Lindee Robinson Photography
Brian Boynton, Cover Model

Cover Design by Christina Hovland

First Edition January 2023

To all those who can't find the words when you need them most.

Chapter One
SAMANTHA

"NOBODY TOLD me Twister was a bad idea," Samantha "Sam" Johnson mumbled under her breath as her right hand went to green, left foot to blue, and her ass in the air. She balanced precariously, so she didn't tip over into Great Aunt Etta Jane, the reason she'd come to work at Purple Peony Assisted Living.

Thanks to her great aunt, Sam's reputation as the premier activities director for the over-eighty crowd continued the upward trajectory she'd begun at The Plains in Newark and continued at Hillsong in Birmingham.

Of course, that was all after the whole Sami Jo fiasco that had landed her with—

"Tits up, sweet cheeks," Betty announced in Sam's general direction.

Crud, what had she missed during her little near-tumble down memory lane?

"Right foot yellow, Sammy Lamb-y," Mertle mumbled out of the edge of her lips.

Sam stilled at the quirky nickname, her blood draining unreasonably from her cheeks. Dammit, she was over this. Why did it still bug her? *Sami Jo...*

"Sam," she corrected quickly, with all the cheer she could muster while in an awkwardly fragile downward-facing dog pose. "Just Sam." Always, just "Sam." She shivered.

Yeah.

"Sam the ma'am, bam, bam," Mertle sang, as she handled the pose beautifully. Like a swan playing Twister without a care in the world. What would that be like?

And where the heck had a woman of her... uh... age learned to be so limber? Seriously, the woman's ligaments must've been made of rubber.

Sam's were not. She'd sort of hoped when the women in her care had requested *the twister*, they'd meant the movie with Helen Hunt and Bill Paxton from 1996. Or perhaps a dance party featuring Chubby Checker.

Luck was not hers, since they'd meant the *activity* she'd accidentally created based on the classic children's game.

"Left foot, red!" Nadzieja hollered from her perch on the edge of a chair. She came to the United States from Russia ages ago, and her accent remained true to her heritage. Also, Nadzieja's stash of vodka that Sam had negotiated to a more reasonable level.

Everyone moved their left foot to red.

Of course, Sam didn't have the elderly women in her Tuesday group class all on one large plastic Twister board—that would be dangerous. No, she set them up on multiple carefully crafted, non-slip felt alternatives. She'd used special Velcro strips to adhere the dots to the plum-colored carpet.

All the latest literature suggested that the elderly in these communities benefited from daily activity. Things like yoga and outside walks when the weather allowed.

The assisted living crew scoffed at her idea for all of that, but Sam was not one to give up. So she'd tricked them into doing some yoga via Twister. The walks? She made a scavenger hunt around the neighborhood that ended at the cookie shop. They loved her ideas so much that they insisted not only on playing Twister 2.0 but also her participation. This required her to hand over calling duties to Nadzieja.

Nadzieja, who was a master manipulator and the Monarch of the Purple Peony. That's what Sam had called her in her head, anyway.

"Left hand yellow," Nadzieja announced, cackling a little since that was going to really shake things up. There was not a way for Sam to move her arm in that direction without toppling over.

Instead of moving her palm, Sam spared her dignity and stood. She clapped her hands three times in quick succession. She always did this to give notice to the residents that she was ending the activity and they were moving onto the next. "Nice work, all. Let's call it a day?"

Dammit. The moment those words slipped from her lips, she knew she shouldn't have phrased them in question form. These women found loopholes in everything and had no issue climbing right on through those holes to get what they wanted.

As could be expected, the participants all fussed an array of "no!" and "we've barely started."

She sighed, internally. But it was nearly time for the backgammon tournament to start in the other rec room. It couldn't start without her there to set it up and then harass the seniors to play. What could she say? Her job wasn't exactly easy now, was it?

Nadzieja stood from her walker with the arrow still in her hand. And the look in her eyes—that flash of mischief and confidence?

Oh, no, no, no. Sam didn't like it.

She wasn't wet behind the ears here. Working the retirement home circuit for years had taught her a few things. So she'd had her eye on Nadzieja from the first time the woman "slipped" on a puddle in the dining hall the night they served kale chips with turkey burgers, and Nadzieja demanded a hot dog with crunchy sweet potato tots instead. Nadzieja loved her tots.

Unfortunately for her, Chef Mike had held his ground.

Nadzieja got the same gleam in her eye and promptly slipped on the puddle, going down, down, down.

At least Nadzieja had said there was a puddle. Sam had opened a report and done an entire investigation and it didn't seem like the puddle existed for anyone but Nadzieja.

Chef Mike still took on that guilt and ensured Nadzieja got whatever she wanted from there on out. To that very day, every meal in the entire community came with optional tots.

Funny thing about that, once Nadzieja got her dog and tots for dinner that night, her hip returned to prime condition, and she had no issues at all.

Though the day Sam told her she'd have to stop dialing the non-emergency police line? Nadzieja got the same gleam in her eye. She'd been calling it often to request the most attractive officers stop in for a welfare check. Not her welfare —theirs. It was a whole thing.

The first time they found it funny. By the fifth time? They weren't amused.

Sam could've sworn Nadzieja had a mat with the grippy bottoms in her room. Sam ensured all the residents had one. But it'd disappeared and Nadzieja went down again.

The officers who arrived with the EMTs? Not bad looking. And Nadzieja had a remarkably speedy recovery from that one, too. Minutes, really. Seconds, even.

So, in this moment, Sam knew what was coming.

This was a blip in time where she had a choice to make— force the issue and call the game, or just play another round so she didn't have to deal with all the blah blah and the reports that came with it.

She went with option B.

"One more game," she said with a perky smile, holding up her index finger.

Nadzieja sank right back down to the chair, wry grin in place, and spun the wheel like the woman had just won the Showcase Showdown on *The Price Is Right*.

The game ticked along and Sam was nearly ready to call the ending—the real ending—when the door to the room squeaked open. She needed to WD-40 that before she left for the night.

Nadzieja let out a *squee* and dropped the spinning arrow board.

Sam was in a modified version of a downward dog, so she had to peer through her legs to the doorway. Of note, she did not topple over at the sight of the most gorgeous man she'd ever seen in her freaking life standing there in the doorway. Thing was, there wasn't truly anything super special about his appearance. Hot guy? For sure. But he looked like he stepped out of a catalogue—unreal and probably fake. Gorgeous men like him were of the processed variety and did not come from natural sources.

His cropped blond hair stood messy-spiked on the top, but cut close on the sides. The black tee he wore strung tight across his chest. The guy wasn't ripped, but he was definitely athletic. And the light denim jeans taut against his thighs? Very nice choice. Those jeans led down to nothing-special sneakers, and still her heart thumped louder in her ears.

Balanced in his arms he held several large, purple candy boxes.

This was like her favorite wet dream come to life because… *charisma*. The guy was doused with buckets of hot guy sauce that he probably tossed all over wherever he went.

Seriously, the way her blood whooshed to her brain and her face flushed was entirely unnecessary. Downward dog, notwithstanding.

His eyes caught hers and her bum was right up there in the air, so she should've stood up, straightened her Purple

Peony polo shirt, turned and said, "Hello." Like the professional she promised herself she was on the regular.

Did she stand up? Oh no. Instead, she held his gaze with hers and smiled at him through her legs. As one does when faced with a hot dude who makes one's cheeks flush.

Good thing that Nadzieja wasn't calling a color-appendage combination because all Sam could focus on was this guy. If he had a vibe, it would shout, "God, yes."

He lifted his eyebrows at her and sort of grinned. Even upside down, the symmetrical perfection of his lips was too much. Too, too much. Somebody call American Eagle because she had a brand-new model ready and waiting for their summer photo spread.

"Hey ladies," he said with a rumble of a voice that made Sam seriously consider what it would be like to play strip-Twister and eat chocolates with him.

Gah, no. Stop it.

Besides, she didn't mean *him.* She meant someone *like* him.

She dated sometimes—not too much. Best not to get too close to anyone, she'd found out. Keeping a comfortable distance was necessary for, well, comfort.

"It's Tanner," Nadzieja shouted, holding her hands together in front of her chin.

Uh-huh, that made sense that this guy would have a hot guy name to go along with his "God, yes" vibe.

The other ladies all straightened, welcoming Tanner. Sam straightened, too, when what she really wanted to do was sit there criss-cross applesauce and grin stupidly at this guy who made her heart pitter-patter like she was a teenager and he was a boy band star.

Which was why she did not do any of that. While he handed out candy boxes, she stood taller and pressed her palms down the front of her shirt, into the pockets of her wrinkle-free, khaki Dockers. She should go say hello. Introduce herself.

But the ladies all circled around the man—whoever this Tanner was. Sam ignored the carnal tug in her low belly and focused on cleaning up the room instead. He had enough company to keep him busy, and the felt dots needed to be put away, along with a few chairs stacked back in the closet. And that backgammon game would not set itself up.

Cautious not to chance any glances in his direction—though, of note, the boxes were filled with truffles—she made quick work of her job. There. Done. But just as she turned to evacuate, and move along to her next task, Nadzieja tossed herself on the floor.

Seriously, she threw herself down like a rag doll. A rag doll being entirely too careful with her box of chocolates. Somehow she managed to set those aside on the way down. That was a pretty neat trick.

Sam had never caught her in the act so blatantly before, but she couldn't exactly do nothing. So she rushed to Nadzieja's aid, even as Tanner did the same. Since he was closer, he arrived first.

"Hey," he said, gentle and kind and—"You okay, Babushka?"

Oh great, he got to call her Babushka. Everyone called Nadzieja that. Everyone except Sam, who had not been invited to use the nickname. Blatantly un-invited was more like it.

Tanner slipped a glance to Sam and something between them opened right up. Right there. He didn't buy Nadzieja's act either.

"It is fine." Nadzieja hefted herself up to sitting. "I am fine."

Of course, she was fine. Even if she wasn't fine things would still be fine, since Sam was a professional who had loads of emergency medical training. One didn't work with senior citizens and not come prepared for all scenarios. Which was why, though Sam knew the ruse, she still started a quick eval for the paperwork that would come with even Nadzieja's Fakey McFakerton episodes. Sam began with a pupil reaction test. Nadzieja, however, wasn't having it.

"Tanner, this is Sam," Nadzieja said, brushing aside Sam's attempts at triage.

Sam glanced around, but no one else was in the room. Where the heck had they all gone?

"This is Sam?" Tanner asked, disbelieving.

"Yes, I've told you all about her." Nadzieja grinned a quick flash of dentures.

Well, that was sweet. Even though Sam didn't know a thing about this guy.

"I thought Sam was a dude?" Tanner sort of said, sort of asked, blinking hard.

Well, no. She was definitely a girl.

"My job is done. You are officially introduced." Nadzieja stood, snagged her chocolates, and waved between them. "I'm off. Enjoy your talk."

Though she said this, she did not leave. Instead, she stood there stuffing a truffle in her mouth while she observed.

"You've got to stop doing that," Sam whispered, still crouched down. She stood, rubbing her forehead.

"Agreed," Tanner said, also standing. Then he sort of breathed what sounded like it was supposed to be a greeting, turned the color of a ripe cherry tomato, and seemed to choke on his tongue.

She pointed to herself. "I'm Sam."

Dammit, they'd already covered this part.

"I guess you know that," she continued with a quick side-glance to Nadzieja.

"Uh-huh." He looked at the floor. Closed his eyes like he was woozy.

"You okay?" she asked. Maybe *he* needed a quick triage.

Wouldn't that be a fun pickup line? Let me check your pupils! How are your reflexes!?

He seemed to have some quick internal gut check, and then he pierced her with his gaze.

"I'm fine," he semi-stuttered. "Now. Now, I'm great."

She didn't buy it. And, yet? The way he looked at her like he wanted to nibble her neck? Dear goodness, it made her stomach flutter, and she seriously considered tossing herself on the floor if it meant he'd keep talking to her.

Any argument she'd made about why this—he—was a bad idea deflated right there.

Getting close to anyone is a mistake.

Especially someone with the ability to wreck her heart. Someone just like him. A guy with staying power who would make her consider staying when it came time to leave.

The red still flamed against his cheeks and the thread tethering him to the moment seemed shaky. "It's nice to meet Babushka's famous Sam."

Famous. No. No, she wasn't famous. Not anymore.

God, no. Her heartbeat quickened, and the intense desire to bolt took hold.

She rocked back and forth on her toes. "I…uh…gotta go back to work," she said. If she hurried, she could finish the rest of her shift and be out of there by the time Chef Mike started baking his tots.

$$\overline{\hspace{8cm}}$$

Chapter Two
TANNER

$$\overline{\hspace{8cm}}$$

NOT EVERY DAY a guy walked into a room and fell in immediate lust with a woman playing Twister. Then again, Tanner's life hadn't been normal since the band Dimefront had recruited him as their new drummer a couple of years ago.

Drummer for Dimefront.

Would that thought ever stop making him grin like he'd just won billions on Powerball?

"You cannot go," Babushka stepped forward to Sam. "Tanner has just arrived." She gestured to him like an elderly showcase showgirl presenting a bedroom set. Or an RV. Or a trip to Greece. "Have a chocolate."

He tried to open his mouth to say something about how he'd like Sam to stick around. He'd heard so much about her —granted, he hadn't known it was *her*. But now everything clicked into place. He'd been under the assumption that she was a new staffer doing an excellent job. Honest to hell, he'd expected her to be a man. Given the way the Purple Peony worked, he figured Sam was a muscled bodybuilder who liked the attention of the older crowd.

He hadn't realized she was *Sam*. There was something

about her that went deeper than surface. A pull he wouldn't mind investigating.

She was pretty personified with those pink lips and the brown eyes that made him want to dive inside, brown hair that he seriously wanted to reach over and touch.

So he wanted to ask her to stick around with him, but his tongue just wouldn't work.

She stared at him funny, like the ball was in his court and now was his time to say something.

This was always his worry. The thing that kept him up at night. Put him in front of a stadium of thousands of fans? He'd play the hell out of Dimefront classics. Put him in a room with elderly women? He'd make a new best friend in five seconds flat.

Put him face-to-face with a pretty girl? His tongue seized and wouldn't work. Then embarrassment would sink in, and he'd turn all kinds of interesting shades of red.

"Stay," Babushka said, gently, to Sam. "Please."

Thank you, Babushka, because he hadn't made a sound, and yet, the last thing he wanted was for Sam to walk away. Not yet. Not before he got to know this mystery woman.

Sam looked to him and he couldn't quite make eye contact.

Shit. Damn. Fuck.

"I need to prep for backgammon," Sam said, pulling the edge of her bottom lip between her teeth. And something about that motion seemed to tickle a part of his brain in a familiar way he could not put his finger on. A way that made him taste purple Spree candies with a side of mozzarella sticks, and wish he was on a Ferris wheel.

Unfortunately, since Tanner was Tanner, he said nothing.

"Tanner comes to visit vhen he is in town. He travels much, but vhen he is here he stops by all the time." Babushka not-so-subtly cleared her throat as though this was the spot where he picked up the slack and ran with it. "He brings us treats. He tells us stories. He—"

Sam grabbed a truffle from the box. "Thanks for the candy. It's great to meet you, Tanner," Sam said, heading for the door. She seemed to wait two-thirds of a second to see if he'd say something.

He tried. Honest as all hell, he tried.

"See you around," she said.

This was enough. He had to break free from the perpetual feeling of peanut butter holding his tongue in place. Unfortunately, that didn't work.

Sam left and he still hadn't said anything.

"Vhat are ve going to do vith you?" Babushka asked, shaking her head. "Sam is good person. You are good person. You come together. You have good time."

"Why didn't you mention Sam is a girl?" he asked, tipping his head to the side.

"Because you needed to meet her first." Babushka lifted her eyebrows. "Now you know she is for you."

The way she said that? A little bit of manipulation seeped into those words.

With an eyebrow waggle, Babushka left the room. He figured he had two choices. Go play backgammon red faced while embarrassment seeped into his bones. Or leave and figure out how the hell to talk to Sam without tripping over his own tongue.

So Tanner left the Purple Peony, stopped by the auto body shop to say hey to his foster dad, and beat it home to the house he shared with his buddy Mach.

Mach was more of a brother from another mother and the house was more of a mansion. Tanner didn't get too bogged down with the details—that's where a guy could get tangled.

When they'd joined up with Dimefront, the band had already established a wicked strong following. The guys—

Linx, Bax and Knox—all took Mach and Tanner under their wings. And when Mach and Tanner proved themselves sticky, the guys bought them a house on the same street where they all lived.

Apparently, that's what rock stars did—blew their money on big houses with connecting backyards so everyone could hang whenever.

No, the place they bought for Mach and Tanner wasn't just a house. More like five houses all mashed up into one massive mansion.

Tanner pulled up the drive and parked his Mustang GT500 in the garage. Then he stopped, dropped his skull back on the headrest and wished he could just be normal.

Mach moseyed through the door from the kitchen to the garage trash bins with a compactor bag.

Tanner didn't move as Mach dropped the bag in the bin, lifted his brows in Tanner's direction, and headed his way.

Mach knew. Mach was one of two people before Dime-front that Tanner could count on. They understood each other better than either wanted to admit.

Tanner unfolded from the car. "Hey."

"Hey." Mach crossed his arms. "Back so soon?"

Tanner nodded. "Yup."

"Huh." Mach headed back inside with Tanner.

"What huh?" Tanner asked, dropping his keys and wallet in the bowl on the table right inside.

"Somethin' happened." Mach shrugged. He pulled open the fridge, tagged two beers, and slid one across the counter to Tanner.

"What if I don't want to talk about it?" Tanner asked.

Mach gave him a look like he'd grown two extra heads. Fair, because Mach knew him and understood that Tanner liked to spend time at the Purple Peony because—aside from the band—it was the one place he could be himself. Complete a sentence.

A safe space where he'd made friends.

"Fine. I met a girl," Tanner said. "Turns out their new activities director, Sam? Is a chick."

A slow grin spread across Mach's face. "Yeah?"

"I like her." Tanner nodded as he popped the top off his beer.

"Yeah?" Mach said, his tone increasing in pitch.

"She's pretty, sure, but she's also got this thing about her that just makes me want to get to know her. Like when you meet someone and you understand they're special, but there's no way to put that feeling into words," Tanner said.

Mach nodded. "Yeah."

"And I couldn't talk to her." Tanner tossed the cap to the trash can in the corner. It hit square in the middle.

"You finally met a woman you want to talk to, and your tongue did the seizing thing?" Mach asked, not like a dick. Like a brother confirming some shitty news.

"There have been loads of women I'd like to talk to," Tanner said.

"But not like this one, right?" Mach asked, gentler than he was generally known for.

Tanner nodded. *Not like this. Not like a magnet pulling them together.*

He took a pull of his Coors.

"Fuck," Mach said, doing the same.

"Maybe I should talk to Becca," Tanner said, the pressing defeat of his inability to deal with this himself weighing heavy.

Becca, Linx's wife, was also a counselor. The non-judgmental kind who genuinely seemed to care.

"Not a bad plan." Mach smacked his lips. "But you don't want to do that."

Tanner nodded again.

"One thing I don't get," Mach mused. "You get laid on the regular."

They both did.

"You've hooked up with women on the road," Mach said.

All the guys—except Mach—had paired up and found love. Tanner sort of figured that wasn't for him given his history. So, yeah, he'd hooked up. The whole Dimefront gig rarely required talking. Groupies wanted a notch on their lipstick tube. He hadn't had a problem handing it over.

"How the fuck do you communicate with them?" Mach asked. "The ones you… you know."

"I don't use words," Tanner said. "Not really. I let them talk."

Things went quicker that way and everyone got what they wanted.

"I could see that." Mach smirked. "Does your dick take over or something so your brain doesn't have to think? Is that what it is? That's probably what Becca would say it is."

No, that's not what Becca would say. Becca would say that Tanner wanted more for himself and got nervous because he didn't feel like he was good enough for more. He knew this because she'd had this conversation with him.

Mach wasn't interested in more. Not into anything permanent, so the whole falling-for-someone bit was not for him. He'd never been a "run away from the shit of life" person or "seize up when shit got hard" person. Not like Tanner.

Their stories were similar. Ditched by the parents and heaved into the foster circuit. Tanner's parents got into illegal shit. They'd taken off. Then they went to jail.

Tanner and Mach found each other and became brothers quickly. A different kind of family.

So, yeah, Mach didn't run. Not like Tanner. No, Mach just made sure everyone knew he didn't fucking care.

Tanner knew better. Tanner understood Mach felt shit deeper than the rest of them—pretending not to care was easier than admitting life could suck so badly.

"I pretend I'm not me." Tanner shrugged. "That's how I do it." Why'd this feel like a confession?

Fuck it. Mach already knew the crap of Tanner's life. This wasn't anything new.

"It's like role play. I'm a drummer. They don't want Tanner. They want the Dimefront drummer." He pursed his lips. Acknowledging that sat funky in his stomach. "That's what I give 'em."

Since he was in a rock band, he'd pretended he was a *real* rock star, not the play pretend one he felt like most of the time.

Mach said nothing. That's how Tanner knew he agreed. Understood.

"How many of those women go home and say they had sex with Tanner Penton?" Tanner shook his head. "No, they say they fucked the drummer for Dimefront."

He'd heard one of them in the bathroom after, making a call and saying that exact thing.

It should've made him feel gross, but it didn't. Because in that moment he wasn't Tanner Penton, he was the drummer for Dimefront. The drummer for Dimefront didn't care.

"You pretend to be someone else." Mach pulled his lips wide. "I can see how that'd work."

Tanner shook his head. Dropped his forehead to the mouth of his beer bottle. "How the fuck do I talk to someone when I'm only me?"

Mach rubbed his thumb along the neck of his beer. Thinking, "Maybe don't pretend you're someone else. Pretend she is? Pretend she's one of the ladies you can talk to —like Babushka."

That wouldn't work.

"Then I wouldn't be attracted to her." Tanner heaved a sigh. No offense to the elderly crew, there was just no attraction there. That's why he did so great with them. Why he spent time there. He could be Tanner Penton there and no one knocked him for it.

"This sounds like a problem," Mach said, a clear attempt at adding inappropriate levity.

"No shit."

"Pretend to be me." Mach lifted a shoulder. "I don't have a problem talking to anyone."

Ha. No.

"Or one of the other guys—pretend to be Bax or Linx. Or even fuckin' Knox." Mach grinned. "Pretend you're them, talking to their wives before they were their wives. Then you're not a fuckboy drummer. You're not taking advantage."

Tanner did know. And maybe that was the only way to make this thing work.

Pretend he wasn't him.

Like role play. But different.

$$\overline{}$$

Chapter Three
TANNER

$$\overline{}$$

TANNER STOPPED at the outer door of the Purple Peony. He'd come back. With more chocolate because bringing a gift at least gave him a reason to stop in that wasn't only… *I want to see Sam!*

Though he had called ahead to confirm with Babushka that Sam worked this afternoon.

Yeah. He'd done that. And then he'd prepared to channel one of the other guys: Bax, Linx, or Knox. With only a small sliver of their ability to play the dating game, he'd be able to seal a deal with Sam.

No, that wasn't right. No deal sealing. He simply wanted to talk to her. See where that took them.

Standing at the door, waiting to step inside? He had to decide which one to go with.

Linx, he'd go with the nonchalant bass player here. Linx, who had no problems with communication—Becca wouldn't allow it. Uh-huh, he could pretend to be Linx. Linx, who said whatever the hell he wanted. And when he spoke to his wife? The gentle way he kept his tone? The other women in the room all got a soft look on their faces like they wanted a little slice of that.

He strode inside.

Be Linx. Be Linx.

Sam stood at the counter there. She glanced up and he was all Tanner. All tongue. No swagger.

"Hi," she said, bright sunshine in a purple polo shirt.

Be Linx. Be Linx.

Linx would apologize for all the awkward. That's what he'd do.

"Hi," Tanner heard himself say, infusing as much gentle into his tone as he could. "I brought you chocolate. Figured it'd be a good way to apologize for last time. I get awkward sometimes."

She paused whatever she was doing, hitting him full on with her bright light.

Be Linx. Be Linx.

"You don't need to apologize," she said, a sweet smile hitting her lips. He wanted to taste it. That smile. "But I'll still totally take the chocolate." She held her hands out with "gimme" fingers.

He handed it over.

"So I wanted to ask… do you like coffee? Dinner?" he asked, leaning onto the counter in a move Linx could've patented.

Huh, Mach wasn't wrong.

When pretending to be Linx, there was no increased blood flow to his cheeks to make them warmer or that familiar quickening of his heart, like it was running away because a pretty girl stood across from him. The King of Awkward might be ready to retire. All he had to do was pretend to be someone else.

"Yes," Sam said. "Yeah. Of course. I drink coffee and I eat. Sometimes at the same time."

Look at him making small talk with a pretty girl. He'd thank Linx later.

"You are here," Babushka announced from the hallway.

"Sam and I were just discussing her enjoyment of coffee." *Keep it light. Keep it chill.*

Babushka glanced to Sam and made an "ahhh" sound.

"Uh-huh," Sam nodded a confirmation. "We definitely were. What can I do for you?"

Babushka looked down the hallway. Frowned. Then turned her focus to Sam.

"I came to tell you that I have gift for you," Babushka said to Sam, totally wrecking their current thread of making plans. "You may now call me Babushka." She lifted her hands as though announcing, *Huzzah!* But with hands instead of words.

"That's unnecessary," Sam said, but something about the way she said it made his chest ache. As though she was saying she wasn't necessary. He understood that feeling. He didn't like that for her.

Unless he was reading into things that weren't there. That was probably the most likely scenario, because—other than him—who would say they weren't necessary? Especially Sam, whom the residents here adored. Clearly, the woman was *necessary*.

"It is necessary," Babushka said, reaching to pat Sam's cheek with her right hand. "My dear, you are ready. I am so proud."

"Sorry, what?" Sam asked, eyebrows drawing together. "What are you proud of?"

"That you are ready, of course," Babushka said.

"Better not to make it a thing," Tanner said under his breath, using the same cadence as Linx when he started in with the sarcasm.

Sam really shouldn't make it a thing because this was Babushka, and she tended to be overdramatic on a good day. He wouldn't read too much into any of this, so neither should Sam.

What would Linx do at this point? He'd probably try to track down a bakery to find some cake.

He sure as fuck wouldn't spend too much time reading into things that didn't deserve the attention. Linx would know this was just another of those things that didn't need increased scrutiny.

Not when he had this possible date about to agree to coffee-slash-dinner.

"Vell, they are ready now. I am sure." Babushka gestured for them to follow as she headed toward the hallway.

"Who's ready?" Sam asked, hurrying after Babushka.

Babushka, who had picked up her pace.

If he hazarded a guess, Babushka was going to rec room two, where who knew what was planned.

He didn't particularly care though since she'd taken off and that left him alone with Sam to walk together.

"She's headed to the rec room," he said, hoping for the nonchalance of bass player Linx, adding in half-a-dash of lead singer Bax's confidence.

Look at him Frankensteining the perfect personality.

Sam nodded and looked at him, wide eyed. "I'm a little concerned. Whenever she gets that pep in her step it usually means more work for me."

"But sometimes it involves cake," Tanner said with a Linx-esque grin.

"This is true," Sam agreed, her thick brown hair falling across her shoulders, tracing her back to the middle of her spine. "You come by a lot?"

"Yup," he nodded. "This crew keeps me on my toes when I'm in town."

"How have we not met?" she asked.

"I was out of town," he said, hoping that was safe enough.

When a guy wanted to get laid, he opened with the whole

drummer for a mega-band thing. When he wanted to truly get to know a person, he went with the more subtle approach.

He should ask her something. What would Linx ask?

"What are the odds of cake?" he asked.

"Not great," Sam said, giving him a funny look like he'd dropped a cracker or two.

"I like cake," he said, still channeling Linx. Truth of it was he preferred ice cream. But he'd already got himself invested in the whole Linx-loves-cake-so-I-do-too sitch.

"It's too quiet for dessert," Sam said, picking up speed to move double time down the hallway. "Nothing good comes when this crew gets quiet."

He didn't disagree. That's why he played instruments instead of attempting to wrangle them by applying for a job at this joint. A person might think it'd be simple to take care of his friends here at the Purple Peony. A person would also be wrong. Very wrong.

"They are here," Babushka flung the door to the rec room open and clapped her hands together.

Everyone else joined in on the applause.

Literally, everyone else. A solid twenty men and women from the retirement home had all joined them for whatever the hell this was.

"What…?" Sam asked under her breath.

She frowned.

There was a whole lot of clapping going on. Hoots and hollers like they'd just got onstage or just finished tying the knot. He could handle this, because Linx would eat it up.

Linx would bow.

So that's what Tanner did.

Honestly, nothing much surprised him with this group anymore. But Sam? Sam seemed surprised, what with the quick startle and the small step backward.

Once she worked here longer, she'd get over that. Because this place was always a surprise. That was part of the magic of the Purple Peony. Part of the reason he enjoyed stopping by.

"You are right on time," Etta said, winking heavily at Sam.

"On time for what?" Sam asked, more than a little confused.

"For the puppet show." Etta said, rolling her eyes loudly—if that were possible. "We have our handsome prince." She gestured to him.

"Huh?" he asked, forgetting to channel Linx, who would've said something like, "Damn straight. It's time somebody figured that out."

"And you, my dear, get to be the magical princess." Babushka practically sailed through the air as she moved.

"Today is checkers day. There are no princesses in checkers," Sam said, sliding her gaze to Tanner as though asking him for help. A small crease formed between her brows.

The crease thing was adorable, even if it meant she was frustrated.

Just like that, the assignment here clicked into place. The way this whole thing had unfolded between them was intentional.

The residents at the Purple Peony had shipped him and Sam.

If he had to guess, pretty soon they'd be sending him direct messages on TikTok to prove how serious they were about a Tanner-Sam mashup.

"If Sam isn't into this"—he gestured between them—"let's not force it, yeah?"

"Into what?" Sam asked. "Precisely."

"I think they're working on a solid set-up," Tanner said, under his breath only for her. "Pretty sure."

"You knew about it?" Sam gave him a look he didn't enjoy.

He lifted an aw-shucks shoulder, then his hands. "My hunch started about thirty seconds ago with the applause."

There was no use fighting with these women when they put their mind to something. Something like a puppet show set-up.

"This is vhy ve do the show. So you two get to know each other." Babushka took charge and herded Sam to the back of a makeshift cardboard puppet stage. Sam kept glancing behind to Tanner.

Unfortunately, he didn't have a moment to consider how these nonsensical scenarios would play together. A set-up, a puppet show, his new ability to form a verbal sentence. There was a lot to unpack here.

No, there was no time to process, because he also found himself herded to the back of the theater, where a crocheted princely puppet—crown and all—got shoved on his hand. The puppet looked a little like a crochet version of him.

The puppet à la Tanner was a little extra, but totally fire. The other guys would be super jealous they didn't get one.

The two chairs placed behind the mini theater had no one sitting there. Clearly, they were meant for Tanner and Sam, so he figured he should go along with it. That's what made the most sense when he came to hang with his Purple Peony friends. Roll with it and enjoy the ride, because this crew threw a helluva party if a person didn't ask too many questions.

He sat in the chair next to an absolutely bewildered Sam. She had a knitted princess on her right hand.

"Are you good being set up with me?" she whispered.

In the tight quarters behind the puppet theater, her face was right near his. Intimately close in a way he did not hate.

"Yeah," he stared at her, soaking in the warmth of her brown eyes. "That's why I asked you out."

"You didn't ask me out," she whispered, again with the frown lines and the bewildered, glassy gaze.

Tanner's tongue got a little stuck. *Channel Linx.*

"I was getting there," he said, stumbling only a little over the words.

This is where he complimented her with a light shade to himself. Said something with the ease of Mach, minus the assholery Mach embraced on the regular.

He didn't get the chance because the curtains to the puppet show opened and there was Betty Jane, sitting near the little window with a handful of index cards.

"Look, if you want to make an escape, I'll cover here." The rush of blood hit his cheeks and he didn't need a mirror to know they'd turned crimson.

No, he didn't want her to go. He also didn't want her to stay if she didn't want to be there. Didn't want her to be uncomfortable.

"Do you even know how long I've been trying to get them to do stuff like this?" she said, under her breath, gesturing with her looks-like-Sam princessed hand. "They fight me on everything. But then they just set *it* up? Because they want to set *us* up?"

"Yeah, they do that," he agreed, moving the mouth of the puppet because there was an audience here and he did still understand the assignment. Also, puppet Tanner didn't stumble over his words. "But they mean well."

"That's why I'm so frustrated." Princess Sam moved her mouth as real Sam gave some evil eye to those sitting in the rows of chairs. "Who do you think bought this theater?"

Prince Tanner turned his hand-head toward the twenty-something people observing the entire exchange. "Not them."

That got him a few chuckles. Even Sam's frown disappeared.

"Ve have questions," Babushka shouted.

"You want an out?" Prince Tanner asked, totally serious because he'd get her out of there if that's what she wanted. "Or you want to see how this plays out?"

Betty Jane adjusted her glasses. "Yes. First question is for Tanner."

"Hit me," Tanner said, using the puppet.

"What do you think of Princess Sam?" Betty Jane read slowly from the card.

The heat rose in his cheeks. And a sticky feeling in his mouth made it impossible to speak.

I think I don't know her yet, Tanner replied in his head. *But I'd like to.*

He did not say this. Because… sticky tongue. So instead he let the puppet talk.

"I don't know her much. Not yet. But I can tell you all care about her," he said, turning to give her his gaze, so she'd understand that he meant every syllable. "That means she's probably amazing."

"Sam." Betty Jane looked at Sam over her glasses. "Same question."

"I like princes." Sam used her puppet to speak, but she snagged Tanner's gaze with her own. "This one seems…"

There appeared to be a struggle going on in her brain. He could 100 percent relate. Usually, he'd step in and help her out—and using Linx as his model, he totally could do that—but he got the intense feeling she needed to do this on her own. So he'd let her.

"Prince Tanner is the type of person who makes me think that the decisions that brought me here might be for a really good reason."

Yeah, that's why he didn't step in.

He nodded. A brief flutter in his belly that he hadn't experienced in years brought him up short. But he dug it. Dug her.

"Prince Tanner. What is your favorite *legal* activity?" Betty Jane read again so slowly it was nearly painful.

He could've sworn Samantha dropped an f-bomb under her breath on the word "legal."

He ran his hand over his jaw. Maybe he should do the scruff thing like Linx? Since he was doing so well at pretending to be the guy. Yeah, he could grow his hair long and grow some scruffy stubble.

"Legal activity?" he asked, using the puppet.

Linx would say something like—"Eating."

One word covered so many bases, all at the same time it tested the waters. Wasn't too basic, but not in your face, either. As he spoke, he hooked Sam's gaze with his own, lifting his eyebrows the subtlest bit to see what she thought about eating.

They sat close enough he caught it when her pupils flared the smallest amount, and she squirmed a touch.

"Follow-up question." Betty Jane made a note on the card. "Favorite thing to eat?"

Of all the questions, so far, this was the most dangerous. Linx would probably say "cake," but Tanner didn't want to throw too much kindling in that direction, so instead he said, "I like to try new things."

He'd given up on the puppet at some point in that quest for an answer, so he only spoke to Sam.

Sam, who laughed.

That's the moment everything slipped into focus. He saw a quick glimpse of how things could work between them.

Sure, they had loads of shit to sort. He came with so much baggage he might as well rent out a storage unit. But here was this gorgeous woman. He could feel her capacity for caring without even having had a genuine conversation. Not yet. Another something to look forward to on the journey to Sam. Something he realized he wanted pretty damn bad.

"Same question for you, Princess Sam," Betty Jane said.

Samantha stared at her puppet for a beat too long.

Tanner? He was a runner. He'd been a runaway as a kid, and he knew the signs. The little ones no one else would catch — how the pulse at her neck kicked up and her breaths got thready. More than that, there was just a sense that only a runner could catch. Sam was gonna bolt.

"I think we're done," he said, pulling the crochet Tanner from his hand. He glanced at Sam, hoping he was reassuring.

She nodded. He held his hand so she could hand over Princess Sam.

He had a foster dad—a man who had also been a runner. When he got the tingly sense that Tanner was ready to bolt, he led the way. That way Tanner could run, and he'd still not forget all the things he deserved.

That's why Tanner stood and moved to the door of the hallway, opening it. Letting Sam pass, then catching up.

"That was the most unique first date I've ever been on," Tanner said, keeping pace. She led the way, and they were going the same direction—headed to the front. He could hit the door if that's what she wanted.

Sam tucked a piece of hair behind her ear. "That wasn't a date."

"How do you figure?" he asked, keeping his tone light. Safe. Sarcastic Mach. "What about that did not scream first date?"

"We literally got thrown together," she said. "And there was an audience."

He winked. "Doesn't mean it's not a date."

She glanced up at him from under her eyelashes, pulling her lips into a grin that hit him right in the gut. "Yes. Yes. It does."

"What was your favorite part of our not-a-first date?" he asked, keeping a light skip to his step.

She stopped. Turned to face him. Her expression turned serious. "That somehow you said nothing and everything, all at once."

"Yeah." He glanced at his shoes, unable to keep the grin from his mouth. "Ditto."

"Listen, I have to go deal with a few things." She jerked

her thumb toward the side hallway. "I'm pretty sure some of the guys are ditching my organized activities to start a real-money bingo game. They're not allowed since, you know, gambling and all that."

Of note, there was not a frown line at all between her eyebrows.

"Okay," he said, grinning. Knowing this wasn't the end, but it was a pause she needed.

He had shit to do, anyway. He didn't mind waiting. Hell, he'd spent most of his life waiting. Until now, he hadn't known what he'd been waiting for. Not until Sam. Now he had a hunch he understood where all the waiting and running had been leading toward.

She strode away with a purpose and confidence he seriously got off on.

Thing was, he watched her the whole time, and she never looked back. That sat funny in his chest.

⚹ ⚹ ⚹

Samantha

DAMN. Damn. She'd liked it.

She wasn't allowed to like it. Like him. Like being in front of all of those people.

So she left. Which was worse than staying.

Sam's heart beat quickly, so she slowed her pace. Took some deep breaths.

Now was not the time for her to think about Tanner and coffee and the way his cologne smelled like pine and salt and musk. No, now was not that time. Not when she was 99 percent certain Harry had a clandestine bingo game going down in his room.

The three usual suspects of the underground gambling ring at the retirement home hadn't attended the puppet show.

Which meant she could track them and ignore the butterflies in her stomach that fluttered around the thought of Prince Tanner.

Tanner. He was only a guy. Just a normal guy who showed up and got thrust into a puppet show.

That's all. That's all it was.

Chapter Four
TANNER

WHAT DID he do about Samantha Johnson? He'd rolled over the events of the afternoon. Rewound them. Rolled over them again.

Clarity was being an elusive fucker on this one.

"What do you think, Harley?" Tanner asked after telling Bax and Courtney's baby all about Sam.

Harley wasn't talking yet, which made her an excellent listener. Wasn't great with the advice though—given the whole no-talking thing.

One of the bonuses of the Dimefront guys moving Tanner and Mach into the neighborhood was they got a built-in pair of babysitters for little Harley.

Uh-huh. That's also why they shelled out for Mach and Tanner's house, he was pretty sure. Tonight when lead singer Bax and his wife Courtney hit him up to chill with baby Harley, he agreed. He was a sucker for Harley, so this was not a hardship.

"I should text Linx," Tanner said, dropping his ass to the leather sofa Mach had picked up for the great room. "Don't you think?"

Harley shoved the play-keys in her mouth instead of answering.

The quiet sometimes got overwhelming. The house was too big. Too much space for a person to get lost in. But since it was also home, and his makeshift family had offered it, he did his best to ensure everyone knew he was grateful.

Even if the ceilings were too high and the finishes too expensive. He'd get used to it. Someday. Maybe if there was something to come home to other than a generally grumpy-as-hell guitar player/brother?

That could be what the house needed… not a place to be home. But someone to make the place a home.

Like what Linx found with Becca. Bax with Courtney. Knox with Irina.

He shot off a quick text to Linx, since he'd spent part of the day pretending to be the guy.

Tanner: How did you know Becca was the one?

Linx: Who's asking?

Tanner: It matters?

Linx: Yes

Tanner: Me

Linx: …

Tanner: Quick answer. Don't break your brain thinking.

Linx: You met Sam, didn't you?

The flow of blood to Tanner's brain stopped because, hold up, how did Linx know about Sam?

Mach knew about Sam, but Mach wouldn't say anything. Tanner stared vacantly at the phone. Who else knew?

Babushka.

Of course.

He ran his fingertips up along the bridge of his nose. This had Babushka written all over it.

> Linx: You met Sam! Be right there.

> Linx: Becca's coming. She wants details.

Tanner: How do you know who Sam is?

Tanner glanced to Harley, who hadn't moved from her play yard. "Uncle Linx is coming to our playdate. He's bringing Auntie Becca."

That got him a giant, toothless smile. He loved this kid.

His phone pinged with an incoming message.

> Bax: You met Sam?

The number of people who knew about Sam continued to grow.

Tanner: Yes

> Bax: Headed back.

Well, if they were all stopping by, Tanner should probably start fixing food or order something. He briefly contemplated telling the guys not to hurry, but they would be wasted words. Whatever. Fine.

He lifted Harley so they could head to the kitchen and start some grub. "You feeling some loaded potato skins or mini pizzas? Maybe a few veggies, so we can pretend to be healthy?"

She grabbed at his nose, pulling at it with her little hand.

"Good call. No veggies for the adults. But you've gotta grow strong." He tickled her tummy.

She laughed and reached for his chin.

"So you gotta eat loads of those veggies," he continued. "Until you get big like Uncle Tanner."

Bax would be hangry since he missed dinner. Linx was always up to eat. Mach enjoyed food. And Knox didn't care either way, but he'd appreciate when Tanner tossed in some frozen apps.

He'd barely got Harley settled in the baby seat when his phone pinged again. Then again. One after another, after another.

He didn't have to check out the screen to know they'd started up the group thread to discuss Tanner. He tagged his phone. Took a glance. Yeah, they had.

Not bothering to read the messages, he added his own:

Tanner: Food in oven. Bring beer.

Then he tossed his phone on the counter, grabbed a couple of green beans for Harley, and cranked up the oven.

Bax and Courtney showed first. Nobody knocked because they were practically family.

"Tanner, you've got some splainin' to do," Bax called from the front door.

"Stop it," Courtney said. Tanner would bet she elbowed her husband in the kidney. This was their way. "Be cool," she added.

"Parents." Tanner looked to Harley, who shoved a green bean in her mouth. "Whatcha gonna do?" He shrugged.

Since Harley was their kid, they probably wanted to relieve him of duty before he got put on the spot by every-freaking-body. Either that or Bax was just that hungry.

Knox stomped through the back door. "Sorry I'm late."

"You aren't late," Irina said, coming right behind him. "You weren't even invited."

"I'm always invited," Knox said, slinging his arm around her and pulling her against his side.

Tanner had seen them do that a million times before, but he'd never been jealous that he didn't have someone to tug against his side. Never even wondered what that'd feel like—to just have someone who was automatically good with it.

Linx and Becca arrived next. Then Mach.

Then they all descended on the oven-baked, makeshift dinner like a pack of ravenous rock stars. Knox messed with his new smart watch in between slugs of his beer. Grumbling and cussing under his breath.

"You gonna do this shit, or do I need to get it going?" Bax finally asked Knox.

"This is my moment," Knox said. "Don't fuck it up. Gimme a second."

"Your moment?" Tanner asked.

No one answered.

What the hell was going on here? "Is this the moment you tell me that Babushka put you all up to this? That she is the ringmaster of this little circus?"

"Uh…" Knox froze like he got caught with his pants down on stage pissing into a guitar case. He glanced around.

"Who told you?" Mach asked, a picture of fake innocence.

Hold up. Mach knew? He already knew about Sam the whole time Tanner spilled his guts about his inability to talk to her?

"I have a brain and two eyeballs. I put it together all by myself." Normally, he'd be super stoked about that. But tonight he was weighed down by the fact his friends were all in this without him.

"We may have known about Sam for a little bit." Irina made a whatcha-gonna-do expression.

"Babushka looped them in," Mach said. "You're right. And I'm sorry, man, can't break a confidence. Hers or yours."

"How long have you all been waiting for me to meet Sam?" he asked, serious as all hell.

Mach pulled his lips to the side. "Eh. It's been a bit."

Suddenly everything clarified. Like a cartoon character with a lightbulb over his head everything made sense.

"I've been set up," Tanner said, jaw slack.

"You like her?" Mach asked, leveling Tanner with a stare.

Tanner nodded. "Yeah, 'course."

"Then ignore the shit that went down behind the scenes to make it happen." Mach winked. "You're welcome."

"You're stealing my thunder," Knox said, growling at Mach. "Stop talking."

"Your thunder is taking too fucking long," Mach countered.

"He's having technical difficulties," Irina said, trying to help him with the watch but not seeming to have much luck.

"I worked this whole thing out," Knox grumbled at his phone. "I put it all on here so I can read it."

"Ad lib," Irina suggested.

Tanner agreed with Irina.

"It's too important." Knox continued tapping on his screen.

"Anyone want to tell me what the hell he's talking about?" Tanner asked, going for no-big-deal.

"You goof, it's upside down." Irina rolled her eyes at Courtney.

"Should I read it?" Bax asked. "So we can move the fuck along?"

"Children. *Your* child. Present," Courtney said. Which was sorta funny, because Tanner had heard her cussing it up in front of Harley and everyone else was dropping f-bombs like it was a fucking rock concert.

"I'm ready." Knox held his wrist up and squinted.

"By all means," Tanner waved him on.

· · ·

"YOU MAY BE WONDERING why we're all here." Knox glanced up to Tanner.

"Not so much. Not anymore," Tanner said, cutting a look to Mach. They'd discuss this later.

"It's important not to give up," Knox read from his watch screen. "You're gonna screw shit up, and that's okay."

"*That's* what you've been working on?" Linx asked, scowling even though he munched on a fry.

Mach handed him a beer and Tanner took it, leaned against the fridge. This seemed like it might take a while. Harley would probably need a few more green beans to get through it. Maybe even a cookie. Fuck, he'd probably also need a cookie to get through this.

"Hold on." Knox pulled off the watch and held up to his face. "Okay, so it's important not to give up. We all have your back. You're doing great."

"What the hell are you talking about?" Tanner asked, shaking his head.

"We're your Samantha Support Team," Knox said. "I named us. Courtney ordered T-shirts."

"Oops. Forgot to do that," Courtney said. And the way she said it? She didn't forget. She simply didn't do it.

"Why are you all my support team?" Tanner asked.

"Babushka told us to be," Becca, the voice of reason, said.

"Just dove right in with that, huh?" Linx asked.

The guys all gave Becca a look like she should be more chill about the whole thing.

"Yeah, Babushka asked you?" Tanner asked, even though he didn't need to. Of course, Babushka asked them to have his back.

"Uh-huh," Knox said, still poking at the watch face. "Oops. I found more notes." He cleared his throat. "Try making your clumsiness with women into something she'll enjoy."

Irina laid her hand over the watch's face. "Honey, no. We're past that now."

Knox frowned. Scowled. Crossed his arms.

Irina rubbed at the base of his neck. "You'll do better next time."

"Could everyone focus for two seconds?" Tanner asked. "Only two. Then you can go back to your ramblings."

"After you met Sam, which apparently already happened, we're supposed to help you. So you don't fuck it up," Linx said, holding his hands wide. "This is us ensuring you don't fuck up."

Well, that was an interesting turn of events. But that's not what he needed. Not really. "I asked Linx how he knew Becca was the one. I didn't ask for you to help me not fuck it up."

"Linx can tell you all about buying Becca a Slim Jim, but prepare yourself because the fucking it up part is probably coming next," Knox said with a shrug. "Just prepare yourself. That's all I'm saying."

"Hey." Irina stepped forward toward Tanner. Then made a time-out T with her palms. "You should probably know that there's a whole machine here in motion for you and Sam. You pretty much only have to show up."

"Turn it off," Tanner said, meaning the words. He didn't need a whole machine to meet someone. To make her like him.

Wait. Did he?

No, he didn't. This would make Sam want to run. They clearly didn't see that.

"You don't like her?" Linx asked, popping another fry in his gullet.

"She doesn't want a machine, dude," Tanner said. "Look, I could like her. A lot. But she won't appreciate this whole pre-planned set-up." Given her opinions about the puppet show, this was a pretty safe guess. "I've gotta do this on my own."

"That's the worst idea to come out of tonight," Knox said, pulling his mouth into a line. "Rethink that one."

"We've been worried you might have a hard time talking to her," Becca said in that sincere therapist-y tone of hers. The one that made her so successful as a counselor because when she pulled it out, a person would tell her anything. "How did that part go?"

This was a fair question, given his success rate until that afternoon.

"We talked," he said.

"Get out," Linx said, a half-grin plastered on his face. "The puppet show worked?"

"We talked before that," Tanner said, not loving the direction of this conversation. What he'd wanted? Some solid advice.

What was he getting? Not solid advice.

"You talked to a girl?" Bax said, a slow grin spreading. He pounded a fist against his heart. "So proud."

Tanner grabbed a plate to load it up since this seemed like they moved through the food quicker than usual. "Yeah, man. I did."

"How?" Bax asked, a disbelieving edge to his tone.

You know, Tanner should tell them now, since eventually he'd tell them. That's how the band stuff worked. Everyone overshared on the regular.

"I pretended to be Linx," Tanner admitted. Then he stuffed the guilt pocket that tried to sneak back up his throat right back to where it belonged—safely in his stomach.

"Shut up," Linx said, the grin on his face epic now. "That shit worked?"

"Yeah." Tanner nodded. Maybe there was a little pride with his guilt.

Linx suddenly became very invested in this conversation. "What did I say?"

Tanner thought back. "You apologized for being awkward. And then—"

"I'm going to stop you right there." Linx held up a hand. "I'd never start with an apology."

"Linx." Becca shook her head. "That's not helpful."

"It's true, though," Bax chimed in. "Linx doesn't believe in starting with sorry."

"What do you mean you wouldn't start with the apology?" Tanner asked, now questioning his ability to authentically channel Linx. "Then you mentioned coffee and dinner and asked if she liked them."

"I don't know who you were being, but it wasn't me," Linx said with an authority that made Tanner believe him.

"Well, who the hell was I being then?" Tanner asked.

"No idea." Linx popped another fry in his face.

"Tanner, if you like her, then you have to be *you* when you're around her," Becca said.

Yeah, that wouldn't work. It didn't work. Next, please.

"We're here for you," Courtney added. "And we're all pretty excited the wheels are in motion. Roll with it. Let it happen."

"You've got this," Irina added with a smile.

"Isn't that literally exactly what I said?" Knox asked, frowning.

"They said it better," Bax said, grabbing four fries and rubbing them in ketchup before throwing the whole mess into his mouth.

"So I go back tomorrow," Tanner said, deciding on the spot that's what he'd do. Go back and remind her he was as amazing as his friends said. "Talk to her again."

"You still stuck in 1975? You could text her instead," Linx suggested. "They tell me that's what the kids do these days."

"I can't text her." Seeing as he didn't have her digits.

"You didn't catch her number?" Linx asked. "Serious?"

"No." They'd been dealing with a puppet show.

"I thought you pretended to be me?" Linx gestured to his chest. "Rule number one of being Linx, get the number."

"You didn't get my phone number?" Becca said, well, sort of accused.

"You were in my car, and I drove you to your house, so I didn't really need it." Linx shrugged. "I'd also like to suggest that we take this opportunity to remember that Tanner's got a girlfriend, but that doesn't mean we have to rehash all the parts of our relationship that I've fuc—funged up. Are we doing the cussing thing in front of Harley until she can talk or are we stopping now?"

"Now's a good time to start," Courtney said, cheerful.

"Funged." Irina pulled out her cell and typed something on the screen. "To rehash Linx's fuck-ups."

"Kid's still right there." Courtney pointed to Harley, who smeared a fry around the tray of her high chair, oblivious to the surrounding adults.

"Right. You don't have her number," Bax took over. "You know where she works. What else do you know?"

"Nothing," Tanner said, not really liking that he was ready to invest in a relationship with a person he barely knew at all. "Just that Babushka isn't usually wrong."

"Get her number from Babushka," Linx suggested. "That's what I'd do."

He could do that. Good call.

"I also know Sam's kind. She cares. I wanted to fall into the warmth of her eyes and stick around for a while. She felt like she could be home for me," Tanner said. The words were a bit of a surprise coming out of his mouth. A familiar burn of embarrassment hit his cheeks when he thought about her.

"Why do I have the feeling this is going to be more complicated than necessary?" Irina asked. He wasn't sure who she was speaking to or if it was more of a blanket statement for everyone.

"Because relationships are always more complicated than

necessary," Mach said. "That's why I stick to my way of doing things. So I don't get screwed. And before you get on my ass about the fucking word screwed, I'd like to point out that I filtered out the fuck." He glanced to Courtney. Grinned. "You're welcome."

"I believe in you, Tanner." Becca moved to him and wrapped him in a hug. "You've got this."

"Why do you all keep stealing my speech and saying it better than me?" Knox asked.

"Get the number," Linx said, tapping twice on the counter as he moved past. "Always get the number."

"Be yourself," Becca called after him as he moseyed down the hall to the living space with the television.

He'd get her number. But not because Linx told him to.

Fine. Because Linx told him to, *and* it made sense.

Chapter Five
SAMANTHA

SAM DIDN'T HAVE a normal apartment, and not because she used her apartment to hide. That was only one perk of living in-residence at the Purple Peony. Nobody ever looked for anyone other than the residents there.

Another perk? She could work 24/7 and no one questioned it. She loved her work. It fulfilled her and kept her mind occupied.

The apartment wasn't anything super special, but it was hers. A one-room studio with a kitchenette and a bathroom. It shared walls with the residents, but they were thick, and the residents mostly let her have her space when she was off duty. Which wasn't often.

There was room for her double bed and a small dark blue loveseat facing the television. But she made the place cute with fun decor—a chess set mounted to the wall with magnetic pieces. A bust of a cat blowing a bubble-gum bubble she'd found at a thrift shop two summers ago. And her guitar she couldn't give up. She may not make music outside this room these days, but she couldn't stop. That was the kind of thing that was in her blood. In her soul.

She needed nothing else.

"This is your mystery guy?" Sam's best friend—Ashley—asked in disbelief, letting out a low whistle. "Hello, Hottie Pants."

Hottie Pants, for sure. Tanner played in a band.

Samantha's palms got sweaty.

A quick online search and he came right up. An excessively popular music group with hits a girl couldn't help but hear everywhere she went.

Her head went fuzzy.

Ashley lounged on the loveseat, her legs dangling over one arm as she flipped through her phone. Ashley had moved to Denver, which—along with Great Aunt Etta—was why Sam settled here for a bit.

"I can't date him," Sam said, hating that this was the truth of the matter. Despite the fact that he was a legitimate rock star, he wasn't the person who would make a good fling. He was the sticky kind that could challenge and change everything.

Not worth the risk.

"I think it's time," Ashley said, kicking her feet up and sitting. "Time to take the risk. Time to give him a shot."

"One of us would hurt the other," Sam said, sitting cross-legged on her bed with her guitar hugged to her chest. With her history, it'd likely be her that got stung. She didn't enjoy getting hurt. Sue her.

"You can't know that," Ashley assured her. "No one knows that. You think Babushka and this crew here would fix you up with someone they think would hurt you? They adore you here. They want you to be happy."

"I am happy." Sam didn't need to defend her happiness level. From one to ten, she stayed at an easy five all the time. Unfortunately, Ashley knew and understood this. Which was probably the reason for the push toward Tanner.

"You are content, sure," Ashley said. Then she held up

her phone so Sam could see the image of Tanner at a concert. "But are you this?"

He didn't wear a shirt, and his abs were c-u-u-t. Most of the background was inky black, but there was some kind of goo on the drums and it glowed as he hit the head with his drumstick. The electric blue goo shot into the air, like some kind of performance art mixed with music. His expression was one of pure bliss.

He was the antithesis of her. Everyone loved Tanner.

No one loved her—well, aside from Ashley and her family.

But there had been no coming back from the MyTube video seen by millions all over the world. Not an exaggeration, either. When she was ten, she'd written a three-minute song. An ode to mozzarella sticks. That was ages ago, since today she barely kissed the edge of twenty-four. Naïve, she'd posted the song online when viral videos were more of a rarity than an everyday occurrence.

"You are the only person in the world who would panic because a rock god asked you to go to coffee," Ashley said with a sigh.

"I like my privacy," Sam countered, knowing deep down that was only the tip of the reasoning.

"I'd say you can't spend your life running away, but you've proven me wrong on that so far, so I'm not gonna say it." Ashley flipped through her phone. "But it's been two months since anyone even posted a Sami Jo sighting."

Uh-huh. There was a website for those mega creeps who tried to track her down. Thankfully, she'd evaded them for nearly a decade.

Some might say that changing her name—Sami Jo was now only Sam—and running away from her one-hit wonder might be overkill. They'd probably be correct.

She'd still do it again. Because the lesson that being a

nobody was hands down better than being somebody was hard learned.

Being a nobody had extra perks of anonymity. Being a somebody meant everybody saw everything—the good, sure. But it was the bad that got the masses excited.

When her song became popular, it wasn't because she was good. No, the ridiculous lyrics and the auto-tuning kept listeners coming back. They weren't fans. They were bullies.

She did not know when she wrote a song about cheese and plucked it out on her guitar that it would become an iconic cult video. Of course, ten-year-old Sami held onto the certainty this would be a number one hit. So she posted it online.

When it wasn't a hit, she forgot about it.

Until years later, some guy found it, posted it on his socials, made it into a joke and suddenly Sami Jo was a hot commodity… as comedy. Not even a good joke. A crusty, smelly joke that the internet trolls took hold of and didn't let go. They attacked everything about her like she was truly an enemy.

The urgency of the consistent mean messaging was more than disturbing. How did they cancel a ten-year-old for writing a song about cheese? And why would they?

She'd never know because when she got the opportunity to drop out of sight, she did.

This started a years long person-of-interest hunt by the public, so she ran. She ran, and she worked where the people did not care or know anything about Sami Jo. People who didn't look for Sami Jo sightings. Sightings that were never her.

And when she'd taken herself away? Well, that made the demand for her even stronger.

"It sucks that my best friend is an urban legend who attracts sexy drummers—"

"Singular," Sam corrected. "Only the one drummer."

"So far." Ashley rolled onto her back, draping her arm dramatically across her eyes. "As I was saying—it sucks that I can't tell anyone about it! About how awesome you are! About how I know where Sami Jo is!"

Sam shook her head. "You don't know where she is. Sami Jo doesn't exist anymore."

And she never would. Sam tucked her away where she belonged—in the past.

She wanted that. But the heated bile of fear inched up into her esophagus. "What if everyone knows who I am. They figure it out. And then what?"

"And then they know," Ashley said. "That's it. Then they know. Period."

Sam shook her head. If she ever dated with the intention of a long-term relationship, she would date no one with a fan base. No! Because someone would start looking at her, recognize her, figure out where Sami Jo disappeared to—hiding out by working in retirement homes because the residents didn't care about a girl with a song from the early 2000s. The song they made up to the tune of *her* song still hurt.

WHERE THE HELL *has Sami Jo gone?*
Probably somewhere as a pawn.
Maybe she went off to Cancun,
To hang out with auto-tune.

UGH. It wasn't even good!

"I want to meet this guy," Ashley said. "Can you introduce me? I seriously love Dimefront."

"You just want to meet him 'cause he's hot." Sam strummed a few chords on the guitar from a song she'd written that wouldn't leave her alone. A song about hiding. And then being found.

This was nonsense that a little trickle of unease made her want to hide away. She didn't want Tanner to fall in love with Ashley, instead of taking a shot with her. But he couldn't exactly fall for Sam, so maybe she should introduce them. That would be the nice thing to do.

"I see the little wheels in your head." Ashley made a wheel motion with her index finger. "I do not want to date this guy. No, I want to meet him because he's with Dimefront. He's hot. Yes, that's why I want him to ask you out again. I'm a little annoyed that you told me he was boy band pretty." She held up another photo in the blue paint series. "This is not boy band pretty."

The boy band-esque aesthetic had turned out to be a decoy. Because there was nothing boy band about Dimefront music or Tanner in those photos. He was 100 percent hot adult male in every single image.

And he'd asked her on a date. Then did a puppet show with her. And then had the audacity to be so kind that he assisted her escape. And then she made sure he left before coming back out, proving that she was awful. A questionable person who made bad choices even when she tried to make good ones.

"What do I even do about him?" Sam asked, actually opening her mind to the possibility that maybe she should give it a shot.

Gah. No.

A shot was possible when he was only Tanner the hunky puppeteer. She could've gotten over this massive hurdle and actually convinced herself to do it. Convince herself that maybe—only maybe—she could consider putting down some roots here in Denver.

But then—*then*—she'd Googled him.

And he was not an accountant. He was not a lawyer. He wasn't even an instructor over at the gym up the street.

No, the Google search was an easy one because he had loads of articles about his recent addition to Dimefront.

"I've gotta go." Ashley stood. "Work will eventually notice that I'm not there."

She worked a few blocks over at a brokerage firm.

Why couldn't Tanner sell mortgages? That would be so much more convenient.

Ashley stopped at the wall-mounted chess board and did a quick maneuver with her queen. She turned to Sam. "Check."

Ashley stopped on her way out the door, pausing with her hand on the handle. "Don't overthink. Just do."

"That doesn't work for me," Sam said in a whisper.

"It didn't work once. Give it another shot." Ashley winked, then scurried out the door.

Sam's phone pinged. She glanced at the screen and the image of Tanner that Ashley had airdropped.

Only once before in her life had Samantha truly known she was toast. That was ages ago, and she learned her lesson.

Bagging a drummer for the most in-demand rock band would mean exposing herself to more of that same ridicule she'd already escaped once. Resurrecting the ghost of Sami Jo and her adoration of mozzarella sticks.

Yuck. God. Ew.

Lunch break over, now was time to get back to work. So she set aside her guitar, checked herself quickly in the mirror, and headed toward the front desk to sort the Sharpies and the pencils for tonight's artistic activity.

Each light thud of her footfalls on the commercial carpet of the hallway tapped out a different message:

He's not worth it…

He might be worth it…

What if he's not?

What if he is?

Dammit. This was nonsense. The two of them didn't even

swap numbers. Even if she wanted to reach out to him, she'd have to track him down.

Lies. Lying to yourself is a bad idea.

So is talking to yourself.

The number thing was not a deterrent. Not really. Nadzei—Babushka would know how to reach him.

Gah. Why was this hard? She clenched her fists, then released them, absolutely refusing to pick at her nails. She hadn't done that in ages, and she wasn't about to start up again now.

Okay, so when life started being an asshole, she took stock and formed lists. Pros and cons. Since she sat right on the center line, and Ashley was Team Go For It, she needed someone to give her an unbiased review. See what they thought.

Uh-huh, she needed an outside opinion. She stepped up to the front desk where Betty Jane was accepting a delivery.

"You find a better grilled cheese in Denver, and I will eat my words." Ted, the delivery man for Denver Sandwich Co., grinned at Betty Jane. "Have a good day, then."

Someone entirely uninvested in the situation… or her.

Ted was a fifty-something guy who owned the sandwich shop. He loved the residents at Purple Peony, so he always made the deliveries himself.

"Hey, Ted?" Sam called.

The insulated delivery bag tucked under his right arm, he turned. "Yes, ma'am?"

What was the best way to involve someone in a person's internal conflict? Just go for it, just do it. "Can I ask you a question?"

"Absolutely. Ask away." He grinned because he probably thought she'd ask him about Swiss cheese or rye bread or something like that.

"Are you single?" she asked. Darn, that did not come out like she'd thought.

"No," he said, furrowing his brows. "All married up."

Well, that wasn't the best start.

"I mean, I'm looking for relationship advice, and you always seem so happy." So much better, that was so much better.

"Fifteen years together last May." He grinned a little wistfully. "Wouldn't change a thing."

"Okay, so—" She gestured for him to sit at the high-backed chairs by the door. The spot that served as their makeshift waiting area.

She sat in the opposite chair and smoothed the fabric on her thighs.

He moved to the chair, but didn't sit. He leaned against the side.

"Whatcha got?" he asked.

She blew out a breath. "I met this person, and my friends all think we should, you know, get to know each other."

"Uh-huh." He nodded.

"But I'm really happy on my own."

"Uh-huh." He nodded again.

"So I don't know if it's a good idea to fit someone new into my routine."

"You wake up in the morning and look forward to the day?" he asked.

Well... "Most of the time. I mean, I think I'm happy. I move around a lot, and we all have things to deal with. So it's not like I'm that unusual."

"Uh-huh." He didn't nod at this one, but that was fine.

"But here's this person who has the ability to totally wreck my peace, or he could be awesome. But I don't know if he's awesome because if I find out, he'll wreck my peace. You know?"

"Uh. Huh."

"Shit. I know what to do." She stood, waiting for an immense wave of relief to splash over her. It didn't show up yet, but she knew it'd make it, eventually. This was the right thing, so of course the relief would come. "Thank you so much. This is so much clearer. I'm going to let it go. Let him go."

The idea of him.

"Huh," Ted said, readjusting the delivery sack under his arm. He gave her a salute as he walked to the door. Then he stopped, like he wanted to say something more.

"Glad I could help," he said, finally.

"Me too." She strode to her workstation at the counter to get going on the Sharpie sorting. The colors wouldn't un-mix themselves.

Ted moseyed out the door, the someone's-leaving jingle bells tinkling as they moved against the glass of the inside door. She focused on the task at hand.

Life was so much simpler when a girl could focus on one thing at a time.

Do you wake up and look forward to the day?

She frowned. Sometimes. Not always. But sometimes. And she'd worked very hard to get to this point… to be more than Sami Jo.

The string of jingle bells on the door tinkled again as she boxed up the red markers.

"You forget something, Ted?" She glanced up.

Glanced up and her gaze collided right with Tanner's.

Her traitor of a heart thunked in her chest and she couldn't help the smile that kissed the edges of her mouth. Tanner walking through the door felt like that wave of relief was supposed to feel. But this time, she genuinely experienced it.

Which was why this had to stop.

Chapter Six
TANNER

LUCK WAS NOT an asshole today because Sam stood at the front counter with a crap load of markers tossed into piles. She sorted them by color. Presently she worked on the reds, burgundies, and pinks.

"Hey," he said, pulling the door closed behind him so the bells didn't clink so loud to alert Babushka and her crew that someone had arrived. They'd figure it was him. He didn't know why or how they'd figure it, but they would.

Sam glanced up. A little smile hit her lips, and she paused. He adored the smile. Felt like it was for him and only him.

Then she seemed to realize she was smiling at *him* and a startled shock hit her expression. Hard blinking.

His cheeks started to get warm.

One thing about Sam, she wore her feelings where everyone could see them. Didn't even seem to put on a mask or pretend to be a bass player so she could communicate.

Just be Linx.

"I feel like we didn't get the chance to connect yesterday." He stepped up to the edge of the welcome desk, leaning his arm there so he wasn't in her space but not standing oddly at the door.

She set the markers aside. "I know. It was nuts."

"Sometimes the craziest things are the best ones," he countered, forcing himself to ignore the burning in his cheeks and the way his tongue felt heavy.

He was pretty certain she wanted to smile with the way her lips twitched at the edges, but she stopped herself.

"I don't know." Her lips parted the slightest bit. She sighed. "The whole puppet thing was a little bizarre."

The tip of her tongue traced the seam of her lips and his nerves all buzzed with anticipation. He wanted to know how she tasted. Know how she felt in his arms. He'd bet she tasted like gumdrops and felt like heaven.

Then she lifted a pencil to the sharpener—the old school kind that mounted on the edge of the desk and had a crank to turn the barrels.

"That's why I came back—"

She turned the crank, and the crunching of wood and lead interrupted his words.

"Sorry," she said, pulling the pencil from the hole. "It's pencil sharpening day."

Sam was nervous. Her hands a little shaky.

He should be the nervous one. She was the one all put together with that tug that made his body want to be near hers.

"No worries, I was only going to ask—"

She started another pencil. Studying the crank handle as she worked.

Okay, well, preferring to give her attention to the pencil was not promising. He waited. She was busy. He got that. But he also didn't stay where he wasn't wanted.

Which meant... what would Linx do?

Easy. Linx would walk away. Linx didn't fuck around with anyone who didn't appreciate his presence or want him there. No matter how pretty the woman was, or how much he had an intense pull to that person.

That's what nearly broke up the band. Linx's demand for everyone to be their best. They started screwing around and Linx said no. Moved on.

So, yes, history indicated that's what Linx would do.

Tanner tapped a quick knock on the counter.

"See ya later," he said, even though she couldn't hear him over the grinding of the wood.

Might as well make the trip worth it and visit his friends. Issue a cease and desist so they could all move along with their lives and stop pushing him and Sam together. Clearly, that's not what she wanted.

A heavy weight pressed against his chest.

Hell, without Sam in the mix he could even try out his new talk-to-pretty-women superpower and see where it got him. Spend one-on-one time with Linx to get a better idea of how he ticked. What he'd do, so Tanner could mimic that. Push this game of pretend a little further.

He stopped. Paused. Swallowed.

He didn't want that.

He wanted to give in to the magnetic tug between them. But what he wanted, he couldn't have. He'd never know how Sam tasted, what she loved, hated, wanted.

"Tanner!" Babushka caught him at the door to the dining room. "Velcome."

"Hey." He stuck his thumbs in his pockets. What was the best way to start with this? The best way to explain that they needed to lay off?

"Everything is perfection vith Samantha, yes?" Babushka asked. "A vedding vill be soon?"

Ha. Uh. They hadn't even made it past the pencil shaving stage of things.

"No." He shook his head. "Look, thanks. She's not into it. So let's let it go? Spread the word so everyone else will let it go, too." This wasn't a question. This needed to happen.

Babushka's eyes went wide. "Vhat happened?"

He glanced at his sneakers, then back to his friend. "Doesn't matter. She's not interested. I respect that." He paused. "You and everyone here need to respect it, too."

Babushka frowned. "I do not care for this."

Well, he didn't either. So, yeah.

"It's not yours to care or not care for." He shrugged. "It just is. Promise you'll leave her alone about it?" And him, too.

Babushka harrumphed. "I have things to do."

He just bet she did. Perhaps she had a grandchild who needed some of her non-requested help. That would make things much easier for him and Sam, honestly.

Tanner turned to the dining-room door to let himself in and check in with Etta and Betty Jane, Agnes, and Carla. Maybe join them in a game of Skip Bo. His hand was on the door handle when Babushka let out a screeching wail. This one did not seem to be fake. He glanced behind and she leisurely laid down, then sprawled on the hallway carpet.

Did he catch her readjusting her left leg for better sprawl? She did that. Right in front of him.

"My hip!" She laid her hand on her right hip. "So much pain!"

"Shit," he said, pulling open the door to the dining room.

She moaned with a decent impression of agony.

"Hold tight," he said to her.

"I'm down. Assistance!" Babushka yelled. "Assistance!"

He pulled open the industrial door and called into the room. "Can one of you call for some help over here? Babushka fell."

"Again?" Agatha asked. "That's the fourth time today."

Well, when she had something that got attention, she milked it.

"Is she really hurt, or does she just want the fire brigade to come?" Betty Jane asked over her glasses, putting down a three of diamonds on the stack of whatever game they played.

"Get Sam!" Babushka wailed.

"Fire brigade," everyone at the card table agreed in unison.

"She prefers the crew from Station 21," Etta said, laying down the King of Spades.

When he first came to the Purple Peony after the crew got themselves evicted from a Dimefront concert at Brek's Bar, he fell in love with the place. He'd never had a grandmother figure in his life, and suddenly he had five. He never expected what they'd come up with next, and whatever it was they'd all have a helluva good time.

Once they went on a clandestine mission to Walgreens for Pixie Sticks and Butterfinger bars and somehow landed on a plane headed to Muskego, Wisconsin. That was an adventure.

He missed these women when he went on tour, honest as all fuck he did. But right now, he wished he was on stage in a big city, dropping a beat for the band.

"Can one of you please call the front for some help?" he asked, stepping back into the hallway to check on Babushka.

Babushka, who did her best impression of a model for a chalk outline as she called, "Sam! Get Sam! Only Sam!"

Tanner shook his head. The woman channeled Meryl Streep with this performance and her dedication deserved an award.

Except...

Fuck, maybe he'd been wrong.

Maybe he saw things wrong, and she really hurt herself. A woman of her age couldn't continually fling herself on the ground and not suffer some eventual damage.

He hurried to her just in case he'd been wrong about what he'd witnessed. Kneeling down, he checked her color—all good. Lips still pink. He held the back of his hand to her mouth to ensure; yeah, she breathed normally. Chest rising and falling just like it should've. He reached for her wrist to take her pulse rate.

"Vhat are you doing?" she asked, pushing his face back with her hand.

"I'm checking your pulse," he said.

"No need." She waved him off.

"Tell me you are faking?" he asked, demanded, so he could assess the situation appropriately. "So I can stop worrying."

Babushka broke character for only a split second. "Believe vhat you vish."

Yeah, that's what he thought. "You've got to stop—"

She held her fingertip up to his lip and whispered, "This vill be fixed."

"Your hip?"

She gripped her left hip. "Ay. So much pain."

"Ten seconds ago it was your right hip," he whispered. "Now stop trying to fix things that aren't broken."

She gave an efficient shake of her head. "Your Sam situation is in *peril*."

Well, yes, it was. But... Shit. Fuck. Damn. "She's not *my* Sam. And there is no situation."

Not one that needed a fake broken hip or the fire department. Any situation they had only required that they avoid each other.

"She is perfection for you," Babushka assured, letting out a loud, "Help!"

"Could you stop doing that?" he asked, in a tone he thought sounded pretty nice given that he wanted to strangle her.

The defiant look Babushka threw his way?

She wasn't gonna stop.

"Let this go," he said, glancing up the hallway where he suspected Sam would emerge at any second.

"Yes. Of course," Babushka said. She waved him off and began moaning once more.

Dammit.

As expected, Sam hurried around the corner with a handful of blue Sharpies in her grasp. She paused only long enough to do a quick mental triage. He could nearly follow her thoughts as she moved from head to toe.

"I fell. Help. I fell." Babushka laid her hand on her right hip this time. "It's broken. I think it's broken."

Given that Babushka was playing this up royally, and Sam cared for her, Sam bought the charade.

Tanner would've believed Babushka too, if he hadn't seen with his own eyes this was all fake pretend.

"Tanner, you've got her for a sec?" Sam asked, going into that calm, detached mode of those excellent in an emergency. "I'll get one of the nurses."

"Yeah." He sure as fuck hoped Babushka would can it before they called in the fire department.

Sam tossed the Sharpies on a table as she bolted back down the hallway she came from.

"You're embarrassing me," he whispered to Babushka. "Please stop."

Babushka ignored his pleas. "My arm!"

"Two seconds ago, it was your hip," Tanner said, accidentally reminding her.

"My arm! My hip! My shoulder!" Babushka cried.

"Anything else? How's the nose?" he asked. "Did you maybe break it sticking it in my business?"

She gave him a know-it-all look as she added to her list of ailments. "My heart. You are breaking my heart."

"You agreed to let this go," he said low.

She moaned, then whispered, "I agreed to nothing."

Sam hurried toward them with a nurse he only knew a little. Katy. Her name was Katy. He moved out of the way as the two of them took over.

"Sam, she's okay. Katy, she's fine," Tanner assured. "I promise she's okay. This isn't real. She's playing a game—"

"There's no way to know when it's real or not." Sam's

gaze caught his and the gravity of her words hung there in the air. "So you always have to move ahead like it is."

"She's got good movement," the nurse said. "Do you think you can walk, Nadzieja?"

"No," she said, entirely too fast.

Instead of arguing, Tanner turned his attention to Babushka. "Can I carry you?"

"Yes, please." Babushka lifted her hand to his cheek, and he would swear on a five-dollar bill she smiled like an evil cartoon villain. "This is very heroic thing."

Sam huffed. "That's not a good idea. Something could be out of place—"

But Babushka already had her arms around his neck, and he hefted her up. Some might expect a woman of her life experience to be frail with bones ready to crack without effort. But the woman was sturdy as an oak.

And clearly enjoying the attention.

"Let's not make this a standard thing, yeah?" he asked.

"Shh, you are making good show. Vomen love heroes," Babushka admonished him. "Take me to front office." She pointed the direction.

"You want an ambulance?" he asked.

"Vhat for?"

Clearly, she didn't need an ambulance.

He got her settled in the little clinic they had on site so the nurse could monitor her.

"What happened?" Sam asked, reaching for his biceps, and pulling him to the side right outside the clinic door.

The slight touch was all it took to increase that magnetic pull he'd agreed with himself that he'd avoid.

God, this woman was pretty.

"She's faking the whole thing. You get that, right?" Tanner figured she did, but just to be sure.

Sam nodded, letting her arms fall beside her. "She's very persistent."

"She didn't like that I told her to leave you alone about the whole set-up thing she started between us," he said.

Sam sighed, pursing her lips. "Babushka doesn't listen to anyone."

Oh boy, did he know that. "I don't want her to bug you about something you don't want to be bothered with."

"Tanner?" She nibbled on her bottom lip. "You're not a bother."

"I get it," he said, lifting his hands in surrender. "You aren't into this thing that she's forcing on us. I'm disappointed, yeah, but I don't want you to feel you have to spend time with me if you don't want to."

"You're disappointed?" The frown lines were back between her eyebrows.

"Yeah, Sam. I am."

"What if I want to be bothered with it, but I'm nervous?" She swallowed.

She what? "That is not the vibe I've been getting."

"I want to spend time with you. It's not that I don't." Her chest heaved as she breathed heavily. "You terrify me."

That made about as much sense as Mach teaching kindergarten. Sure, it sort of worked, but it made little sense. "Why?"

"You play the drums for Dimefront," she said simply.

"Yeah?"

She pointed to her chest. He didn't look to where she pointed, swear to hell he didn't.

"I work in a retirement home," she said, as though this made sense.

He squinted at her—mostly because she still pointed at her chest, and he was seriously trying to be a good guy here and not check out her girls. "And?"

"One of these things is not like the other." She gestured to herself, then to him, startling when her hand brushed against the front of his shirt. But she didn't move it. Which was nice because the little hairs along his arms prickled at the touch.

He wanted to move his hand to hold hers there in the indent between his ribs. Could she feel his heart beating? Sense how the air crackled.

"We don't match," she said. But she gripped the front of his T-shirt, letting her hand stay there.

He moved his hand to hers, letting it settle over the top.

"I don't live in your world. I live here," she said.

"It's not like we're on different planets. Believe it or not, I spend a good deal of time here." He stopped speaking so that could sink in for them both. "I'd like to get to know you. Apparently, you might want the same?"

She nodded. "I do."

"Then what does the rest of it matter? We have coffee. See where that takes us. Maybe it'll take us to dinner or drinks. I don't even know if you like the bar scene. Or if you're a vegetarian. Or if you like pickles and cilantro."

"Not really. On the bar scene." She crossed her arms over her chest. "And I like steak, so the other isn't really me either. Yes on the pickles. No on the cilantro."

"Noted." He swallowed hard, letting his thumb trace along her knuckles since it made her smile.

"Are you always this amazing?" she asked.

Ha, usually he was one of many shades of red.

"No." He shook his head. "Sometimes I seriously screw shit up. But, I just… I don't let it define me. You know?"

She nodded, the little kiss of a smile on her lips making him appreciate the fact that he'd put it there.

"I should go check on Babushka," Sam said. "Make sure she doesn't need a doctor."

"Or the guys from Fire Station 21?" Tanner asked with a wry smile.

Sam snorted. "They're a nice crew, at least. Good guys."

The clinic was empty except for Katy.

"Where's Babushka?" Sam asked, peeking behind one curtain.

"She felt better, so she left." Nurse Katy rolled her eyes. "This is the fifth time today she's done this. I'd say let's reach out to her family for their support, but you and I both know that won't help."

"Keep me posted if she comes back?" Sam asked, then turned back to him, rocking a little on her toes.

"Why don't you come over to my place? After work? Too late for coffee, and I think I hit my quota of people today. But I can order in steaks, and I've got a pool table."

"You probably have an actual pool, too," she said.

He did. "Well, it came with the whole Dimefront package."

"You have a pool?" She stilled.

"I mean, Mach and I share a pad, so we have a pool, but yeah. I do. You swim?"

She nodded. "It's my favorite."

Look at that. He now knew multiple somethings about her. Many things: she liked steak, didn't do the bar scene, cared a lot about the residents here, and she liked to swim.

"Bring your suit," he said.

Funny thing, this whole time talking to Sam, he hadn't been nervous once. He hadn't even had to pretend to be Linx.

"What time do you get off?" he asked, and with that question, he was no one but himself.

And that was only mildly frightening.

Chapter Seven
SAMANTHA

"HI." Sam kept a skip in her step as she approached Tanner.

Of course, he waited at his car like the teen idol he should've been ten years ago. She met him down the street in front of the flower shop, so Babushka and the others wouldn't get any ideas about stalking them and getting involved. More involved.

Sam had pulled her hair into a low ponytail that fell over one shoulder. She hoped it'd project that she'd tried, but not so hard anyone needed to be disappointed when this didn't work out.

If. If it didn't work out.

"If. Not when," she said under her breath.

"Huh?" Tanner asked, that grin of his probably costing thousands in orthodontia to be so perfect. "I missed that?"

"Nothing." She shook her head, clenching and then unclenching her hands. "Talking to myself."

He grinned. "I talk to myself, too." He totally eye-fucked her as she approached.

That was fine. She did the same to him, so even Steven or whatever.

"Sometimes talking to myself is the only way to have a

good conversation," she said, adjusting the long strap of her purse. Maybe she should wear it cross body instead?

"Then you're probably talking to the wrong people," he said.

"Probably."

Butterflies trounced around her stomach and the air between them sizzled like an electrical storm brewed.

His eyes trailed over her again with that same heated gaze from before. Each of the fine hairs along her arms seemed to stand straight at the perusal and a knot of anticipation she hadn't had in forever tied itself up in her stomach.

Her Ashley-approved yellow shirt and jeans went with the Sam-approved plain Converse. Under it all, she'd gone with a black bikini. One with the extra coverage on the tummy, but that also lifted the ladies up, so they stood at attention.

The small black bag she brought along dangled over her arm, falling to her hip. Ashley had made her swear on a whole bucket of mozzarella sticks that she wouldn't cover up with the jean jacket, but Sam brought it along, anyway. Just in case it got chilly.

She stepped closer, right into the storm.

"Hey." Tanner hadn't changed from before. Same tee. Same jeans. Same sneakers.

He lifted a finger to brush the edge of her jawline.

"Hey," she replied, since she didn't know what else to say and she'd already said, "Hi."

Drat. He dropped his hand.

"You have a sports car," she said. Of course, he had a fancy car like this. The guy made loads of cake and he probably liked to go fast.

"I do." He patted the hood.

Sam knew next to nothing about cars—she didn't even own one. The bus worked fine, and it's not like she ever left or went far enough to need one.

The one thing she knew about cars is that the ones with

the spoilers and the special rims and the shiny paint drew attention. Not like she expected him to dive into an old Chevy van, but would it have killed him to pick out a Prius or go with a Tesla? Was a muscle car totally necessary?

"You ready to head out?" He held open the door for her to slide in. She did, situating herself in the passenger seat. There wasn't a backseat. Probably because a backseat would ruin the muscle car appeal or something.

Tanner climbed in. Buckled up. Checked to be sure she buckled—she had. That was super sweet and very attentive. Also, practical, and sensible. All good things.

"Your place?" she asked, rubbing her palms on the jean fabric of her thighs. Then she stopped herself. No nervousness allowed. This was Tanner. He was only a guy with a nice car and an impressive body. That those things made her tummy flutter, and he played in a rock band, meant nothing.

He nodded.

"Figured we'd lie low." He flicked the blinker to hang a left at the light. "Go back to my place. Eat in. Jump in the pool." He glanced her way, as though checking to ensure this was an acceptable arrangement.

Did he have a game plan? A guy wasn't this attentive unless he had nefarious plans. Wasn't that what her grand aunt Etta always said?

"Men are nefarious, Samantha. Don't trust 'em when they're nice. Don't trust 'em when they're mean. Just don't trust 'em!"

Then again, Great Aunt Etta was involved in this entire set-up, so the message was definitely mixed.

"That work for you?" Tanner asked, frowning.

What?

Right. Staying in. Movie. Food.

"Yes." She toyed with the end of her ponytail. "Works for me. Lying low. You know my views on swimming."

"You brought your suit?" He glanced at the small bag, like

he didn't believe it.

"Uh-huh," she assured. "I'm wearing it under."

His cheeks pinked at that. He pulled his bottom lip under his teeth and, oh boy, she wished she could taste him.

She settled in as he tapped out a rhythm on the steering wheel with his index fingers and thumbs.

"The guys sometimes stop by. You want me to ask them not to?" He paused, lost in thought for a moment. "Then again, if I ask them not to come by, they'll want to know why. They'll figure out you're with me, and then they'll definitely make it a point to come by. So that's probably not the best idea."

"The guys? As in… your band?" She choked a little on the last word.

"Uh-huh." He nodded as he pulled up to a stop sign and flashed her a smile. "They're great. Sort of like Babushka's crew—they mean well, but they get their noses stuck in everyone else's business."

"Dimefront?" she asked, for clarification. "The guys from Dimefront *might* stop by? And will *definitely* stop in if they know I'm coming?"

"See, you already know all about the guys from Dime-front," he said, grinning.

"I mean, everyone knows Dimefront." Literally, everyone in North America who ever visited anywhere with a working radio, stereo, or karaoke machine. "I remember when Bax and Linx and Knox all went on tour for the first time. Getting tickets was bananas."

"You've seen the band?" he asked, tone carefully curious.

"Ages ago." Way back when she hadn't been hiding out, Dimefront had their first big hit about a woman's mouth and the things they liked about it.

"You're a Ten?" he asked. His expression went oddly neutral and impassive, as though her answer to this question mattered a lot.

Ten was the pet name the band used for their groupies. She was *definitely* not that.

"No." She shook her head. "Only the one concert and I was in the nosebleeds. But my best friend, Ashley, is totally a Ten, and she's already super jealous. Now, if you can introduce me to Irina Carmichael? I'll lose my mind. She's amazing."

Irina was an actual movie star, and she was brilliant.

He glanced from the road to her. Only a little look, but it made her warm all over.

"Irina's not in town right now. But she'll be back, and we'll get everyone together another night. Invite her over. The guys are cool. Their girls are awesome. You'll like them. They'll like you. Since they'll like you, they'll absolutely like Ashley."

"You haven't even met her," Sam said.

He gave a little shake of his head. "Don't need to to know she's awesome. I mean, you don't need to meet Irina to know she's the shit, do you?"

"Are you always this perfect?" Sam asked, situating herself so she could see his profile without having to crank her neck.

"No." A bashful look crossed his face.

"I don't know that you're being honest." Was she teasing him? She was totally teasing him. And it made her chest swell and her cheeks hurt from smiling.

"I'm always honest." The glimmer in his eyes as he said this was absolutely wicked.

"No one is *always* honest," she countered with a dash of innocence.

"So you're not *always* honest?"

"Well, sure. But we've only known each other for like a minute. It's not like I've had time to have a reason not to be." She chewed on that for a second. "I guess it also depends on what it means to be dishonest. I mean, sometimes we have to keep things to ourselves, so we don't hurt others." *Or ourselves...* "Sometimes the truth hurts worse than not knowing."

"I can't think of a time when that was true."

"Like if you miss a beat at a concert—of course, it doesn't sound good. But telling you that won't help. It's best to keep that kind of thing to oneself." She toyed with the ends of her hair, realized she was doing it, and forced herself to stop.

"Or tell me so I can fix it." He glanced to her lips.

Did she have something there? She tested her top lip with her tongue, then lifted her fingers to check the edges.

His pupils flared

"I think honesty is important with the big stuff," she assured, not finding anything wrong with her lips at all. "There are also some things from the past that don't need to be brought up in the present. That's not being dishonest, just protecting yourself. You know?"

"The little stuff can add up to be big stuff." He cleared his throat and his words were rumbly and rough.

"Maybe," she said.

He raised his eyebrows and a low pull tugged deep in her belly. A good pull. The kind of arousal that felt like all of this talk was foreplay for something more.

She focused outside the window for a beat to recollect herself. They'd merged onto I-70, just passing Coors Field where the Rockies played.

"I think the past is important to understand, for the future," he said, finally.

Nope. She shook her head. "The past should stay in the past."

"I guess if that's the case then the present is where we should focus." He moved his hand to grab a water bottle in the cupholder between them, his fingers brushing against the skin of her arm and making all those fine hairs perk to attention.

He drank the water.

Honest to hell, she'd never been turned on by a guy drinking water but the way his Adam's apple moved and his lips got wet? He might as well have taken off his shirt and given her a lap dance.

Whew, had someone hit the heated seats in this thing?

Nope, that was only her reaction to Tanner and a water bottle.

They drove up to the garage, but he didn't pull inside. Instead, he parked right at the path leading to the front door.

"This is me." He jerked his chin to the mansion.

This wasn't a house. This massive lair of bricks and stone was overwhelming. Gorgeous, too.

She climbed from the car to get some air and hopefully give her body some perspective on reactions to Tanner. "It's massive."

The house sat back a little from the road with a circle drive up front paved with bricks. Another drive led around the side of the house—where they arrived. They took the cobbled path to the front door.

"C'mon, yeah?" He gestured that direction and waited for her to catch up. Then he slid her hand into his and she forgot for a minute what she was supposed to do.

Grip his hand, dummy.

He looked at her hand, then lifted his eyebrows.

Crud, she was being a wet fish. She squeezed his hand, met his gaze, and the kaleidoscope of colors all slipped into place. Her breath caught but he didn't let go. Instead, he rubbed light circles at the fleshy spot between her thumb and forefinger. Was she in middle school again? Because she had a sudden urge to giggle. To blush. But there was something comforting about his touch. Which made no sense at all, but she didn't care because, for the first time in a long time, she looked forward to what came next.

Tethered together he led the way through the thick wooden front door through the marbled entryway that opened up to a posh gray and black living room. The vibe here was rock star famous. Leather and a shaggy white carpet that looked a little like Rod Stewart's hair.

"You live here?" she asked. There wasn't a stray mug, sock, or… anything. The place looked magazine perfect.

"Yeah." He nodded. Tilting his head to the side. "Kitchen's this way. Figured we can either order in or cook ourselves? I'm okay in the kitchen, but my American Express is a better chef."

Hands still linked in a comfortable way that was as if they were always supposed to be like this, right now in that moment. The two of them and only them.

They rounded the corner to a large kitchen. More black —everything was black. Tile floor, countertops, even the appliances. The walls were all a stark, contrasting white.

A shirtless guy with decent abs stood at the counter, pulling a tray from the oven with a mitt.

"Fuck," he said, dropping it on the counter.

There were pizza rolls and chicken nuggets and a bunch of fried appetizers that looked super yum.

"Shit." Shirtless guy blew on his thumb.

"Thought you had plans?" Tanner said, gripping Sam's hand tighter.

Shirtless dude glanced up quickly from the tray and his jaw went slack.

"This is Sam." Tanner squeezed her hand. "Sam, this is Mach."

Mach rubbed his hands along his board shorts. He waved. "Hi."

She waved back. "Hi."

"Everyone's here. They're all in the back," Mach said, jerking his thumb toward the wall of windows looking over the oversized grassy backyard. The pool area was a solid eighty feet away. Not so close that the pool noise was loud in the kitchen.

Half-a-dozen people currently played a game of water volleyball.

That looked like fun. Though, not as fun as a one-on-one with Tanner.

"Seriously?" Tanner ground his teeth together. The muscle in his cheek twitching as he glanced outside.

Mach held up his hands. "Nothing weird going on. We didn't know you'd bring home a date." He glanced at Sam, then at the linked hands between her and Tanner. "He never brings home a date."

"Oh, yeah?" Sam asked. That was some interesting intel.

"Because you're special," Tanner said. Then he turned his attention to Mach. "I'll take Sam somewhere else."

"Oh, hell no." Mach snatched up one of the fried things and tossed it in his mouth. He opened his mouth as he spoke around the food. "Fuck. That's hot."

"Yeah, be careful with it. Just came out of the oven," Tanner said with an eyeroll.

"Everybody's gonna lose their minds that you're here." Mach seemed to attempt to blow on his own tongue.

Uh.

"Why?" Sam asked.

"Because…um…" Mach seemed to be thinking exceptionally hard.

"Yes, Mach, do tell?" Tanner seemed to be issuing a dare.

Mach didn't bite. Instead, he said, slowly, "Because you arrived when the food finished cooking, and everyone is hungry."

Sam worked in the elderly industry long enough to know when to call bullshit. She was calling that here.

"Sam and I are gonna slip out the front," Tanner said, already starting that way.

"Nope," Mach said, surprisingly loud for a guy trying to cool off his tongue. "Can't let you leave, now that you're here."

Tanner gripped her hand harder. "You wanna stay or go, Sam?"

"I think I should meet your band." Sam said, grinning at him. "Check out what it would take to be a Ten." She nudged him with her hip.

Tanner cut a clear warning glance to Mach and pressed the pad of his thumb against his lips. "Okay."

"You wanna handle this"—Mach gestured to the oven and the pan—"while I go outside and let 'em know?"

"Sure." Tanner dropped Sam's hand to skirt the edge of the counter.

Sam immediately missed the connection of his touch. Which was odd, since this was only a first date.

Mach jogged to the door and down to the pool. Tanner pulled open the oven and slid out a tray of mozzarella sticks.

Sam's reality sort of closed into a pinprick in front of her. Which was unnecessary. These were only mozzarella sticks. They weren't some kind of sign or some kind of omen or a message from the past. They weren't a nod that the Dime-front guys knew who she was or anything. Only that they had great taste in appetizer choices.

It's not like she had to sing about them, or anything.

So why was she having a hard time breathing?

Scratch that. Breathing was going fine. The oxygen merely didn't seem to make it all the way to her brain.

She sat—sort of fell—to one of the bar stools, gasping for air like a freaking grouper tossed on the pier. Tanner was saying something to her, but she was too focused on herself to really hear him.

No. She shook her head. Then she pushed back the wave of whatever-the-hell this was going on inside her.

Enough.

She blew out a breath. Sometimes mozzarella sticks were simply cheese with breading, and nothing more.

Chapter Eight
TANNER

SAM WENT PALE, then turned a greenish-gray. He was definitely not an expert on first dates, but that wasn't supposed to happen.

Tanner set the tray of food off to the side without even coming close to burning himself.

Something about the way everything shifted when he pulled out the tray didn't make sense. She'd been good with the first tray. Seemed happy to dive in.

What the hell was it about this one? He looked at the unimpressive cheese logs Mach had dumped on the sheet without laying them out first, so they'd cook evenly.

Tanner wasn't an ace in the kitchen, but he knew to do *that*.

He hustled to Sam, kneeling a little, so they were face to face. He didn't even have to try to pretend to be Linx as he said, "You okay?"

Then he immediately berated himself for asking such a stupid question when she was clearly not okay. Probably lactose intolerant and here he was serving up fried cheese right in front of her.

Still, she nodded. "I'm fine. Sorry. It's stupid."

"You're fine?" he asked, still kneeling in front of her.

"Uh-huh." She continued nodding.

"Is this one of those little untruths that doesn't hurt anyone?" he asked, placing his hands on hers.

Perhaps if he kept this light she'd smile.

She did. "I just… it's just…"

"We can go somewhere else," Tanner suggested, still himself. And not tripping on his tongue. He'd need to evaluate that later.

For now, they didn't need to stick around for Mach and the rest of the band. That could wait for another day.

"It's not a big deal," Sam assured, still nodding her head as though attempting to convince herself.

"Seems like it might be a medium deal?" he suggested, gently. "And you said you're done with people today, so I know another place without all the distraction of cheese and the band. It's cool. I don't mind."

He started to stand, but she reached to his wrist and stopped him. He liked that—

the touching without hesitation.

"Do you want me to meet them?" she asked, her complexion going back to her normal shade.

He nodded. Fuck, yeah, he did. He wanted her to stay right there, meet them, get to see how epic the crew was, so she'd see there was more to stick around for than only Tanner. Once she met them, she'd want to stick around.

"Okay." She took a breath and squeezed his hand. She eyed the cheesy tray with definite aversion.

"I can fix you something else?" he suggested.

She slid her gaze to the trays of food. "This is fine."

"It's not exactly gourmet," he said, waggling his eyebrows. For the record, Linx would never do that. Not in a million years. Linx was entirely too slick to do anything with his eyebrows.

She laughed at his antics, a small sound that seemed to mean a whole lot.

"What's not to love about a good mozzarella stick?" She said it, sure, but she also flinched a little.

Nah, that was only him reading too far into things again.

"You'd rather have a sandwich?" he asked. "Something not deep fried then reheated?"

That got him a full laugh. He wanted to hear it again. Hear her laugh because he'd said something funny.

"A sandwich would be great," she said. "I can make it. Order it. Whatever."

"Two things I can handle in the kitchen? Reheating shit and making a sammich." He started toward the fridge. "You good with white bread?"

She nodded.

"Sam wants a sammich," he sang. Again, not something Linx would do and still Tanner's tongue worked just fine.

The mood from whatever had happened before definitely lightened up and Sam returned to sunshiney and bright.

He pulled the fixings from the fridge and continued with a little ditty about Sam and her sammich, adding percussion with a couple of butter knives. Even imitating a drum solo. She hummed along, but didn't sing.

Her pitch on the humming was spot on. And the way she tapped out the beat with him made his entire stomach feel funny. Stomach-flutter funny. Good funny.

"Sing with me, Sam." He pointed to her with a pickle spear.

She didn't sing. She only shook her head and pulled a *yeesh* face. "Trust me, no one wants to hear that."

Oh, but he did.

"You don't have to sing good to belt it out in the kitchen," he said. "It's all about the effort."

"Hah." She shook her head. "Still no."

He slid the finished sandwich across the counter for her, then started one for himself.

"Listen—" She cleared her throat. "About before. I—"

"You don't have to tell me what happened." He kept his focus on the spread, not the girl. "With the 'you turning gray' thing," he continued.

What he wanted to add? *But please be honest about it if you do.*

She nodded. "Thank you."

The silence covered them like an itchy blanket. He scratched at the back of his neck. How did he get things back to rights with her?

Becca had a suggestion once that wasn't bad for this situation…

Be Linx. Be Linx.

No… he was going to be himself on this one.

"You want a code word or something?" he asked, finishing up the smear with a flourish of the knife. "So if it gets to be too much, too many people, you say the word and I'll know we need to step out?"

Of course, that's what Linx's girl Becca had done for Tanner on the first tour. She gave him a code word, so if he started stumbling, she could help him with an excuse to leave. Or just help him.

Sam's eyes softened at the suggestion. The ever-present magnet between them tugged him to her. He wanted more of that. Liked the tingly feeling he got all over when her mask melted away and the defense systems lowered. She had a familiar quality that made him feel ten years younger. Sorta funny, since ten years ago wasn't the best time in his life. He preferred not to think about it.

But… God, why did he feel like he knew her?

"A code word would be great," she agreed, lifting the sandwich in her hand. Checking it out. "Maybe something easy to slip into conversation, but that isn't super invasive?" She took a bite, savored it, chewing, swallowing, and basically making him hard with the way she gave all her attention to the task.

"So nothing like Armageddon or Beetlejuice?" he asked, keeping things light and trying not to let the excited-to-bring-her-to-meet-his-family vibes seep out too much into the comfortable cadence of their chat.

"Or pineapples or pumpernickel?" she asked.

He chuckled and caught himself staring at her mouth. This was a simple answer—

"Roses." Because her lips were like rose petals and he'd guess that if he leaned in and brushed his lips against them, they'd be as soft as rose petals, too.

"Roses," she agreed. "I like roses."

One more thing to add to his arsenal of things he knew about her.

He glanced at the pool, but the crew had all stayed put. Wasn't that the surprise of surprises? "Expected 'em to start this way as soon as they heard you came along."

"They're giving us space?" she asked, wiping the edge of her lips with a napkin.

"Nah, that's not like them. They're probably just really into this game," he said, but he wasn't entirely certain he believed it.

Knox went for a spike of the volleyball, but Becca was across from him and got there first, hurling it back. There seemed to be some disagreement about whether it was a foul.

The rest of the meal was kind of amazing. He only chan-neled Linx twice when he started to get stuck in his head and his cheeks began to burn. But Sam laughed at his stupid jokes, and they might still be in a world that had always tried to screw him, but right now things looked pretty damn good. They talked like they'd known each other for ages, not only a few days.

He didn't touch the mozz sticks, but Sam kept eyeing

them like she worried they might stand up and march out the door in a line.

"I think I'm gonna have one," she said, reaching her hand to the tray. "I'm gonna do it."

"Don't eat 'em if you don't like 'em."

"That's the problem," she said, grimacing. "I sort of love them. Like *love* them."

He did not expect that. Not one bit. "Then go for it. I'm pretty sure Mach didn't lace them with vegetables."

"You're funny." She went for one. Then pulled her hand back.

The crew at the pool made a shit ton of noise as the game finished and they all pulled themselves from the water.

"Incoming," he said, as Sam went for another. Then stopped.

"You need an assist?" He snagged one, took a nibble to ensure it wasn't too hot. Then held it to her.

He stared hyper focused on her mouth as she parted her lips and took a bite. Then the entire universe tipped a few degrees off center.

Because fucking hell... those lips. He'd know them anywhere.

Everybody knew the legend of Sami Jo. Hell, he could sing her *mozzarella stick* song word for word. He had sung the song many times to himself, to Harley, but...

No.

This couldn't be her, right? No way.

Sami Jo had disappeared, and everyone still looked for her. Not everyone, of course, but even the tabloids would sometimes still report a Sami Jo sighting.

And here was Sam with the same eye color, hair color, name... everything matched up.

Sam took the rest of the cheese stick. "It's so good. Oh my gosh, I've missed these."

Tanner opened his mouth to ask more questions. Here

was the original icon of social media fame standing right in front of him and—

"Little buddy brought a girl home," Mach announced with a ta-da motion as the rest of the crew filed in and absolutely shattered the moment.

Sam set down the rest of her mozz stick. Chewed, swallowed, and gave a jaunty wave. "Hi." She pointed to herself. "I'm Sam."

There was the general chaos of multiple greetings occurring all at once.

Tanner pointed out the couples: Linx and Becca, Courtney and Bax. Irina left for a curtain call in L.A., so she wasn't there. And then there was the happily, forever-single Mach.

"Tanner, I would like to announce something," Bax said, once the intros were through and he'd passed out beers all around.

"Is it gonna embarrass me in front of Sam?" Tanner asked, since he'd sort of prefer they didn't do that.

"Maybe," Linx said, pulling himself up on the counter and dangling his legs off the side.

"We're ready to give you, Tanner Alexander Penton, your official Dimefront name," Bax said with some seriously faux sincerity. "I'm gonna need a drumroll." He glanced around the room.

Courtney pointed to Tanner. "You're gonna have to go to the source, I think."

"Tanner?" He glanced pointedly at Tanner's hands. Then he looked to Sam and said out of the side of his mouth, "Usually, the drummer does this part, so it's a little kink in the plan."

Tanner did a quick beat on the counter. They might talk a big game, but this was his family and they wouldn't do anything to make him look bad in front of Sam. He trusted them.

"Tanx," Bax announced with a loud boom like he was in a stadium and not their kitchen.

"You're welcome," Tanner said deadpan. "Now what's the name?"

"Ha!" Bax draped his arm around Tanner's neck. "You are now Tanx."

"No Tanx," Tanner said, ducking from under Bax's arm. That's what they came up with? For real?

"Dude, Tanx, it is not your choice," Knox added. "We were the triple-x, now you're official. We're the quad-x and… Mach."

"Doesn't have the same ring to it." Bax pulled his lips to the side. "Ah, well. Live and learn."

"Why?" Tanner asked. Why couldn't they come up with something better than Tanx?

"We're going to make T-shirts," Courtney said, painting the air with her hands and pretend paintbrush. "Mugs and keychains. All kinds of swaggy stuff."

"No, I get that." He did. The other guys all had merch. Even Mach had some with his name. Tanner's tees all had his face on them or a pair of drumsticks. "I mean, why *Tanx*?"

"Because we just thought of it." Bax shrugged as he tilted the beer to his lips. "Four letters, ends with an X."

"Your name has three letters," Courtney pointed out.

Bax frowned. "Well, fuck. It's still Tanx."

"That's fun," Sam said, playing with the label on her beer bottle. "You all have fun nicknames. I love it."

"I don't get one." Mach played being dejected. He didn't mean it, though. When Mach really got upset, he went quiet, then he rolled around in that quiet for a good long time.

"Cause he was born with a kickass name," Bax clarified. "No need to add to that."

"Mach is a pretty kickass name," Sam agreed. Then she glanced at Tanner. "Well, it is… Tanx."

"Not sure this is my favorite," Tanner said, at the same

time his chest puffed up and he kept repeating that a few years ago he'd found his fam. They'd accepted him. They gave him a nickname. That was the shit.

With Sam here, too? And him finding his voice with her? Didn't suck.

"We should do Sam," Tanner suggested.

"Oh, let's not," Sam's eyes sparkled as she spoke.

And those lips of hers... fuck him the way they made his mouth go dry and his brain go to automatic stupid. He couldn't pull his gaze away. Not that he wanted to.

The rest of the room seemed to dissolve into the background until it was only the two of them there.

"I just remembered that I have a thing to do at a place tonight," Mach announced. "You all are coming, too. Remember?"

"Yes," Becca chimed in. "The thing at the place. Let's go do that."

They all evacuated like a swarm of rockers following their muse, leaving Tanner and Sam alone again.

"I like them," Sam said, still playing with the beer bottle label but not really touching the brew. "They love you."

"They're pretty awesome," he agreed, stepping forward into her space, moving his thumb to her cheek.

She nuzzled it, and the air crackled around them.

Her breaths quickened. His heart beat faster. There was only the two of them at that moment.

Moving into the air over her lips, he understood he had to tell her. She had to know he knew before they took this thing between them any farther.

He didn't care who she was.

Didn't care that she had a history of being Sami Jo.

He cared who she was today. Tomorrow. Next week.

Yeah, he wanted to understand why she ran so far and so long. Why the people who loved her let her keep running without slowing her down so she could see she wasn't alone.

He'd never be able to thank Dan and Mach enough for slowing him down like that. Helping him stop running long enough to see things could be okay.

"What are you thinking?" she asked, their mouths only millimeters apart, their breaths mingling in the space between them.

"I think I know where Sami Jo went," he murmured, the edge of his lips brushing against hers.

Her mouth made a small "O" of surprise.

Then, his lips still a breath away from hers, he hummed a little of the song.

She froze.

He continued humming.

"Stop." She pushed away from him, pacing. Then she put an entire island of distance between them. "Don't do that. Not that song."

"You wrote it," he said, and yeah, he probably should've used a gentler hand with this. But color him surprised that Sami Jo was in his kitchen. Sami Jo was in his arms. And he was falling for her.

"Sam," he said. "Why are you hiding?"

"Because…" She stopped. Closed her eyes. A tear slipped out of the corner of her eyelid.

"I won't tell anyone," he assured. "I'm not that guy. You can trust me with this."

"I can't trust you," she said. "I barely know you."

"Is that the truth?" he asked, seriously. Because they may have only known each other for a little while but it was more than that. What they were was more than that already.

Another tear slipped out of the other eyelid. "I'm a joke. Sami Jo is a joke."

"You're an icon," he countered.

"No." She shook her head, adamant.

He shouldn't push her on this. But he had to tell her.

Wanted her to know that thing he'd needed to understand. "You've been running for years. You can stop now."

That lit something inside her. "What do you know about it? You're this mega star here in this enormous house with this amazing life and I'm…"

"You're what?"

She pointed to her chest with both hands. Then she crossed them there. "I'm me, Tanner. I'm me."

"*You* are pretty spectacular."

"Roses, Tanner," she said, letting out a long breath. "A whole dozen of them. Please. You don't understand."

But he did. He got it more than most people ever would.

"I think I do," he said. "I really think I do. But I promised you roses, and I won't go back on that. Consider it dropped." He mimed dropping a mic.

"I'm confused." she said, her tone soft but with a low edge. "You said you understand, but how can you understand?"

There may have still been the whole kitchen island between them, but somehow the space didn't feel as far as moments before.

"You left. You ran. I respect that. I did my share of running. But I'm on the flip." He couldn't bring himself to look at her. "I'm also the guy who got left."

His parents went to jail and then to prison, and who knew where they ended up now? They weren't exactly a nuclear family, so none of that mattered. Dan had seen something special in him when he was a teen. Mach, too. Tanner had figured out the hard way that family wasn't made of blood. Family ties came from an active decision to open up. To be authentic with each other. (Something he didn't want to think too hard about because he'd been channeling Linx a whole lot around Sam.)

He was broken when Dan took him in. Dan didn't care that his history was fucked. That his ex, Catiana, wrecked his ability to talk to girls. Or that he used to hit the streets whenever shit got hard.

He couldn't go into it all there in his kitchen with her. That was a lot to lay out tonight. Definitely not something he was prepared to dive into right then.

"You wanna go or you wanna hit the pool?" He tipped his chin to the front door. "You called roses, so it's yours to pick."

"Tanner," Sam reached for his arm.

He stopped. Turned. "Yeah?"

"Thank you." She lifted on her tiptoes and pressed a light kiss to his lips.

He stilled even as his heart beat faster and his body went wired.

The simple kiss was nothing that led to anything else, just a reminder that she heard him. Maybe she didn't understand him. Where he came from. Why he felt this way.

But she heard him.

"Thank you," she said, again.

"For what?" he asked, hoping she got the message he meant to send.

"For the roses," she said, with a small, sad smile. "Thank you for letting me have the roses."

"You feeling like a dip in the pool?" he asked. He hoped like hell she'd say yes.

Chapter Nine
SAMANTHA

TANNER KNOWS. *He knows. He knows.*

The mantra played on repeat in her head, and she itched to leave. But she also made the decision there at his house that she was going to enjoy tonight before planning for tomorrow.

There were times in a woman's life when she had to decide if she was going to sacrifice her happiness for what was right, or go ahead and make a horrible decision because it sounded more fun. Sam would be leaving. She knew this. But for tonight she decided to let herself have that fun.

That's why she picked the stay-and-play-in-the-pool option.

Tomorrow would be the day to start working on the future. Planning her next steps would be the simple part. Actually making the cut and leaving? It'd gotten harder as she'd made connections each place she landed.

Disappearing used to be so simple, but it'd gotten more complex each time. Now, when she ran, she had to clip ties with new people she'd grown to care for—and Ashley wouldn't understand. She hated the upheaval in their friendship when Sam started over.

Sam chewed on her lip. Great Aunt Etta would not be thrilled, either.

Her parents would, once again, resign themselves to another move. Another place to watch her settle.

She slipped off her shirt in Tanner's guest bathroom. His *guest* bathroom was bigger than her whole studio apartment. The designer had continued the black theme into the bathroom, but paired it with burgundy so it looked a little more brothel meets vampire than the rest of the house.

She made quick work of changing. Then she paused at her reflection in the mirror.

"I have to leave again," she said to the reflection. There was no response. She pressed her fingertips against her eyelids.

Tanner left her a plush burgundy towel that matched the bathroom, and she wrapped it around her waist. Then she stopped. Removed it.

A girl ready to have fun in a pool did not need a cover up.

Her lips twitched at the thought as she moved through the kitchen to the patio. Tanner had already headed down to the pool.

There wasn't anything spectacular about his swim trunks —they were the standard variety. Navy blue with some kind of yellow design. His abs, however? She could even tell from the patio that he didn't miss ab day at the gym.

Her mouth went a little dry because other areas of her body had apparently sucked up all the moisture at the sight of shirtless Tanner.

She took her time getting to the pool, letting the stone and grass ground her as she moved his direction.

When she'd approached, he stopped whatever he was doing to the filter and stared, trailing his eyes down her body with clear approval.

That was fine, given she stared right back at him. The ink along his torso was cursive writing. To read it, she'd need to be closer, but it looked to be lines from "Invictus," the poem by William Ernest Henley.

"I'm glad you suggested the pool," he said, staring so hard at her that they may as well toss off their clothes now and get down to business.

She appreciated the clear admiration of her curves. Her body was of the solidly normal variety. Carrots were a favorite, but she also didn't turn down dessert if it looked yummy. Her hips reflected these decisions, and she had no regrets.

"I think I like swimming more than usual today." She gave him a once-over now that she was close enough to see that the design on his trunks wasn't yellow dots.

"You have rubber duckies on your shorts," she announced.

His cheeks pinked and he glanced down. Pulled his mouth to the side. "Yeah."

"I like rubber duckies," she said, light and airy and all it took was this moment for the heavy weight from before—the Sami Jo one in the kitchen—to lessen.

"Sam." He pulled his lips between his teeth.

If she could bottle the way Tanner said her name, she'd do it just so she could take it out sometimes and smile.

She waited for him to keep going but he shook his head.

"Never mind," he said.

"Oh, come on. Whatever you were gonna say, you should say it."

He shook his head.

She wanted to bonk him on the shoulder, but if she did that she'd touch him and if she touched him then there was a solid chance he might touch her, too.

And if they started with that, they'd probably never get in the pool.

That was not acceptable, so she moseyed to the deep end by the diving board and cannonballed her way into the water.

Warmed by the summer sun, the water enveloped her. She came up for air and Tanner stood on the side of the pool, grinning down.

"You gonna tell me what you neverminded?" she asked, treading water, and loving the feel of Tanner's gaze and the water mixed together on her skin.

"You really want to know?" he asked.

"I keep asking," she pointed out.

He thought for a moment. She gave him that time.

"Don't run," he finally said, so softly she nearly didn't hear it.

They were only two words, but they felt like a ton of bricks tugging her into the depths. She dipped under the water, closing her eyes.

What was she supposed to do with "don't run"?

She emerged from the surface. Stared him straight in the eyes and her mouth took over before her brain could process what she was about to say.

"If I run. You can always try to catch me." She'd said it and it was out there. She couldn't shove it back in her mouth, so she made wide eyes at him and said as coyly as she could. "If you can."

She fell backward into the depths and backstroked away.

Tanner took the bait, though he didn't cannonball into the water. He sat on the edge, pushed off with his arms, and slipped into the water.

Then he breaststroked toward her, making excellent time, swimming faster than she could, and catching her around the waist.

Time stilled when his fingers pressed against her bare back, holding her body against his. The slippery skin of their stomachs pressed together and only wet cloth separated his hard length from her flesh.

"Tanner?" she said his name as a question.

He dropped his forehead to hers. "Yeah?"

"Sometimes running is the answer." Carefully, she pushed off from him and backstroked away once more. This time she made it a touch harder for him to catch up.

But he was faster than she was. He caught her, pulled her to him—her back against his front this time. "I spent a long time running. From everything. I know all about it."

Her body begged her to relax against him. To let him tell her all about it. But—

"You don't need to do this," she said, softly.

Make it his personal goal to get her to stop being who she had to be to survive.

His hot breath played against her ear; the strength of his arms cinched around her waist.

"You mean explain why I understand?" he asked.

Well, no, that hadn't precisely been her reasoning.

"I mean, say things you don't want to say," she said, since that sounded way better than a deep dive into heavy emotions.

They should reserve heavy emotions for like the tenth date. Or even the eleventh. Or even the third... since they wouldn't be making it that far.

He turned her in his arms, so they treaded water face to face again. This time he left space between their bodies. A few inches that somehow sparked the desire she'd been nursing even further.

"My parents. They're criminals," he said, wiping out any trace of that desire with a cold bucket of reality.

"They went to prison. I went into the system," he continued.

The warm water seemed to genuinely get colder as they both treaded water inches from each other.

"First, when they got caught? They ran... without me," he said, his voice scratchy like sandpaper.

She reached for his jaw, ran her thumb there down along the curve of his neck.

"They left me," he continued. "Then I ran… a lot. I used to think that if I ran, then the past wouldn't catch me." He closed his eyes. Paused. Opened them. "I was wrong. I ran from a past that wasn't even chasing me."

She pushed away again. Swam to the edge, holding herself up on the ledge with an arm, turning to him.

"Why'd you stop running?" She didn't really want to ask, and yet, she really, really did.

"I realized the thing I was running from wasn't a pair of crappy parents, or a history of bouncing around. The thing I ran from was me." He met her at the wall of the pool. Seemed to think hard about what came next. "That's the funny thing about running from yourself. You can't ever really get away. It's like playing keep away with a shadow. The light will dim, and the shadow will fall into the dark, but then it's there again. Usually when you don't expect it. You know?"

Oh boy, did she.

And what the hell was going on with her? Her situation was nothing like his. It wasn't like her parents left her—they were always there for her. A steady presence when she needed a place to rest from all the running.

They didn't leave her. She always had a place to land, even if she felt like it was a minefield because of the rest of the world.

That's why it was better to stay in the air.

"I'm sorry," she said, meaning every single syllable.

He reached for her hand, linking their fingers together. "What are you sorry for?"

For so much. But mostly, "I'm sorry that happened to you."

He paused for a long beat before adding, "No idea where my parents are. I thought about looking them up once I hit it big, but decided against it. I mean, they wanted nothing to do with me when I was a nobody, so why let them in when I'm finally somebody?"

"You were never a nobody." Of that, she was certain. A guy like Tanner? With a heart like his? Yeah, he was never a nobody.

"I couldn't even open my mouth to speak to anyone I found attractive," he admitted, and his cheeks turned a little red with the admission. "Couldn't form a sentence or a vowel even. But then you showed up and the stakes got higher because I seriously wanted to be able to talk to you."

She used the wall to pull herself closer to him, their legs brushing as they both stayed afloat.

"I walk into a room and there's this girl playing Twister," he said, holding her hostage with his stare. "And she's the most gorgeous person I've ever seen in my life. It's not even the aesthetic—though I seriously appreciate the aesthetic."

"That's a bit of an exaggeration." Still, she smiled at the compliment.

"It's my story. I get to tell it the way I want to tell it." He dropped her hand to push off and float on his back, staring at the sky while the sun set over the Rockies.

"So you walk in the room and my extreme beauty smacks you upside the head," she confirmed as he floated nearby.

The quiet waves of the water soothed. They always did.

"Just like that." He snapped his fingers. "I think, up to that second, I was still running. Just differently. Then you were there, and I didn't want to run anymore."

"So you literally snapped out of it?" That didn't seem super plausible. But what did she know, really?

"Fuck no." He lifted his head to catch her gaze. "I channeled Linx. What *you* got was the Linx special."

"You pretended to be someone else?" she asked. Yes, she was slightly appalled.

He nodded. Tipped his feet down so he was vertical in the water. "It was the only way I could talk."

"You're saying I wasn't even talking to you?" she asked, because wasn't he the one going on about honesty?

"Oh, it was still me," Tanner said. "But it was me pretending to be Linx."

"I think I like Linx. I think I fell for him a little." The admission would only cause pain later, when she left, but it felt good to leave that little nugget behind.

"He's with Becca. Happily so. I guess you're stuck with me."

"I think I like you more, anyway." She reached and squeezed his arm, letting her fingers linger there against the defined muscles.

"Don't tell Linx that. He'll take it as a challenge. Try to convince you he's the shit and then I'll have to up my game and then it'll be a whole competition, and no one will win. Everyone will be pissed. It'll be a thing."

"Why do I think you're not exaggerating?" she asked.

"No idea."

The silence settled around them again. Not uncomfortable or anything that gave her hives, but the baton was clearly hers now. Her time to share since he'd laid out his heart for her.

But she couldn't talk about the song. The fallout. The fear that it'd come back into her life and remind her she wasn't good enough. Even the water couldn't soothe that ache.

"I still talk to my parents," she said, instead. "I think you'd like them. They are super understanding. I mean, they saw the consequences of Sami Jo. They love me and they are happy to keep my secrets. So, I let them."

"Why do I get the feeling there's more?" he asked.

Because... "There's always more."

She swam back to the side of the pool, pulled herself up on the edge to sit there. Her feet stayed in the water, but she leaned back to allow what was left of the sunshine to warm her face.

"You don't have to tell me," he said, swimming to her,

tracing her ankles in the water. "Everything you're running from. Not until you're ready."

That was sweet, but, "I'll probably never be ready."

"Then that's how it is." He pulled himself up beside her, kicking his feet in the pool next to hers.

He reached for her jawline, moved his thumb along the ridge there leading down the column of her throat. "That's how it is."

"Are you for real?" she asked him.

"For you I am." He continued running his thumb against her skin.

Nerve endings she'd forgotten she had fired up at this touch. She shivered.

"I believe you," she said, turning to him, letting her chest brush against his.

"That's enough of a start for me." He didn't move his hand, didn't move in for a make-out session. He only cupped her cheek with his palm.

Her limbs felt weighted—but in a comforting "stay here" way. Could he really be the reason she stayed?

Pfft, they barely knew each other. This was only their first date. Maybe second if they counted the puppet show, which she didn't but he did. So maybe one-point-five dates? That was hardly a solid reason to stick around.

She wanted to trust him, sure, but wanting and doing were two separate things. And trust took time to build. Time they didn't have.

Her throat got thick because deep inside, she'd already decided to give them a try.

"I can't promise that I won't leave," she said. Honesty hurt, but she needed to say this. "But I won't leave right away. I... I think I want a shot at trying this. If you do."

"Fuck yeah," he said, grinning.

She moved her face to kiss his palm. "You don't have to tell me either."

"Tell you what?" He gave her a look like they forgot to put the patty on her hamburger. "I told you everything."

"Whenever you have to pretend to be someone else. You don't need to tell me."

"This whole time we've been talking out here?" he asked. "I've only been me. I think I'll be okay."

"I like you, Tanner. What if we only concern ourselves with the now and the future? The past was just the way we got here." That made so much sense and was so sage.

"I like that," he agreed, staring at her bottom lip.

"Thanks, I made it up myself." She pulled the band from her hair and let the wet strands fall across her shoulders. She toyed with the hair band, keeping her hands busy with the fabric and rubber.

"You know, I do enjoy spending time with you, Sammich," he said, standing and reaching to help her up.

"Oh?" She didn't like the way her nerves all perked to attention at that announcement. Didn't appreciate how her heart beat a little faster and her tummy got squishy like it did when someone offered her a free chocolate cake with lava sauce on her birthday.

"Is that my official nickname?" she asked, a little hair falling over the side of her face. She pushed it back.

"Don't you love it?" he asked, excited and bouncy.

She loved it. Of course she did. "I'll cherish it forever."

They spent the next hours talking about everything and nothing. And when he drove her home, he walked her to the door. She hadn't been walked to her front door in ages. This was a unique front door, but it still counted. She decided on the spot.

"You're not messing with me?" he asked. "You seriously live here?"

She slid her card against the security reader and waited for the door to click open. Then she opened it and let him in.

"Uh-huh. The commute is great." The joke was stupid, but she gathered Tanner wouldn't hold that against her.

He grinned. "I think I'm gonna kiss you now."

"Well, you better." She turned to him, stepping into his arms.

"Oh, yeah?"

"Yeah," she murmured, lifting on her toes and brushing the tip of her nose against his.

With a gentle movement, he moved his mouth to the air above hers, brushing his lips lightly against the rose petal softness of her mouth. He sighed, and that was the end of the gentle. There was heat and passion as his mouth moved against hers.

She'd expected a lot of things from a Tanner lip lock, but the intensity was not one of them. The way he owned every bit of that kiss. And with it, every bit of her. She opened for him, let him move his tongue into her mouth. Encouraged it with her own as she gripped his shoulders and held him tight. He moved his hands to her hair, and she was nothing but putty he could mold.

When he was through and had his fill, he gave her a quick nose kiss before pulling away.

"I'm gonna be in the studio all week with the guys. It'll be stupid intense. But next week we're gonna have a little concert at Brek's Bar. It'll be small. Nothing big. I'd like it if you came." He grinned a sly grin. "Bring Ashley. You can introduce her to the band."

"I know what you did just there."

"What's that?"

"Well, now I have to come, because Ashley will figure out someday that I got an invitation and if I don't go, then she can't go and then she'll never forgive me." Hold up. "Unless she can come without me?"

"Package deal." He touched the edge of her lips with the

pad of his thumb. "You'll need a wingman, and she gets you, yeah?"

"Yes," she agreed.

How he understood that was precisely what she needed was a tad unsettling.

Nearly as unsettling as the quick glimpse of Babushka and Great Aunt Etta slipping off into the darkness of the hallway.

"I think we had an audience."

"Let 'em watch," he said. "It's just us here."

For the first time in a long time, Sam didn't feel alone. And the safety net of Tanner felt like home.

Chapter Ten
TANNER

STUDIO WEEKS KICKED his ass and drug him like an emotional tumbleweed. He helped Bax and Knox with their lyrics. And since he was the guy who knew how to play bass, keyboard and drums, he became the catch-all in the studio for sound checks.

This was on a week without Sam. With Sam? He was still all of that, but also distracted by his cell.

He texted her nonstop.

She texted him right back.

They talked all the time about everything and absolutely nothing.

Flirty phone calls and even a few FaceTime sessions so she could tell him a joke, or he could sing her some of the lyrics he'd been working out with the guys. She helped him work out a few of the issues, but always humming. Never singing.

Twice he popped by late at night when exhaustion hit just to kiss her before he headed home. She'd invited him in both times. But both times he'd been exhausted. He didn't want their first time together to be a quick shag. So he let the building desire simmer.

But he had plans to solve this. And solve it soon.

Tonight they were gonna try out some of the new beats at Brek's Bar. Small audience, good atmosphere, and Brek brought in extra security whenever Dimefront took his stage. Eventually the line outside would wrap around the block, but Brek kept the inside of the bar light on the Tens so the guys could get the feel of the music without insane distraction.

Becca and Courtney had agreed to swing by and pick up Ashley and Sam. Bring them in through the back and show 'em the break room Brek kept available for the band whenever they played. If shit got too intense on the floor, Sam could hang out there.

"Hans," Tanner called the band manager over.

Hans was built as all hell—hitting the gym like a bodybuilder. The guy could be a bouncer if he wasn't the manager of the band. He kept their shit tight. Knew everything about each of them and had a lock on his lips, so nothing accidentally slipped out.

"What's the ETA?" Tanner asked.

"Any minute," Hans said with a wink. He was totally team Sam, even though he'd yet to meet her.

The band worked through the initial sound check before Brek would open the doors.

"Sam never leaves. She's always here, given the amount Tanx talks about her and talks to her. She's got a permanent recliner in my brain," Mach said, then he shook his head as though trying to remove her.

Tanner warmed up his hands doing some drumstick gymnastics—moving them from finger to finger like Val Kilmer in the original Top Gun. Tossing and catching them. The guys eventually stopped giving him shit about his pre-concert calisthenics because they couldn't argue with the results.

Tanner tapped a beat on the snare, adding a hint of bass. "I had to sit and listen to each of you when Knox was losing his mind over Irina, and Bax waxed on about Courtney and how she hated him."

"But not me with Becca," Linx said, plugging in his bass guitar.

"Because you were in the middle of breaking up the band," Bax said, bringing up history that really didn't belong in the present.

Mach slipped a glance at Tanner, shaking his head because this could be a whole Pandora's box.

"Wasn't me who knocked up my sister." Linx shrugged and lifted his eyebrows to Bax.

"I fucking hope not," Mach said.

Just like that, Sam moved through the back of the bar and right into Tanner's vision and he lost all threads of communication with his bandmates.

She stopped at the entrance, seemed to be soaking in the experience.

"She's here," Hans said, with a chin lift toward her.

"Got that." Tanner jumped up from the stool and headed straight to her. He didn't greet her with words, because they'd used up all the words this week.

He tilted her chin up and poured everything he'd missed about her into that kiss. Everything he'd wanted her to know.

In return, she gave it right back.

Which, he should note, he did not mind. Not one bit.

Eventually, they had to separate. Air was important to survival. Also, the doors would open soon, and he'd agreed to staying away, so no one had a Sami Jo sighting.

Brek's Bar was owned by Dimefront's former manager —Brek.

He'd handled Linx, Knox, and Bax through their breakout years before he found love and settled down in Denver with his wife and family. That's why Dimefront picked Denver for their home base. Brek was the glue that held the band together for so long. He was the one who pushed them to give Mach and Tanner a shot.

In so many ways, he *was* Dimefront.

Brek reserved a booth for Ashley and Sam in the back for extra anonymity. There were no phones allowed at these sets. No cameras. Somehow Brek made that happen. The paparazzi lens didn't make it into Brek's Bar unless Brek wanted it to.

Things moved fast after that. The wives all took their usual booth up front. He couldn't see Sam from the stage, but he knew she was there. Knew Brek and Hans had her in their sights, so she'd be okay.

Focusing was hard, but he'd pull through.

They made it through the first two songs and the audience went berserk over Bax's newest creation—a song about being married that was 100 percent about Courtney.

They'd nearly made it through the last refrain when Mach growled into the mic. Funny, that wasn't part of the song, but it worked with the lyrics. They should probably add that in as a permanent addition.

Lead singer Bax threw Mach a look like he'd started singing Baby Shark in the middle of his set. Maybe not so permanent, after all?

Tanner kept his ear on the beat, not letting it drop. Because Mach might growl like that into the mic and shit stayed together, but if Tanner dropped the beat, it'd all fall apart.

He didn't expect Sam to seek him out right after the first set. That'd put her in the light, and he got she wasn't ready for that. Not yet.

"She good?" he asked Hans when he slid back into the Dimefront booth. He had gone on a Sam check for Tanner.

"I added security," Hans grumbled. "And tossed out two guys who kept visiting their table. You're welcome."

"Thanks." Tanner leaned forward to check out the back, to see if he could catch a glimpse.

Hans shook his head. "Keep doing that and you'll blow the operation."

Tanner lifted his hands. "Fine. I'm gonna go hit the bar. Anybody want anything?"

"He's not hitting the bar," Bax said, arm draped around Courtney.

"Nope," Courtney agreed.

They weren't wrong. He was gonna head to the bar, see if he couldn't catch a better glimpse of Sam.

He nearly made it to the bar top—

"Tanner?"

He'd know that voice anywhere. His body seemed stuck in some kind of stasis loop of uncertainty.

Catiana.

No idea what he expected when he turned to face her, but his tongue held stiff against the roof of his mouth and his cheeks tingled from the blood flow there.

"Surprise!" She made jazz hands beside her face.

The ache in his chest when he used to think about her dissolved into… nothing. They'd been friends first. She'd known him before his parents went away. The shit that happened after? The shit with her? It'd affected him more than he'd like to admit—hell, her actions had a direct correlation to his inability to stay a normal color when talking to women.

None of that mattered anymore, and yet his brain went foggy and his mouth wouldn't work.

"You're not going to say anything?" she asked, nudging his arm with her fist. "How great is it to see me again?"

"What are you doing here?" he stammered.

She moved in, taking some of his personal space.

That was no good. He tried to step back, but the wall of people waiting in line at the bar was too much.

"You are a hard guy to pin down," she said. "I've been trying to catch up with you for forever."

He frowned. "Why?"

He'd put himself right up in front of the world.

"I know we left things bad," she said, and he knew she meant it. Once upon a helluva long time ago, he'd known her better than anyone. "I'm sorry about it. The whole thing. I really am sorry. It's just… I miss you. I miss us. You're my guy, Tanner."

He was not. Not anymore.

"No. You don't get to be here." Mach moved into their makeshift circle, taking Tanner's right flank and crossing his arms.

"Mach." Catiana grinned like seeing an old friend. "Always good to see you again."

"Yeah, no." Mach shook his head. "Not so great." He growled again.

"Is she the reason for the whole growl thing earlier?" Tanner asked, the words coming smoother than before, but still stilted.

Mach nodded.

"It's just me." Catiana held up her hands in mock surrender. "We all know each other."

"That's the problem," Mach said, before Tanner could add anything else.

"She's just saying hi," Tanner said. Then he met Catiana's eyes. "Now she can move along."

And so could he.

"I wanted to tell you I'm sorry, Tanner." Catiana sounded apologetic, which was nice, but years too late. "I've been trying to say I'm sorry since it happened."

He hadn't been in the mood to take her calls after she betrayed him with a guy in a shark costume. Hadn't responded to any of her messages about messing up and needing a second chance.

"I tracked you down to tell you that I am so sorry," she said.

Tanner wasn't sure what to do what that. She'd hurt him worse than she would ever realize.

"Great. That's settled. Time's up. Time to go." Mach tapped his watch.

"Are you going to let him kick me out?" she asked. Flashing her smile at Tanner. She used to toss him that same grin and he'd do anything for her.

Now things had changed. The same and yet different enough that he could see she didn't hold the same power anymore.

"Tanner." Mach shook his head. "Time to take out the trash."

Tanner tried to move his tongue, but it wouldn't budge. "I—"

Catiana's expression fell, her lips falling from a grin to a frown. "Mach, really?"

"He met someone else," Mach said. "Tanner here has someone new. Let him have that without all your bullshit."

She frowned a little more. That was all she gave away. Tanner hadn't shared air with her for ages, so he was a little out of practice, but was she disappointed?

That would be ridiculous, because if she was truly sorry then she should want him to be happy with someone else.

"I used to know exactly what you were thinking." Somehow he found the words.

"I know, right?" She flashed him that smile that used to bring him to his knees.

"Now, I don't care what you're thinking."

"You got company watching you," Mach said, with a slight tick of his head toward the direction of Sam's back booth.

"I gotta go," Tanner said. He'd already began moving toward Sam's booth. "Enjoy the rest of the concert."

He took a pit-stop and hit the john to get himself together. He stepped into the hallway and Sam stood right there, alone. Waiting for him.

"Hey, handsome," she said with a giant grin.

The moment was theirs. There was no Catiana. No past. Just the present and a hope for the future.

He took four giant strides to her and pressed a light kiss against her lips that turned to more.

She welcomed it, hands in his hair and her tongue tracing his. The kiss could've gone on for ages, but he had to call it so they didn't get caught. When he broke the seal, they were both panting, breathing hard.

She stepped backward, pushing the door to the ladies' room open behind her. "Excellent set."

"See you after?" he asked, having no problem at all finding the words.

She nodded. "After."

His cheeks heated, and he was pretty sure he had turned cherry tomato red again. This time, he didn't hate it. No, this time he welcomed it.

Nothing else mattered but Sam and the band. Everything else was simply unnecessary noise.

"Tanner." Catiana caught him again as he headed to the stage.

He got the creepy-crawly ants-on-skin feeling. Didn't dig it.

He sighed, turned.

"*That's* your girl?" Catiana asked, and the intensity of her question did not sit well. "That's her?"

"Sam," he said, nodding. "Her name is Sam."

"You know who that is, right?" Catiana said, whispering. "That's Sami Jo." She hummed the intro to Sami Jo's song.

"No," he said the word too fast, with too much emphasis.

Catiana blinked hard, as though shocked at the vehemency of his response.

"I swear it is, Tanner. She looks exactly the same and her name is Sam. That is Sami Jo," Catiana persisted. "I would bet money on it."

"No," he said again. "Stop."

"I get to submit a sighting." She bounced and clapped her hands quietly. "I've always wanted to do that."

How was this the girl he used to care so much for? They'd been so tight for so long. How was this the same person?

"Don't tell anyone," he begged. Yeah, he begged. Didn't turn red. Didn't stumble over the words.

"This is huge," Catiana said, and she had the same spark in her eyes she'd had at prom right before—no. Wouldn't think of that.

"I appreciate you came here to apologize," he said, swallowing all those years of emotion. Forcing the words to come smoothly. "Your apology means a lot." Not a lie. "It'd mean even more if you could let this go."

"Tanner." She gave him wide eyes. "This is big."

"Please."

"We used to sing that song!" she practically shouted, then she started singing the damn song.

He remembered. Remembered singing the song and remembered singing it with her. And, God help him, making fun of Sami Jo right along with the rest of the world.

"Don't," he said, rubbing his head.

"This is her," Mach said, moving toward them with Hans.

Of course, Mach was protecting Tanner the only way he knew how. Looping Hans in to keep the monsters away.

"I'm going to have to ask you to leave," Hans said in that eerily calm tone he used when he was about to get his way.

Tanner wasn't going to step in and help. No, it was time for Catiana to go.

"Bye," he said,.

"Okay." Catiana raised her hands and then she walked away. Stopping once to glance back at Tanner.

How was Catiana once a girl who used to be his every-thing, and now a woman with the power to ruin it all?

He paused. Willing a rewind on the night.

"You're Tanner," a woman said from beside him.

He turned. "You're Ashley."

"We get to meet." She didn't look happy about that.

He tried to shake the ick of Catiana. "Yeah. Sorry. I'm uh…"

"I heard your friend singing a familiar song," she said.

He froze.

"So I have a question, Tanner," Ashley said, stepping closer. "And that question is, who the fuck was that?"

Chapter Eleven
SAMANTHA

ASHLEY LOOKED like she'd eaten a whole plate of truck stop tacos and they didn't sit well. It seemed like she wanted to be having fun, but inside, it wasn't a good time.

"You okay?" Sam asked, sliding into the booth.

"Uh-huh." Ashley frowned, reached for her Jack and Coke, took a big swallow. Then another. "I'm fine."

"Sorry I took a minute." Sam pursed her lips. But this was a good thing, so she could tell Ashley. Ashley would be over the moon. "Mom had an emergency with her new fern she wanted to troubleshoot with me."

Ashley stopped mid-swallow, blinking hard. "From the bathroom?"

"I stepped out back."

"You know you don't leave the building without telling your wingman," Ashley said, her forehead lines creasing deeper.

This was not the response she'd expected from her best friend.

"You've got to watch out for yourself." Ashley fiddled with her straw, swirling the chunks of ice clockwise, then counterclockwise. "I just... I'm worried about you."

"Well, you worry about me. I need a drink." Sam smacked the table. "I'm gonna get one. You need another?"

"Always," Ashley said, going for another long pull.

The band started their next set, and Sam let the music in. This was the song Tanner had been fighting with. She'd helped him build the bridge and—

There it was. They'd done good.

When she was younger, that was the time when she'd craved the spotlight. Wanted to be in the middle of the show.

Tonight? She sort of wished that had worked out for her. But she couldn't think that far back. Instead, she let herself re-live the hallway kissing session. Tanner could kiss and if he could kiss that well, he probably did other things with the same amount of attention to detail.

Since the band was doing their thing, there didn't seem to be much of a line at the bar. Still, Brek was at the other end, so she pulled herself up on one of the bar stools and waited.

"You are Sammich, huh?" Brek, bartender and owner of Brek's Bar, asked, heading her way and tossing a napkin down in front of her.

"I see you've been talking to Tanx," she said with what she hoped was a welcoming grin and not a maniacal smile.

Brek grinned back. So she probably did okay. "Yeah."

Brek had a whole Thor, God of Thunder thing going on. He probably lifted weights almost as much as Hans, but he had blond hair. Hans kept his hair cut super close, and Brek probably couldn't remember the last time he got a haircut.

"What can I get for you?" he asked.

"Another Jack and Coke for my friend. Chardonnay for me?" she asked. "With a little club soda?"

Her order earned her a lopsided grin from Brek.

Was that a weird order? It's what she wanted, and this was a bar. He didn't say they didn't have it. Ugh. Maybe she should've just ordered two Cokes. But she didn't want one, so there ya go...

"On it," he said, pulling a bottle from a mini-fridge under the counter and making her wine spritzer magic happen right in front of her.

"Not many people order Chard at a dive bar."

"It looks like they're missing out then." Because the brand he snagged wasn't a bad one.

"My wife doesn't like much else. But she digs a good Chard spritzer."

"I think I like your wife," Sam said.

"She'd like you, too."

"You used to manage Dimefront?" Sam asked. Her small talk skills weren't sharp, but they weren't nonexistent. Perhaps it was time to sharpen them up.

"I did." Brek slid the glass to her and said nothing else.

She was way out of practice with small talk for anyone under the age of sixty-five, so she didn't push any harder when he didn't keep going.

No need to make it weird. She started to get off the stool, head back to Ashley.

"Tanner's into you," Brek said, and his face was a void. How did he not move any muscles at all?

"I'm into him," Sam admitted. She ran her fingertip along the rim of the glass. "He's amazing."

"Tanner is a great guy," Brek said. "He deserves the best, you know?"

She wanted to crack a joke about how he needed to go find someone who wasn't her, but her heart wasn't in it.

"Are you the best, Sam?" he asked, and the way he asked it made her want to fight for Tanner. Fight for what they could have if they both allowed it.

"I want to be." She did.

Brek nodded like that was enough of an answer for him.

"Is there anything I should know?" she asked. "Any crazy exes I need to watch out for?"

"Nah." Brek shook his head. "Tanner is an open book when he trusts a person. I'm gettin' that he trusts you."

"That's a really nice compliment," she said. "Thank you."

"I suppose the question is, do you trust him?" Brek asked, continuing on.

Why did he wait until she was off the stool to feel chatty? Ugh.

"I want to." She was there, after all.

Brek nodded, seemed like he wanted to say something else. But there was another customer and Ashley still waited for her and her drink.

To describe the rest of the evening would take one word: odd. Maybe even awkward. At first, Ashley wasn't herself. Two more Jack and Cokes and then she didn't seem to care who she was.

The band finished the set, and they all headed back to the cul-de-sac where Tanner and Mach's place was situated. But they didn't go there. They went to Bax and Courtney's house so they could be where baby Harley slept.

Bax and Courtney had a pretty epic backyard. No pool, but they had an in-ground trampoline and a pirate ship. There was a fire pit with chairs around it and everyone settled in, but definitely didn't settle down.

Becca and Ashley hosted a dance party on the deck of the pirate ship, and they even got Hans up there to do part of Meghan Trainor's latest TikTok dance. Courtney filmed it, but she swore to everyone she would not post it online. This was purely for scientific purposes to prove that Hans could move his hips.

Tanner jumped right in, but Sam wasn't ready for that kind of thing with everyone watching. Especially when there was video involved.

"You're not gonna dance?" Mach asked, dropping to sit in the Adirondack chair next to Sam's.

"No." She shook her head.

"Because you can't dance or you don't wanna?" He tilted the bottle of beer to his lips.

"Oh, I can dance." She could. She hadn't danced in ages, but she could.

"A chick showed up at the concert tonight," he said, out of the blue.

Her small talk skills might be off, but that was a weird thing to say. "Me?"

"No." He seemed to weigh his words more carefully than usual. "I don't know how much Tanner's said, and bro code means I can't get in the middle of it."

"What are you talking about?" She turned in the chair to face him more fully.

"I'm just gonna tell you a story, 'kay? Let's pretend it's not a real story. It's only a story."

"But it is an actual story," she confirmed, so she had a better idea of what the heck he was going on about.

"I'm not admitting to anything."

"Fair enough." Fine. *Let's just see where this goes.*

"There was a kid with a lot of baggage I used to know."

Sam nodded. "Tanner?"

"Let's call him Banner."

"Right."

"Banner was super into this chick. They'd been buddies forever and, finally, they became more than that. Each other's firsts in everything, as far as I know. Not like I did too much digging, if you get my drift." He winked.

A little nugget of anxiety spirals settled in her stomach. She nodded again, but didn't love the idea of Tanner with anyone else. The jealousy was unreasonable. She'd had other guys in her bed before. She totally expected he'd been with other people, too.

"They're at Prom—Banner and… this girl." He pursed his lips. "His parents just went down the river for thirty plus.

You name it, they'd done it at some point. Arson, theft, dealing, too many charges to keep track."

"Okay." That apprehension snuggled deeper in her belly.

"They're at prom, and swear to fuck this matters, but some blowhard decided the theme should be Sharknado."

She laughed a little at that, grateful it relieved some of the tension in her tummy.

"Yeah, sounds funny. I know. I was there, but it wasn't my idea."

"So this girl and Banner…"

"He's all into her. He's ready to talk about marriage and babies and all the happily-ever-after bullshit. But she's… not a great person. Not the person he thought she was. She pretended to be with him. Halfway through prom, she broke it off. Got caught getting it on with a guy in a shark costume on the football field." He stared at his beer. "Yeah. It's fucked up."

"I don't like this story," Sam said, crossing her arms across her chest.

"Tanner was a wreck," Mach said, deep in thought.

She didn't correct him about the name. Didn't seem like the time.

"He didn't blame her. I fucking blamed her. But he blamed the other guy. We had a foster dad who gave a shit, and when Tanner took off after prom, Dan sat him down and explained all the reasons he shouldn't go. Then he started a band for us. Dan's a mechanic and he taught Tanner and me to fix cars. Just in case we ever needed a trade. But he saw that love of music in Tanner, and he turned it to a rag-tag band. That's how I got started with music. Turned out, I didn't hate it."

"Why are you telling me this?" Sam asked, since it was definitely not the thing someone usually shared with a guy's new… what was she? Girlfriend? Girl. Friend? Make-out buddy?

"After prom, Catiana reached out to me. Asked me to help patch things up. That she'd made a big mistake. But Tanner couldn't talk to a pretty girl without getting embarrassed. Without losing his words." He tipped his beer to his lips. "She wrecked him, so I told her to take a hike. Did what I could to protect my brother."

He probably pretended to be someone else…

"You came along, and I hate that you've got the pressure, but you have the power to fuck him up as much as Catiana." Mach leveled her with a stare. "I'm asking you don't do it."

That was… that was a lot. Heavy even. And it felt like that type of sharing required something back from her.

But she didn't really have anything to give. Except. Well, there was the one thing—

"I'm Sami Jo." As the words passed her lips, she wished she could stuff them back inside.

Mach paused, then he reeled back like someone had punched him.

"The fuck?" He stared at her. Grabbed his phone and turned on the flashlight, pointing it at her.

"Please don't take my picture," she said, swallowing a whole lump because she misread this. This was bad.

"Holy shit." Mach set his phone aside. "I won't do that. I'm not a dude in a shark suit."

"I don't want to hurt him," Sam assured. "At all. You should know that I've got a lot of baggage, too."

"Don't fuck a shark on the football field in front of him? Yeah?" Mach asked. "That's what I was going for, but I did not expect this."

"I swear I won't do that. The football field thing." Because ew… and ew. "Can you *not* tell anybody about my alter ego?"

He held out his pinky.

"What's that?" She asked.

"Pinky swear. Can't break the bond of a pinky swear. You

won't fuck a shark, and I won't tell a soul." He glanced at his outstretched pinky.

She linked her pinky with his as though it were a solemn oath between the two of them. "Tanner knows. About me."

"Figured as much." He tilted the bottle up to his lips. "But that's not my business because I know nothing."

"Okay." Good, all settled.

"Catiana showed up tonight," he said.

This time, it was her turn to reel backward.

"That's why I'm tellin' you this," Mach said. "He says it's not fucking with him, 'cause he's got you. But I know him better than that, ya know?"

"She was there?" Sam asked, a little loud, but no one heard given they were all dancing on a pirate ship.

"Uh-huh. Hans saw her out. She wanted to get close to Tanner, but she lost all claims on him on a football field."

This woman was there tonight?

"I would like her email address," Sam announced. "Does Hans have it?"

Mach scrunched his eyebrows together. "Huh?"

"So I can sign her up for loads of spam for things she doesn't need. Erectile dysfunction pills, and AARP, and the *Men's Prostate Health Journal*. They send more promotional emails than you'd expect." There were certain things she'd learned from her employment working with the elderly. "I mean, who does that to a person?" She tossed her hand toward Tanner. "Someone like Tanner doesn't deserve that. And whoever does that to him? Deserves to have their email spammed."

"Are you being real with me?" He didn't seem to believe it.

Clearly he didn't know her well enough because she was dead serious. Sam wasn't one to resort to violence, but what could this person possibly want other than to screw Tanner over again? This was the kind of person who made Sami Jo the laughingstock.

"I've never been more real," she assured.

Mach barked a laugh, full-on hysterics coming from him. "I think I like you, Sammich."

"Ha." Funny, though, she didn't mind that he called her the nickname. "Tanx."

"It's fucking perfection, I tell ya." He lifted his beer bottle to clink against her water bottle.

Her phone buzzed in her pocket. She glanced at the screen. "Oh, damn."

"What?" he asked.

"I have to go to work. Babushka fell again." She breathed out a long, tired breath.

"She hurt?" Mach asked, clearly concerned. "You need backup?"

"No, but I'm going to send her a crap load of Candy Crush requests on Facebook later." Sam stood, not ready to go say goodbye to Tanner just yet, but understanding she had to go see what Babushka was manipulating this time.

"Sam?" Mach asked

"Yep?" She turned back.

"I like you, Sam," he said.

Tanner came up behind her and wrapped his arms around her shoulders. "What'd I miss?"

"Babushka did it again," Sam said, glancing over her shoulder at him. "I have to go back."

"Already?"

Unfortunately, yes. She and Babushka needed to have a talk about timing and she needed some time to unpack all the tea Mach had spilled to her.

Chapter Twelve
SAMANTHA

BABUSHKA HADN'T HURT HERSELF. That hadn't been an enormous concern, but Sam continued to worry that if she kept faking, then someday it'd be real, and no one would believe her. She didn't want that person to be her.

The short version of the night before?

After she and Mach talked, something went down with two residents that no one wanted to discuss. But the crew had no issue vague-posting on social media about it. All that together created a perfect storm where the night manager quit without notice.

Babushka somehow felt like the solution was to toss herself on the floor. Again.

Honestly, Sam was getting a constant headache. She loved these residents, but she had to start a whole burner TikTok account, simply to monitor the elderly in her care. They started tracking TikTok challenges and swear to hell if they ate laundry pods? She was going to quit, too.

Unfortunately, she'd succumbed to social media searching, and there was a hashtag-SamiJoTok. Of course, there was. The thought made her insides twisty.

"The important thing to remember about relationships is

not to spend too much time apart," Babushka said. She studied the chessboard on Sam's wall as she supervised pre-date prep. "Also, don't spend too much time together."

"That makes things complicated, no?" Sam asked, keeping only half an ear on Babushka's advice.

"It is balance," Babushka assured, like the wise woman she sorta was. (Sometimes, when she wasn't on the floor.)

There was no balance in whatever this thing was with Tanner. There was only *them*.

The social media challenges were extra popular and #purplepeony had trended more than once. Sam tried to figure out how to work it in as a responsible activity and not a free-for-all. So far, no dice.

"I promise you vill not be interrupted tonight," Babushka assured, crossing her heart. "Everyone vill be on best behavior."

Sam finished up her eyeliner, dabbing the edges with a Kleenex. She did her best, but makeup wasn't really her gig. Lip gloss and mascara? Easy. Eyeliner? Ugh.

Since she was now on social media to keep tabs on her residents, she checked out a few tutorial videos. Those had helped, so it didn't look like a toddler did the application.

"Does this look okay?" Sam asked, stepping back from the mirror so Babushka could look.

She moved to Sam, gripped her chin and got right up in her face to peer. "It vill do."

Well, that was better than nothing.

"Vhat is the vardrobe?" Babushka asked.

Sam laid out the blue dress she'd picked. Tanner said they weren't going out, which was great because Sam didn't really want to deal with more people. But she still wanted to look nice. To let him know she'd made the effort.

"It vill do," Babushka said, her eyebrows furrowing together. "He vill like."

Sam had bought it specifically for tonight. She'd hit some

late-night online shopping and had it delivered. So much easier than going incognito to the store like she used to do.

"This is fifth date, yes?" Babushka asked, feeling the material of the summer dress. "You shave the kitty for him? Or go natural?"

Okay. First, what? And second… *what*?!

"No, this isn't the fifth date." How did one even count dates when you talked all the time? "And my kitty is no one's business but mine." *Thankyouverymuch.*

"If it's not the fifth date, then you do not slap sheets. Sends vrong message." Babushka said this like she ordered a tuna sandwich.

"Um…" Sam had sort of been hoping for a smidge of hanky panky. "Why? Isn't it the third date rule?"

Technically, they were at the fourth date. And wasn't that the acceptable timeline? First, the puppet show. (She'd count it if it meant they could just get on with it already.) Second, mozzarella sticks at his house. Third, the Dimefront show and the afterparty.

"No, it's fifth date these days," Babushka said, going back to study the chessboard.

"I don't think so," Sam assured.

The math wasn't mathing. Unless if she counted the last date as two—since they'd gone to two locations, that was still considering the puppet theater as date number one. Definitely a stretch. But then they'd be at five. If the fifth date rule was an actual rule, they would simply have to fudge the math, because she wasn't in the past anymore. And in the future? She wasn't celibate. Not with Tanner.

"Vhen is the last time you vent on date?" Babushka asked. "Vith a different man."

"I don't feel the need to answer that," Sam countered. It'd been a while. What could she say? Dating had not exactly been a priority.

"So you do not know. Things change." Babushka

shrugged. "You keep up vith change. Or you bury his bone on the vrong date and send all the vrong message."

"You're telling me you never have sex before date number five?" Sam didn't want to ask. She really shouldn't ask. This was an inappropriate question. "Never mind. Pretend I didn't ask."

"I am an old voman. Rules do not apply after seventy."

"That seems convenient," Sam said under her breath.

She blocked out most of the rest of Babushka's chatter, but she caught a little talk about his sixth finger and the importance of treating it right. So, yeah.

"Being vulnerable is the most vital. Be vulnerable through the fear," Babushka rambled on.

Sam paused, picking out her shoes. "Hold up. What did you say?"

'Cause that sounded like it could be good advice.

"Use caution when playing with the sixth finger. It spits," Babushka said.

No. Gah. "After that."

"Be vulnerable and do it afraid if you have to. It is key."

See, now that was the type of grandmotherly advice that came in handy.

Sam sat on the edge of the bed to think it through. She *was* scared. And she didn't like to be vulnerable.

Every time she'd been vulnerable, she'd run. But now she didn't want to leave.

Where did that leave her?

"That's really intense," she said.

"The best relationships begin vhen you are scared. Not too scared, but enough that it's a challenge to be exposed. That's vhen you know it's the good stuff. Because you open up and you do it scared."

"You really saved that nugget for after the sixth finger, huh?" Sam asked.

Do it scared. She could do it scared. She could be Sam and she could stay and she could do it scared.

"He vill be here soon. You vear that? Or that?" Babushka gestured to the dress on the bed.

"That," Sam agreed. She moved to the bathroom to change, fluffing her hair, and adding a bit more lip gloss.

"Babushka," she said as she opened the bathroom door while loading up an extra lip gloss in her bag. "Thank you for being here."

"Babushka took off," Tanner said.

Sam paused. Slowly, she glanced up from her purse. Tanner sat on the little love seat in her makeshift living room.

They both sort of stared at the other, drinking in the moment.

"She let me in," he said, cracking the silence. "Before she left."

"Of course she did." Sam moved toward him. Not that it was too many steps because he met her halfway.

His fingers moved to the sleeve of her dress. "I like this."

Her blood swished quicker, like she was in that moment of disbelief when a person learned they'd won the lottery.

"I have a question," she asked.

His hands were now at her jaw and she was pretty certain what came next would be him kissing the stuffing out of her. Good thing she packed extra lip gloss.

"How many dates have we been on?" she asked.

He thought about that, counting it out on his fingers. "Three, I think. Why does it matter?"

Well, damn.

"Sam. Why?" he asked.

"No reason." She kept her smile in place, but deep down she understood she'd have to fudge some numbers tonight.

<hr>

Chapter Thirteen
TANNER

<hr>

TANNER HAD PLANS, and they didn't involve anyone but him and Sam. It'd been a helluva week in the studio. He needed a break.

So he planned to do something he never did—show Sam his secret clubhouse. The place most like home to him. The house he shared with Mach was a spot to sleep, hang out with his friends, and exist. But this was the place he came to be just… Tanner.

"What is this?" Sam asked as the elevator doors pinged open on his floor. Her hand in his, he led her down the hallway to the door of his apartment.

"My apartment," he said, sliding a key in the lock and pushing the door open.

"You have an apartment?" She followed him inside. "Your fancy mansion isn't big enough for all your stuff?"

"Har," he said, flicking on the lights. "I didn't want the interruptions of my house, you know?"

She nodded.

The place wasn't special, just a standard one-bedroom flat with a living room, bath, and kitchen. Secondhand furniture that came with the purchase, but he had bought a new bed because… he wasn't really sure why. He had no problem sleeping in a hotel bed, so it wasn't that he wanted a bed only *he'd* slept in.

A console piano wasn't easy to bring up the elevator, so he'd decided to just have a keyboard. And the four different guitars that lined the wall by the television all had special meaning.

One was his first guitar. The other three were gifts.

A drum set would have made sense to bring in, given his profession, but there wasn't room. Also, he didn't want the neighbors to hate him.

"Sometimes I need a spot where nobody will show up unannounced, you know?" He squeezed her hand and then moved to the kitchen to turn on the lights there.

She traced her fingertip along the edge of his guitar where it perched on the stand near the sofa. Then played a few notes on the keyboard.

He didn't hate it. He enjoyed it. The having her here.

He moved behind her, putting his fingers on the keys beside hers. Playing her three notes and then adding a few more to them to blend together.

The edge of her cheek brushed against his, her fingers moved over the keys, and she added another few bars to the song they made together.

A few more notes from him and a handful of bars from her and the song practically stitched itself together.

"How do you keep everyone away?" she asked. "From your apartment."

"I don't tell them I've got it." He lifted a shoulder, then moved away to pull off his jacket.

There wasn't much special about the apartment. Not in a super desirable location, but in a good enough neighborhood that he didn't worry about his car getting keyed when he pulled into the parking garage. The thing was, every inch of the 600 square feet belonged to him. No one would accidentally walk in, throw a pool party, or stop by unannounced.

"Only Dan knows it's mine. He suggested I grab a spot for myself when I was struggling with the whole privacy thing. A place to get creative without the nonsense of the world." An apartment Tanner could escape and just be. "I put it in his name, so no one tracks it to me. Just Dan. He's the only one who knows."

"Now I do, too." She grinned. "You're not worried about me showing up unannounced? Surprise!"

"You're the only one I'd want to show up unannounced." He pulled open the fridge. "There's iced tea, wine, and beer if you want anything. I bought these mixed drink cans, too. The lady at the liquor store said they're good." He pulled his lips between his teeth. "Or there's champagne."

"You stocked up for me." This wasn't a question, but a statement.

"Wouldn't be a clubhouse if I didn't keep it stocked. There's also all kinds of junk food in the pantry."

"Clubhouse?" she asked, flicking her hair over her shoulder.

He wanted to reach over, touch it, run his fingers through it. He didn't, because once he started touching her tonight, he worried he wouldn't be able to stop. "I don't really live here. So it fits."

"Don't you have to have a club for it to be a clubhouse?" she asked.

"I guess you're my club now," he said it, and he meant every word.

"That's oddly sweet." She moved forward, running her hands up his arms to his shoulders, then lifting on her tiptoes to press her lips to his.

"That's me. Oddly sweet." He moved his mouth against hers, appreciating the way she melted into his body, allowed him to take control. Things heated quickly, per the norm.

His breaths came quick, his blood thrummed fast, and he was so hard for her he could've burst right through the denim.

He pressed her against the refrigerator, and she moved her leg to make room for the thick length of him to press her core. His erection strained against his fly, practically reaching for her.

He lifted her, and she wrapped her legs around his waist. That worked.

Her skin flushed red, she moaned deep in her throat, and he wanted her. Wanted this. But not here. Not at the fridge.

A guy could have refrigerator foreplay, but the main event should be more special than that. At least, that's what he figured.

Holding her gaze with his, he set her down, slowed things between them. Took care to inhale, count to five. Exhale, count to five.

He nearly did it, too. Nearly got control. But the defenseless gleam in her eyes practically brought him to his knees as it steamrolled any willpower he had left.

"Tanner," she said his name like a plea.

"I've got you," he assured, as his hand moved to her neckline, then down, pushing the cups of her bra aside so his thumbs could trace over the pert buds of her nipples.

He kissed her again, while he toyed with her breasts. He did a nip and twist at the same time that practically made her purr. Her arms gripped him tighter, and they should probably go slower, but he didn't want to.

"You okay?" he asked, pressing himself against her thigh for a touch of relief, even if it was only an insignificant blip of what his body craved.

"Uh-huh." She reached for his hand, sliding it from her breast. "Why'd you stop?" Then she stilled. Dropped his hand. "Is this because it's not the fifth date? Ugh."

So he was lost here. Totally lost.

Resting his hand against her hip, he pressed light kisses to her mouth. "The fifth date?"

She reached for his shirt and pulled it up to trace his abs with her fingertips. Then she went down to his waistband and, shit, he wouldn't make it to the bedroom if they kept this up. Refrigerator sex, it'd have to be.

"I got informed that I'm not supposed to put out until the fifth date," she said.

That was stupid. Who put numbers on shit like this?

"Do you want to 'put out'?" he asked, stumbling a little over the last two words. Partly because it just felt wrong, and partly because she rubbed the length of him beneath the denim.

"Is that not clear?" She gave him a thick squeeze and enough was enough.

He kissed her again to take back the control, then as their tongues tangled he lifted the hem of her dress and pushed her underwear aside.

"Three dates, four hundred and twenty-five text messages, five video calls, and a dozen or more phone calls," he said against her mouth. "I think we've earned this."

She made a low moan of relief in the back of her throat.

"Yeah?" he asked, mouth still against hers.

"Yes," she agreed, moving to position herself better over his fingers.

Now that? That he liked.

Using one finger, then two, he slid them inside her warm, wet center. She moaned against his mouth and his whole body heated. Not in a cherry tomato uncomfortable way, but goodness wrapped up in Sam hot.

"God, you're gorgeous," he said against her mouth, letting his lips linger against hers as she moved against his fingers, setting the rhythm. She was roses and vanilla and honey—

"Tanner," she said with a gasp.

He moved his fingers up to the bundle of nerves between her thighs, rubbing first and then tapping.

She made a mewl sound that he wanted to hear again, and again, and again. "Keep doing that."

He kept doing that.

"What was that you were saying about a fifth date?" he asked, still tapping, reveling with how her breasts heaved against his chest. Not even caring they were doing this against the fridge.

"I'm there," she whispered, and he increased the friction of his hand. Pressed more kisses to her lips, her cheeks, her neck. Vanilla and honey and Sam… Her body responded to each of his movements, her eyes glazed, and she whispered, "Yes," like a mantra, over and over. "Yes. Yes." She heaved a deep sigh. "Yes."

He did a flick and gentle twist move that made her gasp against his neck, then bit him like she'd gone feral. And the firecracker she was, she went off—gripping his shoulders and making that same mewling sound against his shoulder.

He held her up with one arm, stroking her inner thighs with the other while she slid down orgasm mountain.

"So gorgeous," he said as she came back to herself, and the glazed eyes dissolved into clarity.

Then she grinned. Full-on grinned. "You're very good at that."

He pulled away, only enough to ensure she had her bearings back. She let him.

"Hold that thought?" he asked. There was only a whisper of a space between them. "I have something I want to show you."

A quick kiss on the tip of her nose and he gripped her hand, moving toward the bedroom. He'd come by earlier and loaded the fridge, grabbed some grub for later, and then he'd prepped for Sam.

Two oversized bouquets of roses from The Flower Pot sat

on each bedside table, and he'd had Dan buy out all the candles in the general Cherry Creek area. They now lined the edges of the bedroom.

Without the candles lit, or the light on, the room was all shadows and darkness. But he'd fix that.

He turned, so they were face to face and kissed her again, maneuvering her closer to the bed. Once he got her settled on the pillows, he knelt above her.

There weren't any words between them, but the silence sat comfortably, not awkwardly. Pulling his shirt up and over his head, he tossed it aside. Then he kissed her again, because he could, and she let him. Something had shifted, though. Something good. Something that made him seriously glad he'd bought this apartment, because this was safety for him and for Sam. A place for only them.

Standing, he shucked his pants, so he was only wearing boxer briefs. Then he grabbed the box of matches and lit the candles he'd prepared.

He lit them all, the glow of fire and the scent of burning wax, and Sam gave him the hope of a home.

Yeah, that'd do nicely.

"Tanner?" she said his name, the bedding shuffling with her movements.

The warm glow definitely created the vibe he wanted. That vibe being special. Sam should know how special she was.

The last match burned down to his thumbnail. He blew on it, extinguishing the flame.

Then he turned to her.

She'd ditched the dress and wore only a black bra with red panties. He'd been hard this whole time. When she came on his hand, he thought his body might betray him and he'd join her.

But now? Looking at her like this? He wished he could freeze time and memorize every sensation, every movement.

He moved to her, and she opened her legs to him, let him kiss and nip. Gripping both sides of his face, she pressed their foreheads together. "You didn't have to do all of this."

"I wanted to." He unclipped her bra, letting it fall open. Then he moved it aside. Then he kissed from her neck down to her collarbone, up the heavy curves of her breasts, to lick her nipples. One and then the other.

Then he continued kissing down her belly, over and down to the center of her. He tasted and nuzzled and brought her almost to the edge again. Stopping before the point of no return.

"You feelin' special?" he asked.

"Yes," she said, her hands still in his hair, her head tossed back to press into the pillows.

He pulled off his boxers and reached in the nightstand's drawer, snagging a condom, and dealing with it.

She watched him. Said nothing, but kept her eyes on him the entire time he took care of it.

"Next time it's your turn to plan," he said, climbing on top as she lifted her knees and wrapped her legs around his waist.

He teased her entrance before slipping inside. Then he had to count to five again, so he could see this through.

"I guess you've raised a pretty high bar," she said, squirming against his erection.

"You show up, Sam? The night is perfect," he said, lifting himself over her and thrusting in, then out. She seemed to know just which movements to make and just as she made that noise she made just before she came in the kitchen—the mewling whimper—she ran her fingernails down his chest, over his nipples, and he lost all control of anything.

Holding onto each other, they fell together.

Chapter Fourteen
SAMANTHA

SAM SLEPT OVER.

She hadn't planned on it, but they had sex, then they talked, then they had sex again, then they talked. They reheated the dinner Tanner picked up, ate it in bed, and finally, they crashed. They crashed while still talking. Mid-sentence, it seemed.

Wrapped up in everything Tanner, the safety of the moment assured her it was okay to rest. Take a break. Let him hold that space for her.

She didn't think that it was possible. To be mid-conversation and then just… fall asleep with someone. Tanner even sang to her. A song he'd been working on himself but hadn't pitched to the band yet.

They woke up naked and tangled together in his apartment off of Champa Street. She grinned and stretched, then nuzzled into his chest.

He pressed a kiss to her forehead and before she had even the slightest second to think about morning breath and the need to grab a toothbrush, Tanner caught her up again in a kiss.

This time, he pulled her over the top of him.

"I get to be on top?" she asked, waggling her eyebrows. Not to say she had a favorite, but she loved the top. Loved how Tanner took control, but also gave her a little, too.

Instead of reaching for a condom, Sam wriggled down so her knees were between his thighs. She gripped the long, hard length of him, gave a few strokes, and then pulled him into her mouth. She licked her tongue around the head of him, then down the long length to the soft sacks of flesh beneath.

He wrapped her hair in his hands and gave a little direction here and there while she sucked, licked, and feasted on his erection.

She thought she'd heard all the Tanner sex noises the night before. Turned out, he'd kept a few back from her and he had a whole slew of other sounds to make, too.

His balls tensed under her light grip and he groaned a "holy fuck."

She'd never swallowed before. Never wanted to. Maybe this was the time to try? She could do it. Ashley'd done it and she said it wasn't that bad. Just do a quick swallow so it didn't get everywhere.

Yes, she could totally do—

Tanner flipped her over onto her back. Somehow, he did it gently. Somehow, he had a condom in his hand. Somehow, he slid the condom on and then entered her with one swift movement.

She'd been wet—of course, she'd been wet. Doing that to him with her mouth. Hearing those sounds. They hadn't been for nothing. But now he was inside her, and his body over hers, he rode her and it turned out she really enjoyed being underneath, too.

"You prefer top?" Tanner asked, his vocal cords rough with the effort it took to communicate.

"This is good." She gripped his ass. "Good being the worst possible descriptor ever."

He moved them, flipped them over. Seriously, just like that —so she was on top.

The guy was like a sexual position savant with his ability to make it happen lickity-split.

She didn't make it a habit to watch adult movies, but she'd seen one or two. Or more. Sometimes a girl had to do what a girl had to do.

And that's the only time she'd ever seen such a quick position change without all the sloppy weirdness that came when a couple tried to do it themselves.

She'd had one guy she saw for a while, and he made a solid effort.

Tanner wiped every thought of whoever that was right out of her brain as he gripped her hips, and she rode him. Tossed her head back, and let him buck underneath her body.

His thumb found the bundle of nerves at her center, and that's all it took for her to fall. Both literally and figuratively. The orgasm took hold. Her internal muscles clenched around the length of him, and she dropped her head beside his on the pillow.

He finished two thrusts later, but he didn't pull out right away. He let her stay there, stroking her hair with his hands. Not saying a word, and in the silence saying so much.

"We're gonna be in Los Angeles," he said finally, still inside her. "For a couple months. Then headed to do a few shows in Canada." He kissed, lifted her face so they were nose to nose. "You should come."

"I just came," she said, even though she knew that's not what he meant.

"Come with me," he clarified.

She shook her head, sliding off of him so he could handle the mess. "I can't come."

"Work?" he asked, standing to deal with the condom. Grabbing a Kleenex to toss the whole handful in the trash.

She sat up in the bed. "We're down a night manager, so things are tight there."

"Is that really it?" he asked.

She picked at the bedspread.

"What is it, Sam?" He sat beside her, absolutely nude on the bed and not giving a care at all.

She squeezed his hand. "You know what it is."

If Sami Jo started going to concerts, it wouldn't be long before someone put two and two together and came up with four.

"Don't let the fear of what could happen stop you from living." He lifted the blankets and slipped beside her again.

The room smelled like Tanner, rock star, and sex.

"Tanner…"

"I get it," he said, holding his hands up. "Don't push." He tangled his fingers with hers. "But you are too amazing to hide yourself away."

"Cause of the thing I did with my tongue?"

Around two a.m. he'd kissed her, and she'd done this thing that she probably couldn't repeat if she tried, but it involved her tongue against his tongue. He seemed to be really into it, and the sound he made? She came a little on the spot.

"That was fucking brilliant." He toyed with the ends of her hair. "But that's not what I meant."

"I know what you meant."

"I know you know what I meant." He rolled her to her back, settling up on his elbows so they were nose to nose, body to body. "Come with me, Sammich. Come with me."

Her hand automatically went to his hip, holding him right there in that space between her thighs that ached for him again. Already.

"I can make you come until you agree," he said with a wry smile that seemed a little like a dare.

Her ovaries practically started cheerleading for him to win the match.

"I'm not seeing how I would lose in this situation?" She pulled her bottom lip between her teeth, bit on it to remind herself that there was a reality outside of this bed. This apartment… "I don't want to leave. This place, it's so…"

"I know." He pressed his forehead to hers. "I know, Sam."

A forehead touch turned into more and things heated again.

"I can come back on a weekend or two, but maybe you come hang with me as well?" he suggested. "How about you stop in for a few visits? Come see some of the shows."

She wanted to, yes. But Sami Jo at Brek's Bar in the corner was one thing. Sami Jo at a Dimefront concert was asking for trouble.

"You don't just decide one day that you're ready to make a change." She tried to pull away, but he stopped her. Was he an ass for doing it? Maybe. But he'd do it again.

"That's exactly what you do," he assured. "Especially when you're in self-induced purgatory." He leaned up on an elbow. "What's the worst thing that could happen? Everyone finds out that you're Sami Jo. What is it you're so afraid of?"

"You want a list?"

"Sam, it was a long time ago."

"And yet, it still follows me."

"I want that list," he said, brushing her hair from her forehead. "Because I think if you say it out loud, maybe you'll see that it's not as big as you remember."

She felt like a cat someone poked with a hot match. But she didn't act on it. Didn't screech about all the reasons. Instead, she sat up. Pulled the blanket to her chest. Gave herself a bit of a shield about what she had to face here in this bed with him.

"I am afraid that doing my best will not be enough," she said. This was the truth.

"That doing my best will make everyone laugh," she continued. Also, the truth.

"And then I'll be stuck as the butt of their joke." She turned to him, caught his gaze, and forced him to hold hers.

"I am afraid people will follow me," she said, her voice cracking as she said the last word. "Because that happened. I had a guy who hounded me, just because I am Sami Jo. So creepy. Then he followed my mom. This was at the same time there were people online on the message boards saying that I didn't deserve my share of air. People get so weird about this stuff." She swallowed. "Do you know how hard that is to hear that somebody thinks you shouldn't be breathing??"

Tanner reached for her hand. Held it in his.

"My dad cashed out part of his 401(k) to buy security cameras for the house and take me out of public school. He left work early to go with my mom to the grocery store so she wouldn't be scared."

Ashley knew all of this because she'd lived through it with Sam. But Sam had told no one else. It was the deep, dark secret she kept right down in the pocket of her soul

"And during that whole time, I gave up everything I thought I wanted to be. I stopped singing. I stopped writing songs. Did you know I have an entire book of finished and half-finished songs I think are pretty good?" She pointed to herself. "But I can't put them out into the world because I don't want to be afraid." She heaved a deep breath, then kept going.

"So I work with a generation who doesn't know Sami Jo. They don't care that she ever existed, and they don't worry themselves about my inability to sing." The tears fell now, like a summer rainstorm that didn't want to stop.

"Sam, enough," he whispered, wrapping her in his arms. Pushing his forehead against hers.

"You, Tanner, have had real trauma. Mine is nothing compared to yours."

"Stop," he said as he gripped her face between his palms,

gently but not allowing any movement. "I messed up. This is a big deal. I get it."

Dammit, she was going to snot all over him. But he didn't seem to care. He pulled her against his shoulder. Held her there, making shushing noises like he could make it okay.

If only he could make it okay.

"You can't make it okay," she said as tears chased each other down her cheeks. For the first time in a long, long time, she cried with someone else in the room. Usually, she saved her pity party sessions for alone time in the shower. But Tanner got the full force of it. Her chest heaved against him, and not in a sexy way. Not at all. This was messy and raw and… gah, she needed to get herself together.

But he'd scratched at a wound that opened up, gushing the truth all over them both.

"I got you," he said. "I got you." Over and over he said, "I've got you."

She wished he did. But no one really had her. She was toxic, and he was goodness, and how could something so toxic not poison something as good as him?

Chapter Fifteen
TANNER

TANNER KNEW things must've been bad on her side of things for her to run the way she had. He hadn't known it'd been so awful as all that she'd just shared.

She was only a kid who wrote a song.

At one point, he'd been that kid, too. Had the shit that went down with her happened to him? Well, he'd have been well and truly fucked. There was nothing Dan could've said or done to make it better.

A deep-seated rock sat on his chest because he'd been just like the others in the world—he'd made fun of Sami Jo and her mozzarella sticks.

O-o-oey, g-o-o-ey, che-e-esy and fried!

He and Catiana used to make loads of fun of it.

That realization made his heart hurt, because this girl in his bed deserved better than him. Deserved better than the hand the world dealt her.

"I'm okay," she said, the tears drying up, her voice returning to the usual cadence.

"You are more than okay," he assured, kissing the salty wet of her cheeks. "You are perfect."

She snorted in response, and even her snort was adorable.

"I get it," he assured. "I won't push you to come out to L.A. or on the tour. I'll miss you like hell, though." This last part he said against her hair, and that got a whole new slew of wet hitting his.

"What are you thinking?" she asked, breaking apart and wiping her tears with the back of her hand.

Given that he couldn't exactly spill his guts on this one, he went with something he'd been thinking about since he first found out she was Sami Jo. "That you *can* sing. Like, fantastic."

The girl had pipes. The song was just—hysterical.

Mozzarella sticks on M-o-o-nday.

All the days.

Cheese and batter and melty goo.

At least, he had thought the song was hysterical. But with Sam holding onto him like she was drifting at sea and he was her lifesaver, he realized he'd got it wrong.

"I'll get you a set of keys for here if you want? Need a place to escape the Peony sometimes?"

"You don't have to do that."

"If it means you're here when I get back, I'm willing to make that sacrifice."

That bought him a smile.

"And I'll introduce you to Dan. He's… he's basically my dad. He lives two floors down. If you tell him when you're stopping in, he'll keep an eye out for you. Since I won't be able to."

"Dan lives in the building?" She didn't seem surprised, merely curious.

He nodded. "That's why he got me a kickass deal on this one bedroom."

"Like you need a deal," she said.

"Everybody wants a deal."

Sam had to get back to work, check in with Ashley, and then sort out her schedule so they could have a few more nights together before he left town. But before they headed out, he made a pit stop on the third floor.

"Should we knock?" she asked, cautiously, when he used his key to let them into Dan's place.

"No way. Dan gets pissy when I knock. Says it's my place, too. It's what he does for all his kids—we get keys, the door is open. He's a seriously good guy like that."

"I think I like Dan." Sam's eyes softened in that way he liked so much.

Tanner gave her a chin lift. "Just wait, he's epic."

Tanner pushed open the door.

"It's Tanner," Tanner called, setting some of the crap food he'd picked up on the front entry table. He'd grabbed extra Ding Dongs and Cheeto Puffs for Dan. Dude didn't eat much of that stuff, but these were his favorites. "I brought Sam to meet you."

"In here," Dan said from the office. "Be right out."

They moved through his apartment, past the kitchen and living space. Dan's place was a two-bedroom with a large balcony and an office. He'd had a girlfriend for a while who decorated, so it looked like it came from a magazine instead of from a guy who worked in a garage.

"Check it out." Tanner opened the door to the bedroom he'd shared with Mach. Dan hadn't had any recent foster kids —he was one of the last-resort foster dads. When a kid was about to age out of the system and needed someone to give a shit, the social workers brought him in.

The room was exactly the same as when Tanner had shown up, fresh from couch surfing at Catiana's house. He shook off the thought. Better not to think about things like that.

"I moved in and was not looking forward to having a roommate." That wasn't Catiana. "That turned out awesome, since Mach was who I got paired with."

"Mach doesn't know you have an apartment here?" she asked.

He shook his head. "If he does, he's never said anything."

Sam stepped into the room, seemingly awed. It was just a room. But, she wasn't wrong… it felt like more than that.

Since no one had been in there since the last guys moved on—found jobs and a place to live—the space was musty and yet still smelled like the Pine Sol spray Dan made them clean with three times a week. In return, they got a place to stay, a full belly, and he made sure they knew a skill. Usually, that skill was fixing cars, but sometimes he'd go rogue and create a rock star.

"This is where you grew up?" Sam asked. She obviously meant this as a rhetorical question. But—

"It's where I spent a few years as a teen," Tanner said. "Not really where I grew up."

"I think you're wrong," she said this slowly, clearly savoring everything about the space. "I think this is where the growing up happened."

She probably wasn't wrong.

He didn't enjoy thinking about that time in his life, so he moved to the window. Looked outside. Watched the traffic.

"You and Mach had bunk beds?" Sam asked, her lips twitching with a grin.

That was nice, the smiling.

"A bed's a bed when you haven't had one in a long while," he said with a shrug.

Now she frowned, the happiness from before all but erased from her face. "That hurts my heart."

"Don't let it." He stepped to her, wrapped his hand around the back of her neck to pull her in for a kiss. "I've got loads of cake now. I can buy all the beds."

"No girls in the bedroom," Dan said from the doorway. "You know the drill." He said it, but the huge smile on his mug told the actual story—he didn't mean it.

Tanner was not above giving Dan an enormous hug. The guy earned it, and more. In spades. So Tanner gave Dan his due, then he held his hand out for Sam.

"This is my Sam," he said, and the way saying that made his posture straighten and his shoulders push back… yeah.

She took his hand. The bashful look she gave Tanner made him want to take her back to bed until she forgot to be anything but happy.

"It's so great to meet you, Sam." Dan didn't push her to shake his hand or offer a hug she might not feel great about giving.

Dan kicked off, heading to the living room.

"He is not what I expected," Sam whispered in Tanner's ear.

"He gets that a lot." Tanner had heard it all.

Dan was a mechanic, and he was a foster dad to only he knew how many kids. He'd come off the streets, too. Ralph—the original owner of the garage—took him in. Nothing formal, but he let Dan work at the shop. In return, he gave him an office to sleep in and all-access to the vending machines. Eventually, they bonded, and Ralph handed over the business. That's why Dan dedicated years to ensuring other guys got the same chance as he did.

"Sam might use my apartment a little while I'm in L.A. and Canada." Tanner followed Dan to the living room, where he kept his recliner. He kept Sam in his periphery so he could tell if she got antsy. Got scared. Felt like running.

Not that she'd do that around Dan—nobody did that around Dan. But she'd had a hard morning, and he knew the inclination to take off wasn't easily squelched.

"Sounds good to me. Sam, you know where I am. My door is always open. Tanner'll get you my number?" Dan asked.

Tanner nodded. "Yeah. If that's cool?"

"Totally," Sam agreed. "Thank you."

"Who would've thought." Dan sat in the recliner, leaned forward, and stared right at Tanner.

"Thought what?" Tanner asked, already knowing.

"That I'd have been right?" Dan asked, and the smirk? Un-fucking-necessary.

Unfortunately, Dan was correct and Tanner appreciated that. Dan had told Tanner to stay the course, and he'd find his own reward.

He did not know that reward would have brown eyes and the name Samantha.

Chapter Sixteen
SAMANTHA

THE WEEKS PASSED ENTIRELY TOO QUICKLY, and Sam was looking straight into the eye of the future. That future being without Tanner since he'd be leaving for Los Angeles in only a couple of days. Her stomach felt a little pukey at the idea of this time alone.

Interesting, because she'd always excelled at being alone.

Sam opened the door to her Purple Peony apartment and paused. There were three of her charges lounging in her space. Well, not lounging, but they were there.

Her tiny apartment wasn't even a condo. Heck, they could barely consider it more than a room. A room with a double bed, a tiny kitchen, and a bathroom with one of those walk-in bathtubs for anyone with mobility issues.

They were there for a reason—she knew an ambush when she saw one. Two steps backward was all it would take to get back in the hallway. Then she could pretend she'd never seen them there.

"She's here," Babushka announced before Sam could escape. "You're here."

"Oh good," Betty Jane announced, waving her hand toward the chessboard. "I'm losing the chess match."

"How did you get in?" Sam asked, because she didn't expect a whole heap of privacy, but a little was to be expected.

"We have a key," Aunt Etta said. "Don't worry, we don't use it much."

This was news.

Don't ask. Don't ask. Sonofagun, she was going to ask. "*Why* are you all in here?"

"Catching you up on laundry," Great Aunt Etta said. She'd dyed her hair blue. Something about, "All the kids doing it these days."

"Losing a chess match," Betty Jane announced, throwing her hands in the air before moving the knight.

She really should've rethought that choice.

"Aunt Etta, you don't need to mess with the laundry," Sam said. "Betty Jane, you don't wanna move the queen yet. Babushka? Are you only here to beat Betty Jane at chess? Or…?"

"I am here because I have learned that you did not accept Tanner's invitation." Babushka studied the chessboard as she spoke.

"Invitation to what?" Sam asked. Look, if they were going to be all up in her business she needed to know precisely how much they knew about her choice not to go with Dimefront.

"They are recording and touring and you vant to stay here," Babushka said as she plucked up her own knight and sacrificed him to take out a whole slew of Betty Jane's players.

Don't ask. Don't ask. "How did you find out I said no?"

Of course, it hadn't been a secret she wasn't attending. She'd simply never made it a point to let anyone know Tanner had asked, and she'd said no.

"Do you know what would pair really nicely with this blue blouse?" Great Aunt Etta asked, holding up a sleeveless tee Sam wore sometimes on the weekend when she wasn't working.

"I bet you are going to tell me," Sam said, starting toward the sofa. Then stopping. Then, you know what? There were too many people all up in the small space, so she wasn't entirely certain where she should put herself.

"The ocean," Betty Jane said. "This blouse pairs well with the ocean."

Shit, it sort of did. With the blue-on-blue swirl pattern it had going on.

Sam still didn't know where to go in her own home. But she needed to figure it out faster than this. Because as it was, she only stood in the doorway. Though it was a fast exit if she bolted.

Gah, she wouldn't bolt. Not over this. But if she sat on the bed, that was too close to Great Aunt Etta and she would use the proximity to manipulate Sam.

On the sofa? Well, that was only a stone's throw from Babushka and that was a no go.

Betty Jane was a safe bet, but she was a wanderer, so Sam couldn't tell precisely where she'd end up.

Instead of making herself comfortable in her home, Sam set down her bag and leaned against the wall.

"Take your vacation time," Babushka said. "You have built up vacation."

"Spend the time with Tanner," Betty Jane—the traitor —said.

"We'll do fine without you for a few weeks." That was Great Aunt Etta chiming in as she folded up a pair of Sam's panties.

This was the nudge Sam needed to ensure her laundry was always folded and put away, or hidden in the depths of her closet.

"How did you even find out I said no?" she asked. Because she'd told nearly no one. Other than… oh shoot—

"The same vay I find out everything. People tell me,"

Babushka announced. She reached for a pawn on the wall-chessboard, moving it and placing Betty Jane in check.

"I give up." Betty Jane threw up her hands in surrender.

"I got you," Sam said. She moved to the board and dammit, she did not want to move her queen, but it was the only option. So she did it. "Also, I'm not going."

The crap part was that thinking about going gave her a stomachache. Thinking about staying made her feel lightheaded.

She could not win.

"You have not agreed to go… yet." Great Aunt Etta rolled a pair of yoga pants into a tight swirl that would fit most excellently in the dresser drawer. Where'd she learn to do that?

Screw it, she was going in. Great Aunt Etta could share her folding secrets. Sam reached for a pair of pants and followed along as Aunt Etta did the roll and tuck thing.

"You talked to my mom, didn't you?" Sam said, pointing the leggings at her great aunt. "That's who told you."

Sam had made it a point to check in with her parents daily. Both via video call and text, even a phone call here and there—like it was 1996, and the world hadn't gone to shit.

"Of course, I did," Great Aunt Etta lifted her shoulder like it wasn't a big deal or a slight betrayal in Sam's trust of her mother. "Your mama worries about you."

Oh, well, Sam didn't want her to worry.

"She's afraid if she comes to see you," Great Aunt Etta continued, folding up the pants with a quick flare of brilliance Sam did not quite catch. "Then it'll just mean you pull up the tiny roots you've planted and start again."

"She thinks that?" Sam asked as the guilty thickness in her throat took hold. She didn't want her mom to be worried. That's why she'd left in the first place—so Mom and Dad could live a normal life without… Sami Jo.

The knock on her door came right before it opened, and

Courtney pushed through the gaggle of the elderly. "He invited you! And you said no?"

"Damn," Sam said. Not even under her breath, just out there for everyone to hear.

"I told them to leave you alone," Becca followed Courtney, clearly attempting to be the voice of reason.

"Them?" Sam asked, but it was too late because Knox and Linx—even Bax—squeezed into her little apartment.

"Where's Mach? Tanner?" she asked. Since they were having a party, perhaps she should put out some appetizers.

"They both said that you're private and to leave you alone," Courtney said. "But you should know that you are now part of our crew and that means we don't do that."

"Which is actually what we should do," Becca added.

Courtney glared lovingly at Becca—was that a thing? Sam couldn't say she'd ever seen that before.

"I'm here to remind them that's what we should do," Becca continued. She got shoved toward the little double bed and sat on the other side from Sam.

Becca grabbed a shirt from the laundry bin and started folding. That was sweet, but Sam made an internal promise to herself that she would never again leave out a bin of laundry. She quickly snatched out all the panties and shoved them under her pillow.

If Becca noticed, she said nothing. Which was sweet.

"You and Tanner can use my old apartment in Los Angeles." Courtney held up her hands as though she was surrendering. "We go out there every so often, so we kept the lease. And Knox and Irina live across the hall when they're in town. So you and Irina can get to know each other better. She's really eager to meet you."

That was a touch low, seeing as Sam had told them all of her girl crush on Hollywood starlet, Irina. The woman was hysterical and a kickass actress. Ashley may have been starstruck over the Dimefront boys, but Sam was bananas over Irina.

"If you're worried about the Tens, the security at the building is super great. And Knox and Tanner won't let anyone near you."

Sam wasn't worried about groupies. Well, she was because they might recognize her. But not because of the reasons Courtney probably suspected. Sam let out a long breath, blowing her bangs up with the movement. "Thank you. Really. I just can't come."

"She can come," Babushka said. "She has vacation."

"Thank you." Sam swallowed all the words she wanted to say. "Thank you for explaining that."

"There is compromise here, I feel it in my bones," Babushka announced, moving a rook that once again put Sam in check.

Dammit.

She stalked to the board—which was hard given the number of people in her room. The fire marshal would not like this at all. Then again, he didn't have a particular fondness for the Purple Peony.

Hold up. If she pushed her king one move over... yes, that'd do it.

"Checkmate," she announced, lifting her arms in the air.

Then she glanced to Babushka like, *Whatchagonnado?*

"It is compromise, yes?" Babushka asked, like she'd seen that coming all along.

Fudge, had she thrown the game? No, that wasn't like her. Babushka did a lot of things, but she didn't lose intentionally. Unless, by losing she'd actually be winning. Someone should probably move beside her in case she tossed herself on the floor.

Sam seriously did not have the energy to deal with that right now.

"I'll visit," she finally agreed. "How about that?"

This was Los Angeles, there were loads bigger celebrity sightings to worry about than one with Sami Jo. What good was Sami Jo when there was Lady Gaga and Jimmy Fallon?

"She vill visit." Babushka tossed her hands up in the air as though this was all her doing. Which was fair, given that it mostly was.

"We got a concession." Bax clapped like Sam had given a performance, and honestly? She didn't dislike it.

Actually… that felt good. She liked it. She enjoyed being the center of attention when they were all being awesome. Not calling her names or threatening to kill her parents.

Why did she like it? It's not like she'd done anything other than agree to something totally ridiculous like visiting Tanner in Los Angeles.

"This is going to be fun," she said. "I get to meet Irina."

And see Tanner. Not waiting until he caught a moment and could come back to Denver.

It's not like she was going to go out there and announce who she was. She'd just let the bright lights of Dimefront stay on Dimefront. That could be her strategy. Keep the attention off of herself and onto the boys who had earned it.

Maybe it could work?

Chapter Seventeen
SAMANTHA

A week and a half later

SAM CURLED up on the bed at Tanner's place in one of his Dimefront tees and a pair of ratty shorts she'd never wear in public. This was her first night spending time at Tanner's apartment. She needed a break from the Babushka crew after the latest incident on TikTok involving a blow torch challenge.

The apartment held onto Tanner's scent and was officially her new favorite place because of it. She needed to see him again to remind her she was changing how she did things. Remind her why she might want to stay in Denver permanently.

Her phone buzzed beside her. She reached for it. Smiled.

Tanner: What are you doing?

Sam: Thinking about you.

Tanner: Miss you.

Sam: Miss you too.

Sam: Waiting for food delivery.

Tanner: Did you go to the clubhouse?

Sam: Yes.

They texted all the freaking time. She hadn't expected it to be this hard, being a thousand miles away from each other.

Sam: See you in a few days?

Tanner: Miss you more. Can't wait.

Tanner: What'd you order for dinner?

Sam: Greek

Sam: Kebab night!

Tanner: Yum

Tanner: Going to a press thing with the guys. Talk later? 🤍

Sam: Absolutely. 🤍

THE QUICK KNOCK on the door pulled her from the bed. She was at that point of being hungry where she would break into Tanner's stash of Doritos if the food didn't come soon.

She unlatched, unlocked, and tugged open the door.

The girl on the other side of the door didn't have the normal "warming" bag the Big Eats Delivery Service required of their drivers. That's why Sam used their service—

the food always arrived warm. This person only had a plastic sack tied around the Styrofoam.

Sam was a smart woman who understood that you always checked the door viewer, and on a normal day, she used more caution than the average person.

And yet, today she rode on the post-Tanner text high and flung open the door without checking. The blonde woman there wearing the designer jeans—looked like maybe they came from Rag and Bone—had a smash-you-like-a-bug expression she managed to quickly wipe away into neutrality. She did it so fast, Sam questioned if she'd even assessed it correctly. The tight top the woman wore totally worked with the outfit. Sam just couldn't shake a little tickle in her brain that told her to get away. She wasn't safe.

If she'd checked the door first, she would've requested that it be the contactless option.

And, honestly, with the tip she'd left on the Big Eats app, she would've figured the delivery person would be happier to make the drop.

"Hi," Sam said, holding her hands out to take the delivery.

"This is yours?" the woman asked, balancing the food on one hand.

"I'm guessing so." That was an odd thing to say when making a delivery.

"Samantha Johnson?" she asked.

"Uh-huh. I have the pin code. It's…" Sam flipped her phone in her hand to pull it up on the app—

"Sami Jo." The woman said the name as though Sam didn't know who she, herself, was. But she knew, and at that announcement, everything went numb. Lips. Even her earlobes had no feeling anymore.

"My name is Sam," she said, instead of confirming the woman's use of her former name.

Dan might be downstairs. She could go there, hit his apartment, and hope like hell he was home. Dan was safety.

The woman handed over the food. Thank goodness. Maybe they could be done with this, and she could figure out what the hell came next.

"I knew it was you," the woman said. "Knew it from the second Tanner mentioned you two are together. You really don't look that different. I mean, yeah, the hair's longer. And you got a little fluffy. Not judging, just saying. Tanner has always liked his women a little fluffy, you know? But all-in-all you are definitely Sami Jo."

Sam started to step backward into the apartment. With a little luck, she could kick the door closed, have a private panic attack, call Dan and call Tanner and—

"Hold up," the lady said. "I'm just a friend of Tanner's. I only want to talk."

Mach told her Catiana had been at Brek's. Said she had blonde hair and blue eyes. This had to be her. "You're Catiana."

"You know me." The wry smile on Catiana's lips didn't sit well.

Nothing sat well right then.

"Mach mentioned you." Sam looked up and down the empty hallway. "How did you know about this place?" She stumbled over the words as she spoke.

"I followed you," Catiana said, brightly, as though it wasn't a big whoop. That it wasn't more than slightly creepy.

"Can I come in?" Catiana asked. "So we can talk? Girl to girl?"

"That's not a good idea." Sam preferred not to be murdered by a woman who slept with sharks. By anyone, really.

"Sami Jo, please," Catiana said, again.

Everything in Sam froze this time, the numb disappearing

into ice. How she could be frozen in place and burning up at the same time made no sense.

"My name is Sam. Or Samantha," she said. "I'm not sure who you think I am, but I am Sam or Samantha."

"Can I give you some advice?" Catiana asked. She didn't move closer, but it felt like she did, and Sam took a step back.

"You can do whatever you'd like," Sam said, placing her hand on the door. Another step and she could push it closed. Flip the lock.

Push it closed. Flip the lock.

"Running from your past will only make you miserable," Catiana said, like they were girlfriends sharing tips. "Embrace it."

"Is that what you're doing?" Sam asked, distracting Catiana enough, so she'd get to talking and then she'd be distracted and Sam could slip inside. "Embracing your past, I mean?"

"I loved Tanner," Catiana said. "He was my guy, you know?"

Well, she did. But also, "You hurt him."

"Have you ever made a mistake?" Catiana asked, and any hint of the grinch facade fell away.

Dammit, in another life, Sam and Catiana could've been friendly. But today there was a lot happening in this meet-up, things Sam would be better able to address if her blood sugar levels were more stable and she had some warning.

"I have," Sam said. Because those words from Catiana seemed to bop her upside the head. Yes. Uh-huh. She had made mistakes. Loads of them.

She didn't doubt that Catiana still had feelings for Tanner. It made sense that she'd hang onto something, someone, as good as him.

"He's moved on." Sam adjusted the food in her arms. "If you love him, or you loved him, let him keep going forward. Not drag him backward."

That sounded reasonable.

"I want another shot with Tanner," Catiana said. "I've been trying to connect with him for ages, and I finally got through. I know that's probably hard to hear, but it's true."

The damage she did to Tanner wasn't the kind of thing a person could just bounce back from.

"Here's how this is going to work," Catiana said, and Sam sort of wished she didn't look like a fairy princess when she spoke. Or that she'd ever had a consideration that they could've been friendly. "You are going to break it off with Tanner. In return, I won't tell a soul who you are. No one."

Sam waited for the other shoe to drop.

"But if you don't, then I'm going to tell everyone." She paused. Lifted a shoulder. "*Everyone.*"

Perhaps Sam should stop the continuation of this conversation and go back to the original plan of getting back into the safety of the apartment.

Catiana was a desperate person who wanted an old boyfriend back. She was a lot of things, but Sam didn't think she'd truly hurt her. Not physically. It's not like she'd brought a tarp, rope and a shovel. But, even so, she held more power in her hand than she knew.

"You had a chance with him," Sam said, taking another half step back.

Catiana started forward. Shit.

"Can I please come in?" Catiana asked. "We'll figure the details."

"That's a bad idea. I'm sorry. I wish you all the best, but this isn't my place to let you in. And you really shouldn't be here." Quick as she spoke, she finished the movement backward, pushed the door closed, and flipped the lock.

She could call for help. Maybe the police helped with things like this?

But what would she say? My boyfriend's ex followed me,

delivered my dinner, and then asked me to break up with him?

They probably wouldn't respond to that. Besides, if she did that, she'd have to tell them why it was such a blow that Catiana knew she was Sami Jo.

She did not want to discuss that.

No, she'd text Dan. That's what she'd do. Dan wouldn't ask about it. And if he did, Sam could trust him because Tanner trusted him.

She felt stuck in place as the web of her past caught her, and she hated it. Hated the way it made everything cold again when she'd only just warmed up.

"Tanner told me who you are," Catiana yelled through the door with absolutely no regard for the neighbors.

"Go away," Sam whispered to herself, gripping the styrofoam containers covered in plastic to her chest. The heat of the kebabs didn't bother her. The seeping of the liquid into the plastic where it pooled didn't concern her.

Catiana was the one who bothered her. Catiana and that little voice in the back of her head that said she might be right.

Tanner had cared for her, Mach said. He probably loved her.

"When I saw him at the concert," Catiana continued. "He told me exactly who you are. You should ask your friend… what was her name? Ashley? She was there, too."

"Go away," Sam whispered again. This was only a mind game, and mind games were never real.

"Did you know back in the day he used to laugh at your song with me? He knew all the lyrics. Better than me. Probably better than you, too."

Sam's chest tightened. But why wouldn't he have found a chuckle at her expense? The rest of the world did. It's not like it changed anything in the present.

"Go away," she chanted to herself.

"He's always been able to talk to me, you know? I wrecked it for a bit. But I'm ready to fix it. He deserves that. You know it and I know it, and even that ogre Hans knows it." She was on a roll now.

"Go away," Sam whispered again as she set the food aside.

"That's all I came to say. You know the stakes," Catiana yelled, again through the door. "It's up to you now."

Sam pressed her palms to her cheeks. This was one of those moments she'd faced before—when she had to decide whether she left to protect the people she loved or stayed and risked more than she could handle losing.

But this time, instead of allowing herself to fall into the vat of panic, she swerved left.

Things she knew?

Ashley would tell no one about Sam's secrets. Never.

Tanner cared for her and at some point she'd fallen past the lust and straight toward being in love with him. That part was the one that scared her.

But even if he didn't love her, he wouldn't do anything to cause her pain. He wouldn't tell her secrets. And even as a kid, he wouldn't have made fun of her. That's just not who he was.

Another thing she knew?

Catiana wasn't trustworthy. She'd already proven all of that. And, clearly, she'd figured things out and had an agenda.

Which meant there was only one thing she should do right now. Carefully, she grabbed her cell and forced her hands not to shake.

Then she called Mach.

Chapter Eighteen
TANNER

"HEY, TANNER, YOUR GIRL JUST ARRIVED," Hans said over the intercom into the studio. "Take five?"

"Better make it ten," Mach said. "And group huddle with her once the wives show."

"What are you talking about?" Bax asked.

Yeah, that. Same question, but from him.

"I sent out an SOS to Courtney, Becca, and Irina. They'll be here shortly." Mach slipped his guitar into its case.

"Sam's *here*?" Tanner asked, and confusion didn't even cover the questions going on inside his brain. "In California. In this building?"

Mach nodded. "Yup."

Sam was there. Holy shit. He got to hold her. Touch her. Kiss her.

Sam was there, and he didn't know she was coming.

But Mach clearly did. Why'd that sting?

"Was this supposed to be a surprise?" he asked. Because if it was supposed to be a surprise, they'd fucked it up. Honestly, everyone had been weird since last night. Even Sam. She hadn't answered his calls and only shot off a few texts here and there. Said things were super busy.

As though Tanner had called her into reality, Sam slipped through the door into the studio booth with Dan.

With *Dan*. Dan who rarely left Denver because he had a body shop to run and he hated to fly.

What the fuck was going on?

All he knew was she was there, and he was going to share the same air. They'd sort the rest later. Balancing his sticks on the snare, he stood and maneuvered around the cords and instruments to the foam-lined door.

"Sam?" he said as he pushed it open. "Dan?"

Sam went right to him. Slipped into his arms. "I missed you."

He would've kissed her, but she buried her head in his chest and seemed to melt there.

"I missed you, too," he said. "What's going on?"

In response, she gave him a squeeze and sighed like all the issues in the world would be okay now that they were together.

"Give me a minute to enjoy this," she said.

He understood that feeling since it was pretty much the same one he experienced with her in his arms.

"What the hell's going on?" he asked Dan.

"Catiana figured out Sam," Dan said matter-of-factly. He'd gone into protection mode—Tanner had only seen it once before. When he'd convinced Tanner to stick around after the whole Sharknado prom debacle. "Catiana tracked her down. Made some threats."

"She did fucking *what*?!" Tanner didn't mean to roar, but roar he did.

Sam jumped a little in his arms, which was unacceptable. She didn't need to be afraid when they were together.

"I'll need the details," Hans said from behind Tanner. "If you have contact information, that would be helpful."

What the hell? "What can you do about it?"

"I make problems go away so you can focus on music,"

Hans said. "That's my job. This woman is now a problem." Hans adjusted his cuffs and headed past Tanner.

"You and I are gonna talk," Tanner said before Hans made it to the hallway.

"After," Hans waved him away, which would usually piss him off, but now he had Sam here and a big fat mess he only had the summary about. He had a hunch there would be cleanup needed. He needed Hans's help to do the cleanup—that's where Hans excelled.

"Green Room is ready," Courtney said, peeking her head in the sound studio. "Figured that made the most sense."

"You know what's going on?" Tanner asked her. Sam still gripped his chest like she was afraid he'd disappear. He moved his hand behind her neck, holding her there. Letting her know he had her.

"Nope." Courtney shook her head. "But I got the SOS, so I'm here." She glanced at Sam. "She okay?"

"She's fine. She's a tough one." Dan tilted his head to the hallway. "Let's give them a second. I'll catch everyone up while Tanner chats with her."

Finally alone, Tanner asked, "What did she say to you?"

"God, I thought for a second, in another life, we could even be friends. She's like a chameleon," Sam said.

"I know. I know her." He understood this ability of hers to be sweet and then salt all in the same breath. "What did she say to you, Sam?"

Sam inhaled deeply. "That she knows who I am. That I need to break up with you so she can have a shot. And if I don't, she outs me to the tabloids." Sam shrugged. "Standard variety blackmail."

His heart spasmed at that. Where did he even begin? At the part that involved him, that's where he'd start.

"You understand that she was forever ago. I would not go back to that. To her. What we had when we dated was not healthy." As illustrated by what happened when they broke it off. She broke it off. "We were just kids."

"I wasn't really worried about that part," Sam said, with a distant look in her eyes. "I mean, I'm not willing to break it off. So it doesn't factor."

Why did that make his heart perk up to attention?

"So I-I don't know what's going to happen," Sam said. "And my stomach is in knots over it. I'm trying to be tough. Sami Jo is about to be exposed."

"No matter what she does, it's going to be okay."

"What about everyone around me?"

"You've got me. And you've got this entire team of people out here who have your back. Nothing is going to happen to the people you care about," he assured.

"You can't promise that."

"You're with me. That means you're Dimefront as much as I am. That makes you family to everybody here," he assured. "I can promise it won't be like last time."

"You can't promise that, either."

He couldn't. He understood that. Hated that she was right, and the words were only lip service. He couldn't really protect her, but he could damn well try.

"Why didn't you come to me first?" he asked. The hit his pride took would be fine. He'd get over it. But the fact she hadn't trusted him with this?

"Mach told me about Catiana. He warned me the night she showed up at Brek's." Sam leaned back and glanced up at him. Her eyes never got wet, and her jaw was firm. "I wanted to run. But then I didn't. And I needed to know what I was dealing with, so I called him."

Tanner did his best not to let that fester. He failed, but he sure tried.

"I wanted to tell you," Sam said. "I just... I needed someone outside of *us* to give me a reality check."

"Mach did that?" Tanner asked, hoping like hell his

brother came through for him.

"Mach and then Dan." Sam's brown eyes sparkled with a hint of wet. "They really love you, and they are livid."

They could join the club. The way the thought of his ex made his heart ache for Sam, and the rest of him felt nothing? He needed to not see Catiana for a good long time.

"Are you gonna be okay?" he asked, careful with his tone so he didn't spook her further.

"I am." She nodded. "And I'm not running. Not from you. We're going to figure this out. I'm tired of letting the wrong side win over a stupid song about cheese." She chuckled a little, but her heart wasn't in it.

It was more than a stupid song about ooey, gooey fried cheese—he understood that. He also got that right now Sam needed simple. So that's what he'd give her.

Hands linked, they headed out the door and down the hall to the Green Room. Which was a stupid name for the room, since there was nothing green about it. Just white walls and faux-lux furniture with a mini fridge.

Courtney stood as soon as they entered the room. The fire in her eyes was not something he'd seen before. Not like that.

"She called you fluffy?" Courtney asked and Dan's anger had clearly worn off on her. "I'm going to murder her with my socks."

"It's okay," Sam assured. "It didn't bug me."

"I'm going to get there first and handle it." Irina said, standing beside Courtney and then moving to Sam. She held out her hand. "I'm Irina, and I am pissed."

Very still, Sam took the offered hand. Shook it.

"I'm really more of a hugger, and you are now part of our family, so if you're good with that, I'd like to give you a hug?" Irina asked.

Sam nodded, sliding her gaze to Tanner as Irina went in for a hug. The woman gave an excellent hug. Strong hug. Precisely what Sam needed.

"You left out the part where she criticized your appearance," Tanner said, eyes on Sam as Irina pulled away.

She shrugged. "It wasn't the important part."

He begged to differ, seeing that this woman beside him was the most gorgeous person he'd ever seen in his entire fucking life. Seeing as she didn't know how gorgeous she was, the catty club could get their claws in her and he was not about to stand by and watch that happen.

"We need a plan. She knows who you are, and if she knows about my secret apartment, she probably knows where you work and where you live," Tanner said, running his hand down the back of her hair. He paused.

"Secret apartment?" Bax asked. "What secret apartment?"

"If it's a secret, then we aren't supposed to know about it." Mach gave a curt nod to Tanner.

Of course, Mach had figured it out.

Dan whispered something to Bax, but that wasn't the important part of what they had to deal with, so Bax didn't keep asking.

The fact was that Tanner's hands were tied. Dimefront had a record to cut, and tickets, and logically he couldn't go back to Denver to sort this out with Catiana.

He chewed on his bottom lip. "We'll come up with something."

"I can probably take a leave of absence," Sam said with a sad smile. "It'll jack with my bank account, but Babushka offered to pull some strings at work. I think they'll give me some time off."

He liked that. Liked that she had not only Dimefront at her back, but his friends at the Purple Peony, too.

"You should know Babushka is ecstatic that I want to take a break and stay with you," Sam continued. "Great Aunt Etta is already making ridiculous plans for our future."

"What plans?" Becca asked. "I hope they're good plans. You need a hit of goodness."

"We don't need to go there." She gestured to the rest of the room. "Not now. I told her one step at a time. Though it involved real estate tours of homes for Tanner and me. The ones with a guest house for her to live in."

"Tanner already has a house," Mach said, frowning. "When you're ready, you move in. That's what we do. Family stays together."

Well, they shouldn't get ahead of themselves. He'd be over the moon to have her there, but she had to make that call, not Mach, and not him.

"I have a guest house." Bax raised his hand. "Just next door to Mach and Tanner's place on my side of the property line." Then he stopped, looked to Courtney. "We. I mean, *we* have a guest house. You're welcome to it whenever."

"It's for our parents so they can all come see Harley," Courtney added. "Unfortunately, they have decided that since Bax and I are now happily together, they deserve to go on all the cruises to celebrate. We aren't invited."

"We told 'em they couldn't take Harley on a world cruise without us. It was a whole conversation," Bax added with a shiver.

"Which means the guest house sits vacant a lot," Courtney added.

"Well, the simple part is settled then," Sam said. "But, um… I'm Sami Jo, and I think I'm ready to stop running."

This was excellent. But even in all that excellent, a lump of worry stuck in his throat. Sami Jo had to be safe. Sam had to be safe.

"Courtney," Hans said, doing the thing he did where he took charge of the room. "This situation with Catiana will be handled, but we need to plan for if it blows open." He gave Sam a long stare. "When it blows open because you sure as hell look like yourself. And eventually there will be Sami Jo sightings all around you that will lead to you. You could dye the hair. Maybe change the makeup. But… damn, you look like you."

"Quick thoughts," Courtney said, pulling her lips into a line. "The line between love and hate is super small. Like razor thin. Usually if you love someone you can hate them fast, and if you hate someone you can love them, too."

"Case in point," Bax pointed to his chest.

Dan cleared his throat. Swear to hell, Tanner thought he said, "Let's focus."

"You did nothing wrong," Courtney continued. "You wrote a song. A song people liked." Courtney thought about that.

"No one wants to admit they love a song about cheese," Knox said.

Irina's expression was open and soft and all for Sam. "Because it makes them feel stupid. You know? So they make fun of it instead."

"I don't think that's what happened," Sam whispered.

"Can I tell 'em?" Tanner asked.

She nodded, so Tanner gave the run-down of all the shit that went down after Sami Jo's video hit big. Cyberbullying may have been the term, but the reality was more than two words pushed together. The reality was that things got so bad, Sami Jo wanted to disappear. So she did.

"For goodness' sakes, she wrote a song. She didn't take out a gas station while high on mozzarella stick smoke," Becca announced, and she was not happy. Not at all.

"That would make it harder to sell." Courtney pulled her lips to the side. "I need to think about this. Figure it out."

"I've got work to do," Hans said, stalking out of the room.

Good, Courtney was excellent at the art of the spin. Hans was the fixer they needed.

This would be okay.

He hoped to hell it would be okay.

Chapter Nineteen
SAMANTHA

SAM GOT to be on top this time, and she'd discovered she preferred to be on top *and* on a tour bus. Something about bagging a rock star on his tour bus seemed a little naughty. Apparently, she liked naughty. Who would've guessed?

Tanner's bus was amazing, with a suite in the back for sleeping and… other things. A mini bar up front with a stocked bar, fridge, and pretty much anything a person could want.

All Sam wanted was presently inside her. He slid his hand up her hip to her belly, holding her there at her midsection.

"God, you're stunning," he said as she rocked them both into heaven.

She moaned her reply, given she couldn't quite find any words, but she sure appreciated the sentiment. Tanner sometimes let her take control of their lovemaking, but once he was close, he took it back. Took it back, and she didn't mind one bit.

That's exactly what he did now. Nothing shifted with position or his noises, but the air got thick and he got rougher, and she loved every single second.

Her breasts bounced with each thrust he made and each

responding movement of her hips. With light touches, he trailed the back of his knuckles down, over her hips to hold her in place on the right side.

Tanner tilted her hips and groaned as she took him deeper. He moaned something incoherent, but it kinda sounded like her name, so she'd take it.

Then he pressed right where she loved it. Right at the apex of her thighs, in the one spot that she'd only found a few times herself. But Tanner seemed to have a treasure map or something, given that he hit it every single time.

She came spasming around him and he lifted in one quick movement, holding her against his chest as he finished as well.

They didn't move right away, which she liked. Loved how he liked to take those moments where they came back to their senses and just look at her like she was the most precious thing in his world.

"I'm falling in love with you, Sam," he said, holding her hips still, so they were still connected.

The warmth of his words thawed any residual ice from Sami Jo. This was them. She could have it.

"Same," she said, tipping her forehead against his. The curtain of her hair fell around them, cocooning the moment in some kind of time capsule she knew would always stay clear. Never fade into the background of other memories.

"If I started talking about rings, would you want to run?" he asked, which was absolutely bonkers, given that he was still inside her.

Was she ready to get married?

Gah, probably not. Not yet. Not because of him, but because she was still figuring out what it meant to be *her*. This was all new.

She wasn't hiding. But she wasn't not hiding, either.

Which meant… soon she would be known again. And that left her mouth dry and her lungs seeming to gasp for air.

And yet, the idea of an engagement to Tanner was not a

thought that left a bitter taste. Actually, it seemed like it might be nice to have something that tied them together besides their midnight promises.

"I can talk rings," she said, moving off of him so he could stand and take care of things. "I might need to talk slow."

"That works," he said, his back to her for a quick second. "We talk slow, you know where I'm coming from and where I wanna be someday. Same goes for you, yeah?"

"Yes," she said, moving over so he could pull back the covers and climb into bed.

"You wanna get dressed before sleep?"

She shook her head.

That got her a wicked grin.

She reached up, stroking the pad of her thumb along the edge of his neck. "I love you, Tanner."

He grinned a wicked grin, lining his body alongside hers and kissing her long and deep and… everything. "Same, Samantha Johnson."

"If this is the future, I am really enjoying it," she said.

Then they talked. Talked until they fell asleep together with the sound of the wheels under them as the backdrop to their future. Sam never let herself get too comfortable in one spot. This was the way of life she'd allowed up to this point. Time for things to change.

Being uncomfortable was overrated.

Chapter Twenty
SAMANTHA

"YOU CAN'T KEEP AVOIDING THEM," Sam said as Tanner added more product to his hair.

"Just because Hans hires a whole crew of stylists to come along with us on the tours doesn't mean they know what they're doing," Tanner fussed with his shirt. Tucking and then untucking it.

The stylists dressed him like some kind of doll they got to play with and leaned too far into his—what did Hans call it? Right, his "boy next door" image. Apparently, Hans and Courtney hoped it would bring in some of the fifteen to twenty population. Tanner, however, did not approve of the look.

Sam didn't hate it, though. He made a cute boy next door.

"Just because they want me to play the part doesn't mean I have to do it," he said, going with the shirt untucked.

Good call, since the styling team would've likely made him tuck it in.

He might be able to hold a conversation with a woman now, but every time the stylists got to him he froze like a rocker stuck in the headlights of boy band fashion.

That was why Tanner took care of this part himself before he left the bus. He even took extra time on his hair, so they didn't have a chance to "fuck it up."

He'd found it easier to pass off their "help" if he looked like he put in a good effort himself.

"You comin' to the stage tonight?" he asked, carefully, like he didn't want to let any of the hope bubbles form.

They'd had two shows on the road, and for both shows she'd stayed behind.

This was easier. The best way to prevent a Sami Jo sighting was to prevent the sighting. Easy as that.

"No, I'm good here." She leaned into the shiny mahogany paneling of Tanner's private bus.

"You should reconsider," he said.

She understood that he wanted her there. That he worried because she didn't leave the bus, not since they left Vancouver when they got *on* the bus.

The bus was kickass, but they were at concerts. She sort of wished she could take a peek backstage, feel the energy of a crowd that adored the band. Sink into the experience.

That wasn't for her though.

She had taken little steps one at a time and wasn't ready to dive right into the fray. Not that fray, anyway. There had been one thing from her Catiana meet-up that still rubbed funny.

"Can I ask you something?" Sam chewed at her lip, then stopped. They'd gotten a little rowdy last night and her lips were more tender than usual. In a good way, tender. Fuller from everything they'd, ahem, done for each other, to each other. In his case, on each other…

"Anything," he agreed. "Ask me anything."

"There's this thing that Catiana said to me, and it's totally been in my head the last little bit."

That got his attention. He didn't move to her, which was good because she didn't need that. And she appreciated that he let her have the space so she could spread her wings all on her own. He didn't always succeed, but she'd noted his effort. Appreciated it.

"I only need to know so I can put the entire experience with *her* behind me." She brought her notebook with her and held it against her chest.

"What is it?" he asked.

Sam forced herself to loosen her grip on the notebook. "She got in my head with some of the things she spewed."

"Tell me," he said, keeping his expression impassive. She knew him well enough to know that he, once again, found himself so furious at his ex. That happened a lot since Denver.

Sam took a deep breath, worried that what she'd say would be a wrecking ball to her confidence and everything they'd started building. "She said you told her about me. The night at Brek's. That you and Ashley both knew that she knew—"

"You know Ashley and I better than that," he said. Was that too quick? He seemed to say that really quickly. Almost like he'd been waiting for her to ask.

Gah, no. This was Tanner.

"You know us," he assured.

She did know them. They were both on her team, neither of them would jeopardize that. Sam nodded. "I just needed to be certain." She swallowed hard, because she had another question. This one was the one that really bugged. "She also said that you both used to laugh at me. Said you loved to use the song I wrote and… laugh. At me." She crumbled a little inside as she said the words. "Not about the song. I know the song's funny. But, she said you laughed about me."

He didn't say anything right away. Probably felt like she was putting him on the spot over things that weren't true. Straight from the mouth of a known liar.

"I know better," she said, holding up her hands. "In my

heart and in my head. But I can't shake it. I can't shake what she told me."

"Hey." He moved to her.

She dropped her head to his shoulder, and he held her. Just held her there as she relaxed into him. Let everything Tanner soothe all the past hurt.

"The past is in the past," he said, holding her hand up to his heart. "You know who I am now and what matters to me. I'm with you, Samantha Johnson. It may have started with Twister, but I love all the parts of you that make you, you. Even, and most especially, the Sami Jo part."

She didn't need to ask to know this was honest. Because Tanner was honesty in person form.

"I have this thing." She held up the notebook with her songs. She'd been gripping it so hard that the indentations from the edges left marks on her palm.

"Whatcha got?" Tanner asked.

"Dan said I should show you these," she said.

He held out his hand, and she stared at it for a long second, then she made the leap and handed it over.

"Against my better judgement, I decided to listen to him," she said, her hands shaking because this was a big deal. But she could do hard things.

"Are these your songs?" Tanner asked, his expression brightening like she'd offered him something more than only a notebook with words.

She nodded. Shoved her hands in the pockets of her jeans so they'd stop shaking. "Maybe check them out? See if you think they're good? They could be shit. But Dan said I need to work on my confidence. I got a whole lecture about it." She shivered.

Dan had taken her on as a project, it seemed. He video called daily to check in and texted often, too.

"Did he bring out his PowerPoint on confidence?" Tanner asked. "He's got one."

"No." She shook her head. "But he paced a lot while he lectured."

"That sounds like Dan." Tanner held the notebook in his grip like it was one of the most precious things anyone had ever shared with him.

"You've gotta go," she said, lifting and pressing her lips quickly against his. The familiarity of the movement was a gift she never thought she'd be able to give. And yet? Here they were.

The succession of three knocks that sounded more like someone attempting to pound in through the door was Hans's signature style.

"Come in," Tanner hollered.

Hans stepped into the bus, lugging a rolling suitcase. "You moving in?"

"No." He set the suitcase to the side. "I brought Sam a friend."

"Do it," a voice that sounded a helluva lot like Ashley said from outside the door.

All the nerves from before dissipated and Sam's heart swelled.

"I'm not doing it." Hans gritted his teeth.

"You have to," Ashley said, again. "Or I'm staying out here."

He should probably do whatever Ashley wanted him to do, because she was nothing if not persistent.

Hans pinched the bridge of his nose, said something under his breath about dealing with unreasonable people and then, surprise of surprises, Hans made jazz hands toward the door.

"Ashley!" he announced.

"Ahhhh," Ashley ran on the bus like it was a stage and she was the star. She patted Hans on the arm, which was funny 'cause no one just patted the guy. He was definitely not a guy who seemed like he would enjoy a pat of any sort.

"What are you doing here?" With a bubble of laughter Sam moved to Ashley and wrapped her in a hug.

"I heard a mean lady was awful to my best friend, and then I heard my best friend is not leaving the tour bus. And then Hans here—" She jerked her thumb toward Hans. "Offered me a ticket with backstage passes, a diamond necklace, and all the free food I can eat, if I'll just come get you to leave the bus." Ashley grinned. "So I'm here."

"A ticket and passes, yes," Hans said. "The rest? No." He turned to leave, paused as he stepped down. Stared Tanner right in the eye as he said, "She is now your problem."

"I'm nobody's problem but my own." Ashley started a personal, unaccompanied tour of the bus. Opening cupboards and poking around in the fridge. "Though Sam knows I snore, so I told Hans I need my own bedroom. I mean, as much fun as it would be to have a sleepover sleeping between you two, I'm not into that."

Sam caught Tanner's gaze and gave a subtle head shake. This was Ashley. No filter and always 100 percent herself.

"She's always like this when she gets excited or has too much orange juice. Give her a minute, she'll chill," Sam said.

"Hans assured me the couch pulls out?" Ashley asked.

"It does." Tanner nodded.

As he and Sam continued to get more comfortable together, his ability to speak without starting over had improved. His cheeks didn't even turn red most of the time.

"I asked if Hans pulls out too, and he did not find that as funny as I did," Ashley said.

And there it was. Tanner's cheeks turned more than a little pink as the tornado of all things Ashley swept right in and took hold of all the air in the room.

"I'll get the sofa made up while you are at the concert." Sam said, cutting off the invitation and guilt before it could be issued.

"I'd be good with that, but you're gonna be at the concert

with me, so I will do it when we get back." Ashley bounced onto the sofa. "I also brought earplugs for you both."

"Mach's bus has bunk beds," Tanner suggested. Probably because the doors on the bus were not-so-solid and he had created something of an after-concert routine with her that got a little… loud.

"Mach's bus also has Hans and—" Ashley pulled her lips to the side. "I need some space to crack that nut."

"I'm assuming you mean figuratively?" Sam asked, even though she could see Ashley on a mission was not one to give up.

Poor Hans.

"Either way." Ashley pointed to Sam. "That's what you're wearing backstage?"

"I'm not going."

"See, the thing is, I can't go if you don't go, and I *really* want to go."

Gah. Ashley was not going to let up on this.

"Fine." Sam tossed up her hands. "I'll go get dressed." She headed to the bedroom. "I have to find something appropriate for a drummer's girlfriend, but that also includes sunglasses and a hat."

"You could go sweater with a hoodie?" Ashley called behind her.

"I don't know." Tanner dove in with his thoughts. "It's pretty warm out. Better not to try too hard at incognito or they'll look harder and hope to find Lady Gaga or somebody like that."

"You know, it's so much easier being myself with a group of elderly people who don't know, don't remember, or don't care about Sami Jo. I can just wear my work clothes with them," Sam said from behind the door.

"Dockers and a polo do not a happy life make," Ashley said loud enough for Sam to hear.

To be clear, she didn't have to be very loud because the

thin door allowed each room to hear what was happening in the other. That's why there couldn't be any sexy post-concert time with Tanner unless everyone got super uncomfortable.

"I've never been backstage," Ashley said. "It's much easier to be myself when I am doing nifty new things that involve rock stars."

"Nice," Tanner said. "I approve of this tactic."

"I'll get her there," Ashley assured.

Sam paused pulling the new shirt over her head. "I can hear you, you know."

She quickly finished changing, pulled the lanyard with her backstage pass over her head, and opened the door to the living room. The midriff-baring top she'd selected was fire and she didn't need a mirror to know her hips absolutely owned the jeans. Even so, she couldn't shake the stomachache that always started when she even thought about going out there.

"Do you mind if we walk over with you?" Sam asked. She tried to keep her words steady, but they shook all the same.

"Yeah." He held out his hand. "We'll go together."

Sam gripped his hand like he was her everything, and Ashley skip-hop-walked along on the other side as they headed toward the stadium.

"There's always food backstage," he assured Ashley. "All you can eat."

"Yay," Ashley said. "I knew Hans wouldn't let me down."

Things moved quickly backstage. Tanner deftly managed to slip away every single time the fashion police showed up. Mach, she noted, used the same maneuvers with them.

"You came," Courtney said with an excited squee. She hurried to Sam. "You are going to love this."

Ashley settled in with the wives, but Sam didn't sit. She stood right at the edge of the stage, balanced on that precipice where she was still backstage but only one more step and she'd be in front of everyone.

This should've been terrifying, but the energy of the stadium already started to drift backstage. She seemed to be poised on a cliff of excitement with the rest of the crowd, all through the opening act.

Waiting and preparing for the drop.

And then the Dimefront guys hit the stage. The energy shot to the stratosphere.

Her breath caught and she was under some kind of a spell. There was a moment before the first chord that seemed like a free fall.

Then the roar of tens of thousands of people all cheering at the same time washed over her, lifted her up, as Bax opened with one of the more popular Dimefront songs.

That wave of sound pushed away all of Sam's defenses. The urge to dance. To sing. To be in the center of that spotlight cracked something in the wall she'd fortified around her dreams, exposing all the hopes that ten-year-old Sam had cultivated. What she'd wanted.

And for the first time in forever, she remembered. Remembered why she'd wanted the dream in the first place.

Chapter Twenty-One
TANNER

TANNER'S MOM had always said that when things looked their best, that's when to expect the worst.

But Tanner's mom had been wrong about a lot of things. This was one of those things.

They'd had a few more shows since that first one when Sam stood in the wings soaking in the vibe.

She loved it.

He understood this not only because of the way she smiled when Dimefront played, but also she'd been coming to the concerts. Escaping the busses with Ashley and hanging out with the band.

Tanner's whole world was lighter.

Unfortunately, Tanner was reveling in that feeling and reading Sam's message when he walked straight into the jaws of Hans's styling team.

"Shit," he said, accidentally making eye contact with the head stylist.

He turned to bolt but he didn't get far because Greg, the

reporter doing a spread for *Rolling Rock magazine*, seemed to pop out from behind one of the equipment boxes. Veteran reporter. Doing the Dimefront album creation, release, and tour run-down.

"Tanx," Greg said. "Have a minute for a few questions?"

Boy, did he. Greg could have all the minutes until the styling team got tired of circling.

Tanner stopped. "Absolutely."

"Tell me a little about how things have changed for you with Dimefront since you got started?" Greg asked, amiable as ever.

"The past couple of years things have only gotten better. The group's grown as Knox, and Bax, even Linx paired off. It's nice to have a family like this."

Sam and Ashley trotted toward their impromptu interview. He lifted his chin their direction. "Go on ahead, Sam. Give me five, yeah?"

Sam gave a thumbs up.

"Sam's your new flame?" Greg asked, conversationally giving Sam a solid look that Tanner did not like.

Sam paused at the perusal, gave Tanner a questioning glance. "I'll catch up," he mouthed.

"I'm not talking about personal shit." Tanner tried to smile, keep it friendly. But the words didn't come out that way, not really.

"When one of the new members of Dimefront starts seeing someone seriously, fans are going to want to know," Greg pointed out.

"Personal stuff is personal," Tanner clarified since Courtney had told them all that they had to be extra nice to *Rolling Rock* so the magazine would be extra nice to them.

"Sam?" Greg called Sam's name, ignoring everything that Tanner had laid out.

Tanner pursed his lips.

Sam paused, turned.

"It's all good," Greg assured. "I wanted to meet you. Sam? Sam, right? I've heard a lot about Tanx's new girl."

Sam looked to Tanner. He gave her the go-ahead to come over. She grinned, stepped up to them and shook Greg's hand. "Super great to meet you, too."

"Shoulda worn a hoodie," Ashley said under her breath. "Babushka suggested the hoodie today. She's usually right."

"She lets you call her Babushka?" Sam asked, her eyebrows falling together. "Already?"

"Right." Greg adjusted his press badge. "I understand you also have celebrity status. Sami Jo? Isn't it? I'm hoping I can ask you a few questions about that."

Fucking hell, he did not.

"Dude, what are you talking about?" Tanner asked, stepping a little in front of Sam so she could take off if she needed.

Sam had sucked in a breath and reached for his arm, gripping it tight, her fingernails breaking through the numb and reminding him this wasn't a dream. This was reality. A reality raising his blood pressure.

"I'm just Sam. Samantha if you want. That's all I am," Sam said as though she'd been rehearsing this very moment.

The words flowed so smooth, even if her grip got tighter.

A photographer stepped beside Greg and started snapping pics of Sam. Not like the paparazzi with all the flashes. No, this guy took the pictures like he had a right to do it. He probably did, with having an all-access invitation to anything that went on backstage. That's why Hans told them not to pull any shit once they came out of the busses.

"You ask first before you take someone's picture. She doesn't like her picture taken, asshat," Ashley said, putting her hand up in front of the lens. "Stop being a douche canoe paddling down the river of fuck you."

Tanner blinked extra hard because Ashley called the photographer from *Rolling Rock* a douche canoe. And the reporter knew this was Sami Jo. And Tanner had a concert to put on for tens of thousands in fifteen minutes.

Everything was fucked.

"Hey, guys." Courtney hustled over to them. "What's going on? Greg, you need another beer?"

"Nope." Greg kept his entire focus on Sam like he was eye-fucking her and he better damn well not be doing that.

Tanner wanted to punch him in the face.

Courtney, not being dense, must've sensed this because she stepped right in the middle of everyone.

"What'd I miss?" Bax asked, draping an arm over Sam.

"We've been talking about Sami Jo here," Greg said, clearly intrigued by the dynamics of everything happening around him. He wasn't a dick about it. He was a professional asking about a lead.

"How the hell did he find out?" Bax asked, staring at Courtney.

Courtney who let out a breath like she was a balloon losing all her air.

"I got a tip. Did a little recon. Put it all together and realized my source is correct," Greg said. "This is my job. It's only my job."

That didn't mean Tanner wasn't aching to slug him. Tell him off at least. Fuck it. He was gonna do it. "Sam and Ashley here? They're my guests—"

He didn't get any further in that statement because Ashley flung herself to the ground a la Babushka. Really, she went for it. He could've sworn he heard something crack.

"Ashley?" Sam dropped to her knees beside her friend. "Oh my God."

"Why'd you trip me?" Ashley pointed at the cameraman. "That's not okay. Shit. Shit. Shit." She held her shin. "I think it's broken."

"What's going on over here?" Hans asked, striding into the fray.

So much that Tanner wasn't sure where to begin.

Hans stepped beside Ashley and gave her a onceover that did not seem platonic. Funny, because Ashley was putting on an excellent performance about her shin.

Unless that crack was the real deal. In which case... Damn. Fuck. Damn.

Tanner knelt next to Sam. Even Greg kneeled, too.

"Let's, uh, get you to the first aid tent. We'll get the doctor over there." Hans didn't wait for Bax or Tanner or anyone else to offer to do the transfer. He lifted Ashley with extreme care. Tanner could've sworn he saw a sly grin just touch the edges of Hans's mouth before he lifted her. Hans gave a Sam a cue to come along with them.

Once they were out of earshot, Tanner turned to Greg and the photog. "They are my guests. You won't harass them or take their picture unless either invites you to." Tanner crossed his arms. "You get me?"

"Tanner," Courtney said brightly. "You should go check on your guests." Then her expression turned serious. "I got this."

She better have it.

He headed to the tent, stepped inside and apparently Ashley was illustrating her ability to play hopscotch with both feet.

"See, I'm good," she assured.

"I heard a crack," Tanner said.

"Uh-huh." Ashley nodded. "I took some lessons from Babushka on making it look more authentic."

"They found me." Sam stared into space. "I knew it would happen. But why couldn't it be tomorrow? Or the next day? Why does it have to be now?"

Mach pushed through the flap that acted as a makeshift door to the tent. "Just heard. How can I help?"

"I don't know," Sam said. "I don't know anything right now."

"We're waiting for Courtney to sort things out." Tanner sat beside Sam, giving her a little space but still there behind her if she needed him.

"Are you okay? " Courtney asked Ashley, striding through the tent opening.

Ashley was mid-hop dance.

"Clearly she's fine." Courtney pressed her fingertips to her temples. "This is shit. Totally shit. They're running the story. They want to be the ones to scoop it."

"Okay," Sam said. She dropped to sit on one of the folding chairs. "It's okay. We knew this was going to happen."

"Somebody could deflect the attention," Courtney continued, doing the bit where she spoke to herself. "Good job on that before, Ashley." She paused her thought train to give Ashley a good once-over. "They are worried about getting sued, but they're still going to do the exposé."

Hans cleared his throat. "This is not good."

"That's why I said this is shit." Courtney lifted her hands in surrender. "I'll make my calls, but this just screwed with all my initial plans for…well…you." She gestured to Sam.

"You need somebody to deflect the attention?" Mach asked, like he had an idea for that.

Whatever idea he had, Tanner would guess it wasn't a good one. Probably not a legal one.

"I need to think up some kind of stunt or something that will get all the attention off Sam. I was thinking of doing this thing with the Red Bull guys when everything came out, but I don't have time now to make that happen." Courtney stopped pacing long enough to stare out the window toward the stadium.

"Don't worry." Mach clapped Courtney on the shoulder before moseying from the tent. "I got this."

"He doesn't have this." Courtney stared after him. "But you all do need to get on stage. So let's do that and while you do that, I will figure this."

Hans met Courtney's eyes, and something passed between them.

"Did you get the source?" Hans asked.

"Of course, I did. Catiana is nothing if not a woman of her word." She glanced at Sam. Then Tanner. "I'm so sorry."

His heart dropped and the cold hand of defeat took hold.

"I guess the payout was an acceptable alternative to getting rejected by Tanner," Sam said. He didn't like the defeated sound of those words from her.

Hans stomped out like a bull ready to go take on Pottery Barn.

"You need to do your job," Sam said to Tanner. "I'll wait here. Or in your bus."

"But not backstage," he said, his limbs heavier than a moment before. She loved being at the side of the stage.

Truth was? He loved her there, too.

"You'll be here or there when I get done?" he asked. Damn, but he tried to keep his tone even, but it didn't work.

"I won't go anywhere," Sam agreed. With that, she pressed a kiss to his lips, and he headed to work.

Chapter Twenty-Two
SAMANTHA

TIME WAS an interesting thing as life fell to bits around a person. It happened so slow and so fast, all at the same time. Like swinging on a swing set as a child, slicing forward through the air and then falling back. Weightless, yet somehow still moving.

Sam didn't know how long it had been since the concert started, but now it was dark.

"Mom, they are going to post it soon. So I wanted you to have a heads up," Sam said into her phone. The group moved to Hans's bus once the music started. Honestly, this was pretty much exactly like the one she shared with Tanner, so it didn't really matter where they were.

"Baby girl, they can't scare us anymore," Mom assured.

The infamous "they." The "they" no one really ever knew.

"If it's all out there, come home," Dad said. They did the phone thing on speaker so they could tag team Sam. "We want you home."

"I'm actually in a pretty good place here. Everyone is being amazing." She folded a little inside herself even as she spoke the words.

"That's not a healthy way to live," Dad said.

He clearly hadn't seen the buffet table.

"We're ready when you are," Mom said. "Time to come home."

Sam wasn't certain how she felt about that. Happy, sure. But also nervous? Things could get so bad, so fast.

Goodbyes said, she hung up with her parents. Irina, Becca, and Ashley were all monitoring social media. Waiting for it to drop.

"Sam." Courtney pushed the phone away from her cheek and covered the mouthpiece. "If I get you an exclusive on Entertainment Now, will you do it? If we move quick, it'll pre-empt *Rolling Rock*." She sighed. "Words I never thought I'd actually say, but we will have more control if we do it this way."

"Too late, it's up," Ashley said. Turning her phone, so everyone could see the image of Sam right next to an old one of Sami Jo.

The headline? *Dimefront's Tanx Identifies Sami Jo.*

"Hitting TMZ as we speak, I'm sure," Irina said, hitting refresh on her phone.

Sam hated how that made her feel creepy crawlies all over her skin.

"Tanner didn't do it," she said. That was the most important correction to be made. "Can Entertainment Now make that clear?"

"You're trending on…well…everywhere," Ashley said. She set her phone aside and reached for Sam's hands. "I'm sorry, Sam."

Sam wasn't feeling a whole lot right then. She should be angry. She should be excited to see Tanner. But all she had was numb reality.

"Entertainment Now still wants the exclusive," Courtney said. Then she tapped her phone to her lips. "New thought." Courtney sat in front of Sam. "Hear me out."

"I love it when she does this." Irina moved closer. "Usually she gets the best ideas after those very words."

"Okay." Might as well hear her out, given Sam didn't have many choices at the moment.

"You can sing," Courtney announced. "You're good. Or you were good. I'm sure you're still good."

"She's still good, and she writes music," Ashley added. "It's exceptional."

Did Ashley seriously violate the best friend code of secrets without any hesitation? Sam's mouth tasted funny. Like she'd just been sick.

"I believe that," Courtney said. "So… why don't you become a performer?" Courtney continued. "We pretend that this was all our idea. We're launching your new career. Sami Jo Take Two."

"I did not see that coming," Irina said.

"Curveball," Becca agreed. "But I like it."

"She's excellent," Ashley assured. "So good."

"I only sing in the shower now." Sam shook her head even though she wanted to jump up and own it. *Yes! I am amazing!*

"I've seen you backstage watching the guys. You have the same look as all the other artists who take that stage," Irina said. "It's not a bad thing, at all."

"I can use this." Courtney held up her phone to the exposing post. "I use it. I can't spin the press away. That won't work. So I think we lean into it. Announce Sami Jo is back. Working on a record. Or if you want to be an actress, we get you a few auditions. I hear they're looking for new hosts on a couple of long-running game shows. We could try for that."

"Wouldn't that be a lie? I mean, I have done nothing other than work at retirement facilities for years. I can't just decide one day I'm a singer." Sam was nearly sure.

"Why not?" Becca asked. "Isn't that how it happens?"

"It can be the truth," Courtney assured. "All of those things can be the truth. We make it true, right now. You decided to work on a record? Boom. Done. Hans and I? We deal with the rest."

"I don't even have an agent. A manager." Or the slightest idea what came next. "What if it all goes downhill again?"

"You have Hans. You have me. We have a good team, and we can make this work." Courtney seemed to really believe this.

Why did it sound so appealing to be the one on stage?

"They'll laugh," she said.

"I don't think so," Irina said. She held up her phone to one of the social media posts. "There are mean comments, sure. Some people are just born dicks. But most of them are human beings super glad you are still alive."

"They won't laugh." Courtney assured, stone-cold serious. "They laughed because of how that guy framed your video. Had he framed it differently, they would've taken you more seriously."

"It was a song about how much I love breaded cheese." There wasn't much that could be taken seriously there.

"Maybe not so seriously," Courtney admitted. "And I can't rewrite the history. It's there. But I'm a publicist and when I can't make something go away, I figure out how to work with it." She took a long moment before she said, "I suggest we work with it."

"She can sing," Ashley said. "And she writes songs. And she's amazing."

Sam didn't say anything to that.

"I've been paying attention over the decades we've been best friends." Ashley crossed her arms. "I know you still write. And I know you still sing. Shower or no, you're good. I will fight anyone, including you, who says different."

"I believe she will fight you." Courtney said. Then she turned to Ashley. "The way you tossed yourself on the ground for her. Color me impressed."

"Are these decisions I make without Tanner?" Sam asked, thinking it through, out loud.

"I don't know how to say this without coming across like an ass, so I'm just gonna say it." Courtney pinched her face all up. "Tanner wouldn't ask you about his career moves. I don't think you should have to ask him, either."

"Girl's got a point," Becca said.

"But if we're building something—which we want to be—then we should start talking about things, right? Like you and Bax? I bet he talks to you before he plans a tour or anything?" Sam confirmed.

"She's also got a point there," Irina said.

"I'm on the planning committee for the tours, so it's a little different," Courtney said. "But I see where you are coming from."

"Can I say something?" Becca asked, her tone as soothing as always.

Sam nodded.

"Relationships are give and take. They require communication. It's important that you also make decisions that are for you. You alone. Just like it's important that Tanner does that, too. It doesn't mean you're doing things without each other. It means you ensure you don't disregard the things you need as well."

That was a lot to digest in one small soundbite.

"I don't have to decide right now, do I?" Sam asked, fiddling with the Loopy case on her phone.

"No, of course not," Courtney assured. "This is a huge decision. But it's something that I can work with. Something Hans can work with. We make this go away by leaning into it. I don't know why I didn't think of it before." Courtney's phone pinged. She checked the screen. "The guys are coming back here. Hans cancelled the meet and greet." She frowned. "I gotta send something out on that cancellation so it doesn't look like it's connected to you."

"It is connected to me, though, right?" Sam asked. Tanner hadn't mentioned that they ever cancelled the VIP stuff.

"Well, yeah." Courtney furiously typed on her cell. "But we can't tell the press that."

"Oh damn," Irina said. "Oh hell. This could be bad. Or good. Or very, very bad. Or very, very good."

"What now?" Courtney asked.

Sam would bet ten dollars the woman would either win the publicist of the year after this or get a raging migraine.

"Mach announced a competition." Irina said this as though she didn't want to say it.

"What kind of competition?" Sam asked.

"He is doing a dating competition." Ashley's eyes went big. "Did he think this through?"

The boys all clomped their way onto the bus, each of them heading for their respective partner, smooching it up, and then settling in. Tanner went straight to her, and Ashley made funny faces at Hans, who stayed by the door with Mach.

"Mach." Courtney marched over to him, put her hands on his shoulders. "I want to shake you right now. But I also want to kiss you."

"Shake him. Don't kiss him," Bax suggested. "Otherwise, I'll have to beat the shit out of him."

"I am helping." Mach grinned. "Tanner needed someone to distract shit? I handled it."

"Fuck me." Hans stared at his phone. Then he put his face in his hands.

"No thanks," Mach said. "But I reopened my account on Nocturnal Cupid, then I posted to my socials."

Hans looked at Courtney. "Who gave him access to his social media?"

"It was not me." Courtney was gritting her teeth.

Honestly, Sam appreciated the focus wasn't on her right then. A nice reprieve from the rest of the day.

"You don't have any rules?" Irina asked.

"Rules for what?" Tanner asked.

"Uh-huh, same question," Sam said.

"Why would I need rules?" Mach asked. "It's a simple PR stunt."

"You don't do stunts without permission," Hans said, way too relaxed for Sam's comfort. Given that he never relaxed, this seemed like a decoy.

"What's the stunt?" Tanner asked, carefully.

"I opened my account. I posted on my socials with a link that the thousandth person to match me gets the Mach exclusive Dimefront experience," Mach announced.

"What does the experience include?" Bax asked, more cautious than Tanner.

"Depends on who I get matched with." Mach grinned big at that. "But the minimum is dinner, tickets, backstage passes, meeting all you assholes."

"That's how he wrote it." Courtney pursed her lips. "Word for word, that's how he wrote it including the 'all my asshole bandmates.'"

"It could be anyone!" Irina tossed her hands to the side. "Put limits and fine print on this kind of thing."

Courtney and Hans did the mind meld thing once more, where they seemed to have an entire conversation without saying a word.

"It could be anyone," Mach said with a sly grin that made Sam scoot a little closer to Tanner. "Like that woman from Amsterdam with the tongue ring. Could be her? That wouldn't be bad."

"Or it could be a serial killer Ten!" Courtney pressed her fingers against her eyes.

She was going the migraine route, it seemed.

"I'm choosing to be positive. I posted and I've already got

like five hundred matches to go through." He held up his phone. "It'll be fine. Lucky one thousand wins the prize, and it takes some heat off of Sam."

"I would like to point out that Twitter is reporting an uptick in the number of people who are hoping Mach matches with Sami Jo," Becca said. "That could be fun."

"I'm not on that Nocturnal site." She wasn't.

"Also, you're with me," Tanner pointed out.

That, too. "Yes, mostly that," Sam agreed.

"This is all remarkably unhelpful," Hans said, his glare fixed on Mach. "You had ten minutes before the show."

"I can get a lot done really quick when I need to." Mach shrugged. "And Sam, if you wanna join the site, I'll tell you when I'm ready for the winner. You click the match. Boom. Done. You and me go to dinner."

"You've got to be fucking kidding me," Hans said. He turned and left the bus.

"I'm going to go talk to him." Ashley scurried after him.

Everyone took that moment to let it sink in that someone wanted to follow Hans when he was in one of these moods. Usually he needed a long breather and then he'd craft the perfect plan to extract them from whatever mess they'd created.

"I'm going to go stop Ashley from pissing him off too badly," Sam said, standing and heading after her friend. "Give me a sec."

Hans and Ashley stood super close to each other by a stack of the black equipment boxes. The big ones made of plywood with wheels and silver clasps to keep things inside.

She started toward them, but they headed around to one of the other buses. Was that Bax's or was it Linx's? Crud, she didn't know.

Following them, she stopped at the first step. They were arguing.

That wasn't good. Ashley could argue with anyone, but

arguing with Hans was as bad as arguing with the photog from *Rolling Rock*. Both were poor decisions.

"You need to tell her the truth," Hans said. "My guy at *Rolling Rock* said Catiana told them everything."

"There's nothing to tell," Ashley insisted. "Nothing was bad."

"Tanner told Catiana that Sam is Sami Jo," Hans said this matter-of-fact like it was just standard run-of-the-mill conversation.

But Sam felt those words crushing her heart with each syllable Hans uttered.

"It didn't happen like that. She guessed, and then he accidentally didn't correct her. I was there. I know what happened," Ashley assured.

"Tell her."

"Life has hurt her enough. I will do nothing that will hurt her more and telling her will hurt her."

"The fact that you knew she'd figured it out and still didn't tell your friend? Catiana spilled that too. They'll use it next. This won't end," Hans said.

What? Sam required a second—possibly many—to sort through that.

No, it couldn't be true, because that made no sense. Why would either of them keep this from her?

She stepped away from the door of the bus and hurried to the one she shared with Tanner. She grabbed her purse, a hoodie sweatshirt, and she decided it was time to disappear again.

Not forever, only to give herself some time to think. To get past the anesthetized feeling in her fingers and toes so she could process it all.

Then she'd figure out their future, and if they still had one together.

Her future, and what came next for her.

Chapter Twenty-Three
TANNER

TANNER WOULD NOT PANIC. This wasn't the time.

"She's not with you?" he asked Ashley. "She went to find you."

"What?" Ashley turned a few shades paler than usual, so quickly he could see it even in the low light of the streetlamp outside the stadium where they'd parked the busses. "Oh crap. Let me get Hans."

Tanner shot off a text to Sam.

Tanner: Need to see you.

No response.

He pressed the icon with her photo, putting through a call.

Straight to voicemail.

Fuck.

The air seemed to be thicker all of a sudden. Harder to breathe in.

He texted again:

Tanner: Where are you?

Nothing. No dancing bubbles alerting him she was responding. No read receipt. Nothing.

Tanner: I love you

Tanner: I'm worried

"Hans is here," Ashley said, hurrying back.

"What happened?" Hans asked. "Why isn't she with you?"

"When did she come to get me?" Ashley asked, like this was the important question and not where the heck Sam had gone off to.

"Right after you left. Ashley—"

"Hans and I were arguing." She closed her eyes. "Catiana..."

He wanted to scream at the sound of her name. "I'm so fucking tired of hearing her name."

Ashley nodded. "Me too. But she told *Rolling Rock* that it was you who told her Sami Jo's identity."

"Yeah, I know that part." It was the headline. But Sam understood he hadn't told her. He hadn't. They'd covered it.

He'd already asked that it be clarified by Courtney when she made her plan for clean-up. It'd go out in the press releases. Be a little correction box no one looked at but him. But it'd be there. On the record.

"In the big article coming out in the magazine, Catiana—"

Tanner grimaced at her name.

"—she clarifies you didn't tell her specifically. You simply didn't correct her when she guessed," Hans said, stepping into their huddle. "That is the accurate version, yes?"

Tanner's lips went dry. His mouth, too. He nodded.

"I told Hans about it. Since, you know, I'm an accomplice." Ashley's shoulders sank as she spoke. "Dammit, I was in on this."

"Catiana also talked about how you both made good fun of Sam back in the day," Hans said with a frown.

"Dammit." Why was history so hard to rewrite? And why was it always trying too hard to fuck him?

This was it. He blew out a breath. Scraped his fingers over his scalp. He'd lose Sam because he'd been an idiot. Wasn't that the sad story of lost love always? And he didn't even know if she was hurt. Okay or not okay?

The pressure of all the universe seemed to push on him from all sides.

"Sam is fine," Hans said, as though reading his thoughts. "She checked into a Hilton a few blocks from here. I just heard. Unfortunately, I heard through the wrong grapevine and the paps are all over. It's like she's Justin Bieber in his biggest days. They've gone nuts for her. This is more than Courtney and I ever imagined or planned for."

"She runs. When she's scared or hurt, she runs. It's what I always did, too," Tanner admitted.

"What pulled you out of it?" Ashley asked.

"I finally had a family who wouldn't let me run."

"Then be that for her," Hans said.

"Can you get me into the hotel?" Tanner asked.

Hans nodded. "Through the back?"

Duh. "I'm sure as fuck not going in the front door."

He would not give up on Sam. And if she was ready to give up on him, then he'd be sure she didn't give up on being herself. All of herself.

He choked on that thought. If that's the last thing he could give her, it would have to be enough.

Hans worked fast, and soon Tanner stood in front of Room 315. He knocked.

"It's Tanner," he said through the door. "Hans found you. I asked him to get me here."

The scraping of the deadbolt and the chain, and then the door pulled open.

She was okay. He moved into the room and hugged her so tight.

"Tanner." She put her arms around his middle as the door clicked closed behind them.

"I've been so fucking worried." He didn't release her. Just held on while he could. While she let him.

"I'm sorry," she said. "I needed someplace to think."

This is where he should lay it out that he would back off, but he needed to be sure she understood why it was so important that she—

"Don't do this. Don't disappear. I can't." He pulled back, shoved his hands in his hair. "I can't lose you, Sam. I want to be strong enough to let you go, but I can't. I'm not that strong."

An odd calm descended over her. And a numbness hit him like the world was in slow motion, and the only two people going at normal speed were the two of them.

"Did you know Catiana figured me out that night at Brek's? And you didn't tell me?" she asked.

"I don't want you to run," he said.

"It's not cool that I left without telling someone. I get that. I'd be pretty upset if it was you who took off. I'm sorry about that. I also need you to answer the question." Her face pulled tight with pain as she spoke.

"Please, don't do this," he said.

"That's not an answer," she countered.

"It's the only answer I have."

"Please tell me," she whispered.

"Yeah." He nodded and his heart sank to the icky hotel carpet. "She told me she knew I'd found Sami Jo," he continued. "I asked her to keep it to herself."

"That was your solution?"

In hindsight, it wasn't a smart solution. He knew that now. "That didn't work out so well. I'm regretting that decision."

She blew out a breath. "And then, on top of it all, you didn't tell me."

He shook his head. "I didn't want to lose you."

"I opened up to you. Let you see all of me! The messy and the gross and the—"

"I don't want you to run," he said again. This time, he moved to her. "Because I know how that can end. So I didn't tell you about Catiana. I didn't tell you that I knew your song because I was one of the idiots who made fun of you about it. God, Sam. If I could take everything back and do it differently, I would. I would, Sam. I would."

She didn't back away as he came closer and pulled her into his embrace.

"I'm so mad about this," she said, her breaths uneven. "Mad at you for knowing that *your ex* had figured me out. Mad at Ashley."

"I don't want to be," she continued. "Having you here makes me forget about the mad. But then I remember how you talked about the importance of honesty. Yet, you didn't tell me any of this—not that you laughed at me or that you understood there was a risk in Catiana. No, you didn't tell me until there was no other choice."

"I know. I did that."

"But it's not your choice," she said, holding his gaze with hers. "These are the things you tell someone when you're in a relationship with them."

"Sam… I was afraid you'd leave."

"I would've."

"Exactly."

"That wasn't your decision to make. Then or now."

"Sam, you can't keep running. Because you'll run and run and run and yes, things were shit. But you can't spend your life running away. I know this. I know how it can be exhausting."

"I want to go home," she said. Her tone stayed even.

"Denver. Okay. We'll make it happen." He'd make anything happen at this point.

"No." She shook her head. "I want to go home. Home. There's only one place that's ever been, really."

Now that? That fucking wrecked him.

"Are we done?" he asked, hoping like hell this was just one of those things they'd talk about someday and remember how it made them stronger.

"Do you want to be?" she asked.

Why was she so detached from him? From everything?

"I want to say no." She pulled her lips between her teeth. "But I'm not sure that's the right answer. So I want some time to think about it. Can I have that?"

He had little choice in it, now, didn't he?

"I love you," he said, hoping it would be enough.

"And I love you, too," she said. "I do."

But even with the words, he could tell she wasn't certain love was enough. And he understood that. When you spend your life running? Love didn't really factor.

Chapter Twenty-Four
SAMANTHA

A week later

SAM'S PARENTS hadn't changed her bedroom. It remained exactly as it had when she first moved away. Baby blue carpet, the Selena Gomez poster on the wall by the window, and the guitar stand in the corner all stayed just the same as they had back then.

Sitting cross-legged on her tie-dyed bedspread she now understood that while this room didn't change, she'd changed tons.

Color Sam surprised when the majority of messages Sami Jo received said good things. Stories about how her song had made days better. How parents sang it with their kids, and the spouses, or their moms and dads. How it had mattered to them.

The influx of goodness pushed Sam to nudge Courtney about maybe giving this career a shot.

Of course, the trolls were out in full force, but so were the people who loved her song. She could see the balance now, even if it wasn't always a comfortable equilibrium.

Tanner: 'morning

Sam: hi!

Tanner: Going back to Denver today

Sam: last night's concert good?

Tanner: Bax crowd surfed

Court not amused

Mach still trying to figure out online dating

I'm missing you

Sam: miss you too

spending time with mom and dad

ready to go back to normal

whatever that is

Tanner: see u in Denver

Sam: <3 you

Tanner: i love you

Sam: . . .

Sam typed out *same*. Deleted it. Then typed it again. Then deleted it.

Gah. She wasn't angry at Tanner.

Resigned, sure, not angry. She still loved him, too. And Ashley.

She'd made choices, and they'd made choices. What came next? That was the big question.

Tanner loved Sam's songs. So Sam decided to share them with Courtney. Let Courtney decide for herself if Sam had the chops for the business. Courtney believed she did, and phoned almost daily with ideas about Sam's potential career in music. How they'd position it. Label ideas and packaging. She really believed Sam could do it.

Sam would say she nudged her in that direction, but that would be a lie. Courtney was full on shoving her. Gently, and with a plan.

Tanner believed Sam could do it, too, though they hadn't talked on the phone.

Sam asked for space to sort out this part of her life, and Tanner, forever the good guy he was, agreed to give it to her.

Now that she'd had her time to wallow and process, she was ready to move forward.

They'd texted about mundane life stuff, and her new influx of notoriety.

He seemed to wait for her to make the first move onto something more.

Tanner did ask if he could share some of her songs with Courtney and the guys. They loved them. Bax even messaged her to stop fucking around and embrace her genius.

That had made her laugh.

Linx assured Sam that if she could still hold the pitch—which she could—then she was the real deal.

They all barely knew her, and yet they cared.

The light knock on the bedroom door of Sam's childhood home had her looking up from her cell.

"How's my girl?" Mom asked, standing there with a glass of orange juice Sam already knew was for her. Mom seemed to have a continued concern over Sam's Vitamin C intake. She set it on the nightstand but didn't force the issue.

Sam gave the juice a pointed glance, then her mom. "I'm good, Mom."

"Keeps your blood sugar up," Mom said with that smile she didn't seem to shake since Sam arrived home. "Hypo-glycemia isn't a joke."

Sam would drink it. Because it was her mom and she adored her mom.

"Is Ashley coming over later?" Mom asked.

"I think so," Sam said. She couldn't stay mad at Ashley any more than she could be angry at Tanner.

"You should talk to her, you know," Mom said. She lifted her hands like she was surrendering. "I know. It's not my business, but you two need to have a good chat about this whole mess."

"Do you think she betrayed me?" Sam asked, the question so soft her mom probably didn't hear it.

"No," Mom said without hesitation. "I think she did what she thought was best for you. In my experience when we come from a place like that and it doesn't work out, it only means we need to communicate better. Let the other person know what's going on, even if it might hurt them."

Sam nodded. Mom was correct, per the norm.

Turned out, Ashley didn't get proper approval at work before the Canada excursion, so her boss said she didn't need to come back. That's why Ashley came home with Sam. Things remained stilted between them, but Ashley was her best friend forever and ever. They'd make it through this mess, just as she and Tanner would, too.

Ashley didn't seem too disappointed about losing her job. More disappointed in losing the paycheck.

"I'll make extra snacks," Mom said with a wink.

Mom had taken a different approach to the paparazzi, who hid in the bushes and waited on the sidewalk. That approach?

She fed them. Did what she could to make them comfortable. Took them snacks and orange juice and asked about their parents. Courtney said this could be brilliant because now they all really liked Sami Jo since she had a kickass mom.

Dad drew the line at inviting them inside.

Sam agreed with him.

The doorbell rang. Sam grinned. Another package from Tanner.

"How long are you going to make the boy wait?" Mom asked.

Sam stood, moved to the window, and glanced outside. Only a couple of guys sat in the lawn chairs Mom had put out for them. Waiting. Waiting for nothing, really, except lunch from her mom.

Sam stayed inside.

The initial flare of Sami Jo interest dissipated when Sami Jo didn't actually do anything. She was like a sleeping puppy they kept poking with a stick but who refused to respond. Instead, her mom fed them and gave them a place to sit.

"It's another one for Sam," Dad hollered through the house.

Mom lifted her eyebrows. "Don't make him wait too much longer."

Sam had been home with her parents for a solid week when the first gift arrived. Roses. Of course, there would be roses. They still sat on her nightstand. They wouldn't be going anywhere. Tanner sprung for the preserved kind that lasted forever.

The day after the roses? Tanner sent her a pair of running shoes. In the right size and everything. He supported her and her decisions: *Run if that's what makes you happy. - T*

"Delivery for Sam." Dad moseyed into the room with a package under one arm and an apple in the other hand. He bit into the apple and handed her the package. "It's cold. The package. The apple's not."

She pulled off the brown paper wrapping.

Mozzarella sticks and a note.

"What's it say?" Mom asked, leaning in.

Sam cleared her throat. "Don't forget to enjoy the things you love."

"That's poignant," Mom said. "And the truth."

Fuuuudge.

"I'm going back to Denver," Sam said. A girl couldn't stay angry when a guy bought her mozzarella sticks.

She lifted her phone and typed out a message to Tanner.

Sam: same

Tanner: ...

Tanner: mozz sticks made it didn't they?

Sam: 🖤

"I need to book a plane ticket, apparently," Sam announced.

"I'm sure gonna miss those boys out front." Mom peeked through the window and waved. "I'll make them a sandwich for the road."

"Mom?" Sam asked. Then she held up the frozen cheese sticks. "Make 'em these."

~

"THANKS FOR COMING WITH ME," Sam said, following Ashley through the jetway.

Sam had gone incognito with her hair pulled up in a baseball cap, Clark Kent glasses, and baggy clothes with a hoodie for good measure.

A few people did double takes, but one look from Ashley and they kept their distance.

Ashley came along even though she didn't have employment in Denver anymore. She still had an apartment to clear out, and she didn't want Sam to be alone. Hans had arranged for Ashley's car to be waiting at Denver International Airport when they landed. That was super nice.

"I would do anything for you," Ashley said, pausing as they spilled into the airport. The mountain air greeted them immediately, something that took a little getting used to. Both the altitude that made the air thinner, and the lack of humidity that dried everything out.

"Can we talk about what happened?" Sam asked. She'd been biting her tongue the whole way back. Unable to broach the subject.

When a person ran from their problems, meeting them head on was definitely not an easy skill to assimilate.

"Of course." Ashley nodded. She moved so they weren't in the way of foot traffic.

"It really hurts that you and Tanner kept this whole Catiana mess from me," Sam said, biting her lip because she seriously didn't want to have this conversation.

But Mom was right, it needed to happen.

"I am so sorry," Ashley said, her eyes pleading. "I should've told you right away. As soon as I knew. I just… you were so happy with Tanner. And you deserved that happy. Anything I said about what I saw could've wrecked it. I didn't want that for you. But it wasn't my decision to make. I can see that now."

"So what do we do now?" Sam asked, unsure what a person did when they met their problems head on and didn't hide from them.

"We just keep going." Ashley closed her eyes. Then opened them. "Because you're my best friend."

"I'm so glad you're my best friend, too," Sam said.

"We're going to hug now, aren't we?" Ashley asked, already moving in for a hug.

Sam nodded.

Getting out of the airport and into the car Hans had waiting for them was easier than Sam thought it might be. But somewhere along the way somebody had tipped someone and now they had a fleet of cars following them, attempting to get close and take photos.

Ashley kept up a game of cat and mouse, easily moving out of their line of sight when they got close.

"You want to be my manager?" Sam asked. Yes, it was out of the blue, but it'd been on her mind since Ashley started doling out those stay-back glances to the lookie-loos.

Besides, Ashley was good at managing things. People. Worse came to worst? She'd throw herself on the floor.

"Sure, I could be your manager. I have nothing else to do. What's the pay?" Ashley asked.

"Funny thing, there's no pay. Until I make money. Which, who knows?" Sam shrugged.

"Sounds good. I'm in." Ashley frowned. "Hans probably won't like that, though. He wants to be your manager."

"I can have two managers. Besides, he's already working with Dimefront. And I can pay him nothing too, to keep it fair."

Ashley snort laughed. "See, that's the kind of logic I need to accept employment."

Sam lifted her fist for a bump. Ashley met it.

One of the paparazzi got close again. Ashley changed lanes, maneuvered between an American Furniture Warehouse delivery van and a semi so they couldn't get a picture.

"You think they know we are going to a residential retirement home and not somewhere interesting?" Ashley asked.

"Nope." Sam chuckled at that. Sam still kept her job there, while she figured out how to launch her new career. The residents demanded mozzarella sticks at every meal, in her honor.

They pulled into the circular drive at the Purple Peony, and Ashley stopped.

"Is Britney Spears inside shaving her hair?" Sam asked, stretching to look over all the cameras and paparazzi.

"I don't think we have enough snacks for them all." Ashley frowned.

"We have no snacks," Sam pointed out.

"That's what I just said." Ashley frowned. "Well, I could

call Hans and get some security, or I can park and we make a run for it."

"I'll get out of the car and see what happens?" Sam asked. Maybe they'd give her space so she could get through? That could work, right? She pushed open the door, but the cameras all started clicking and it got super intense. She quickly shut it. "Maybe not."

"I think we have a solution," Ashley said, nodding toward the door.

Babushka marched through the swarms, whacking the paparazzi out of the way with her cane like it wasn't a big deal at all and just a normal day at the Purple Peony.

She moseyed to the back side door. "Vell, open it already."

Sam unlocked it. Babushka climbed in.

"Let's drive," she said. Pointing her finger to the exit.

"Where to?" Ashley asked.

Good question, because it could've been Ottawa. Could've been Walgreens. Neither would've surprised Sam.

"Five minutes and then ve go back."

All the paps had gotten out of their vehicles to take pictures. So when Sam and Ashley took off again, they had to scramble to get back inside.

"Let's pull in here," Babushka said, pointing to the parking lot of Pistol Polly's Gentlemen's Club.

"Sounds good to me." Ashley pulled into the parking lot. A whole slew of paparazzi followed them.

"Now park there." Babushka pointed to one of the pull-through spots. "Do not turn off the car, and you vait for my signal. Then you go, go, go!"

"All right." Ashley gripped the steering wheel.

Sam waited, her heart beating a quick staccato in her chest.

The paparazzis all parked, hopped out of their cars, got

into position to photograph Sam's exit. Babushka pointed her finger ahead. "Now!"

Ashley squealed the tires, leaving a ton of rubber on the asphalt.

Babushka laughed like she'd just seen the funniest thing in her life. "They have to get back in their cars and start again." She smacked her knees. "Next stop, Casa Bonita!"

"That's all the way on Colfax," Sam said, turning in her seat to see Babushka.

"Yes, vell, they need a tour of Denver." Babushka lifted her hands like, *Whatchagonnado?*

Sam pressed her knuckles against her lips because these poor photographers had no idea what they were in for with Babushka.

"You have forgiven Tanner, yes?" Babushka asked nonchalantly.

"Uh-huh." Sam couldn't hold back the smile. "I'm here to tell him."

"Vell, you must do something epic to tell him. Something to make a statement." Babushka slapped the back of Sam's seat as she spoke.

Three more times of the same Babushka stop-park-and-go-maneuver, and all three of them were in hysterics. The last time, the paps weren't taking the bait, so Ashley got out of the car and popped the trunk. Then when they started to get out of their vehicles, she slammed it closed and hopped back inside. Taking off once again.

"I know what I'm gonna do." Sam said. "I do. I have an idea, but I'm gonna need your help."

"Help is vhat I do best! Back to the Peony," Babushka announced. "They are ready."

"Who's ready?" Sam asked.

"Everyone," Babushka assured, as though this was genuinely assuring her of something.

"What are they all going to do?" Sam asked, leery of the answer.

"You vill see." Babushka clapped softly.

"Does it involve those glow-in-the-dark phallic stickers you made last month?" Sam asked. She'd confiscated the first batch, but had a hunch there was more.

"Do not vorry," Babushka enunciated each word. "They dissolve in the rain."

"I'm still worried." Sam covered her face.

"I vill not lead you vrong," Babushka assured.

When Ashley pulled into the circular drive once more, the paparazzi were still there. Still clicking away. But the residents of the Purple Peony had made a human shield for Sam to get inside.

Ashley pulled up to the opening.

"Go, Go! Go!" Babushka yelled. "They can't hold for long."

Sam didn't tuck and roll out of the car, but she also didn't wait for a full stop, either. That miscalculation sort of knocked her off her balance. She did not fall, though. But she ran quick into the safety of the Purple Peony and their security doors.

Then she told Babushka her plan.

And Babushka loved it.

"Ve vill need Dimefront," Babushka announced.

They would. She would. Sam needed Dimefront.

Chapter Twenty-Five
TANNER

TANNER WAS NOT GOOD COMPANY.

Hell, if he could get away from himself, he would. That's how badly his company sucked.

Because Sam was there. She was in Denver and she hadn't texted that she was coming. Hadn't reached out when she arrived. He'd had to hear about it from Entertainment Now and then Mach and Courtney.

Oh, yeah, they'd contacted her and knew precisely where she was. What she was doing. Probably what she'd eaten for lunch that day.

Then Hans decided they had to do a quick gig at Brek's for some event Brek decided to have at the last minute. Usually, Tanner enjoyed a gig at Brek's. But tonight his mood was not of the party variety.

Which was why he was shit company. Mach sat next to him in Brek's little break room because he was the only one willing to tolerate Tanner's crap mood.

Probably because Mach was in his own crap mood. With the dating app open on his phone, he still contemplated how to figure out the thousandth match. The matches came in so quickly and he had so many to sort through. It'd gotten all muddled up.

The order kept getting switched, and Mach couldn't keep anything straight.

The whole thing was almost comical—Mach trying to count women. Ha! Scratch that. Not almost comical. Hilarious was more like it.

The one bright spot in the day.

"Anybody got a happy pill for Tanx?" Mach asked. "Maybe something to get him to stop brooding."

"Fuck off," Tanner said, running his thumbnail along the edge of the cracked Formica table.

He hadn't been sleeping great. His beard had started to look like Linx's, and the only reason he shaved it was because Hans got the styling team to tackle him.

The shaving thing wouldn't have gone down if he didn't have to do anything but sit there and ruminate while they did it, so that's what he did.

"Love sucks," Tanner said out loud.

"Preach." Mach flicked through his screen. Then tossed the whole phone aside.

"I hate it. I hate how it messes with my head, every second of every day," he continued.

Sam didn't screw a shark on the football field, but he felt as lost as he had after Catiana ditched him for Brian Marks at prom.

"You get used to that mixed feeling of impending doom and utter happiness," Linx said. "Takes a bit, but it's kinda nice after a while."

"You think it's over? With Sam and me?" Tanner asked no one in particular, but also everyone present. "That's why she didn't tell me she's in town?"

He could've reached out, but when he tried, he tripped over the bit of pride he had left and put his phone away.

"One step at a time," Knox said, leaning back on a chair

and balancing. "One step. Then the next. You won't know until you know."

Tanner nodded, even though he wasn't feeling it.

The crowd at Brek's was a rowdy one tonight. The vibe from the bar area seeped into the break room where they waited. On a normal night, he got off on it. Loved the way it made his whole body feel lighter. Untethered.

Tonight? He just didn't want to be here.

"You're gonna be good, man," Knox assured. "That is a Knox guarantee."

Knox and Irina had a moment where they'd taken a break and Knox had been a wreck. But he'd still hit the stage. Still showed up.

Tanner could do the same. Then he could head out and not feel like a total tool for ditching the guys who'd always shown up for him.

"If the one step at a time thing doesn't work, you can always help Mach figure out what the fuck he's doing," Bax said. He kicked back in the chair beside Linx, balancing, too.

Somewhere in the last ten seconds they'd started some kind of balancing on two chair legs competition. This was life with Dimefront.

"I will let you handle the whole damn thing," Mach assured, his phone back in his grip, still fat-fingering his way through Nocturnal Cupid.

"Dealing with your dating profile sounds like the worst possible way to start feeling better about shit," Tanner said with a scowl.

"Yeah, I can see that," Mach said, nodding, still tapping at his screen.

"Let me do it." Courtney sauntered into the room, holding out her hand. "And guys, put your chairs down. We don't need a cracked skull before the show, 'k?"

"You want to pick the winner?" Mach asked, frowning.

"I'll go through and figure out the thousandth." Courtney made a gimme motion with her fingers.

"No." Mach shook his head. "Because you'll try to find someone perfect for me. Not do it the math way. I don't want someone perfect for me. I want the math way, so she'll be horrible."

Courtney rolled her eyes. "Whatever."

"Time to hit the stage," Hans said, striding into the room.

"Hans could pick the thousandth," Courtney said. "He doesn't care who you match. There will be no strategy at all."

"Are you still fighting with that?" Hans held out his hand. "Give me the phone."

Mach handed over the cell. Probably because he didn't want to piss off Hans, also because this had gone on for way too long. That's what Tanner figured, anyway.

Hans didn't even glance at the screen as he clicked the matched button. "Whoever that was? That's the thousandth. Deal with it." He tossed the phone back to Mach.

Mach stared at the screen, totally dumbfounded.

Yeah, even Tanner hadn't expected that level of not giving a shit.

"After the show," Hans amended. "Deal with it after the show. Everybody out. Time to make the donuts."

"I still don't know what that means," Mach said as he grumbled.

They clomped out of the break room, through the door into the bar. What seemed like a thousand cameras hit them right in the face. Flashes, shutters, cell phones held up high and flashing like mad.

"Sonofabitch," Mach stepped backward on his heel. "Give a guy a warning."

"No cameras at Brek's. Isn't that the one rule?" Tanner squinted against the onslaught.

"I bent the rule," Hans said, helping them through the crowd. "Quick sneak release was Courtney's idea."

"Nobody told me," Tanner said. He wouldn't have let the stylists fuck up his hair so badly if he'd known there'd be cameras.

"Next time we'll be sure to add you to the text chain," Hans said, with no feeling at all.

Tanner wanted to check his phone once more before they jumped on stage, but then Hans would probably confiscate it and he'd have to beg for it back. Instead, he scanned the front row.

What was he expecting? Her to be there?

Maybe a tiny part of him hoped she'd come to the concert. Was ready to move forward with him. This would be their big ta-da moment.

A familiar face caught his line of sight, and his heart fell to his toes because it wasn't Sam—

"What the fuck is Catiana doing here?" Tanner asked.

"Oh, shit." Mach glared down at Hans. "Too far. Too much. That's a no. Fix it."

Courtney slid between the three of them. "Catiana is here as my guest. Tanner, I told her you wanted to speak to her."

"Why the hell would you do that?" Tanner asked, his blood pressure inching higher and itching for a fight.

"So she'd show up," Hans said, still without feeling. "We'll deal with it after. Get on stage."

"You make no sense," Tanner announced.

"It's my gift." Hans handed him an extra pair of sticks for his back pocket since Tanner had broken a few on stage when he got seriously into a song or started off pissed. Tonight was a night for both, apparently.

"Don't let her near me." Tanner took the sticks, shoved them in his back pocket.

"Consider it done," Hans said, and this time Tanner swore the guy smiled.

Gig to finish. Gig to finish. Tanner did three bounces on his toes like he always did before a show. Knox taught him that—to have a ritual to prep the mind before a gig.

Then he hopped on stage, pretended Catiana never existed, and when the lights came up and the music started? He played like it'd be his last concert ever. The same way he played every concert since that first with Dan.

Music was healing. He understood that before, but playing with the band gave him something to breathe for, and that was the reminder he needed.

He poured everything into the performance.

His sticks hit the drumheads, the cymbals, his solo was epic. After the show, he'd reach out to Sam. Fuck his pride. Fuck this fight.

Time to grow up, Tanner.

The bar was totally wild as they finished the last bars of their finale song. Tanner started to stand to leave, but the other guys weren't moving off stage.

Right. The encore. If Bax wanted to do the encore, he'd give the signal. The guys waited for his signal.

"Not a bad Tuesday night, right?" Bax screamed into the microphone.

The crowd went absolutely bananas and Tanner caught a glimpse of Courtney off the side of the stage with Sam.

The room all stilled for him, even though the insanity of the atmosphere continued for everyone else. His heart didn't actually stop beating, but with the way he went all kinds of lightheaded? It may as well have.

"Sam," he said, even though there was no way she could hear him over the sound of the crowd.

Still, she seemed to somehow know he saw her because she glanced up and caught his gaze. Then she smiled. Then she waved. Like it was just the two of them and there hadn't been a whole slew of a shit storm to weather.

He waved back.

Her cheeks went pink. Pinker.

It seemed the stylists got to Sam too, because she had a helluva lot more makeup than usual. Her outfit was sick—tight shirt that made his mouth water like a creep. Jeans that fit like a fucking glove. And heels—had he ever seen her wear anything other than sneakers before? No, he hadn't.

He kinda liked the new look.

Enjoyed the old one, too.

There was room in his heart for both.

"Are you ready to lose your fucking minds?" Bax screamed into the microphone.

There it was, the cue for the encore song. Their biggest hit they saved for last and only for the rowdiest of crowds.

But instead of the starting chords of Devil's Cut, Linx played the oh-so-familiar beginnings of Sam's mozzarella song.

"I have a friend here tonight," Bax said as the guys continued playing that refrain over and over. "Her name is Sami Jo."

That got everyone on their feet. Tanner hoped like fuck Brek's floor could hold all this stomping.

"She said she'd like to sing a little something." He gestured for Sam to get on the stage.

Courtney and Ashley both stood like a wall behind Sam, but she didn't turn back. Didn't seem to have any inclination to run.

His entire chest puffed up with pride and he paused long enough to catch the beat and get in on the song.

And then the magic of the stage took over, and Sam stood on the stage.

"Hi," she said. "I'm Sami Jo, and I wanted to sing a little something for my boyfriend. I think you might know him." She pointed to Tanner. "He's the cute drummer back there."

Tanner gave a salute of acknowledgment, and then Linx started the song.

Sam belted it like a professional. A song about cheese and

happiness was going to bring down the house at Brek's. Go figure that one out.

The crowd sang with her.

Bax sang with her.

Fuck, all the guys of Dimefront sang with her, even Tanner.

The sweat from the lights dripped into Tanner's eyes as he played for her. Played for Sam.

She thought she sang for him. But he knew better.

Sam sang for herself.

And, with that, he understood that he'd won.

Scratch that. Love won.

He fucking loved being in love… with her.

Chapter Twenty-Six
SAMANTHA

SHE UNDERSTOOD NOW why people did this. The rush of being on stage was like a drug.

"Fucking stellar." Bax wrapped her in a hug, lifted her right off the stage.

That was super sweet, but she wished he was Tanner.

The bouncers were working double time at the moment, keeping the crowd from the stage. Because they were cheering and clawing at the air. They were cheering for Sami Jo. For her.

Bax set her down, and the grin on his face was magic.

"I did okay?" she asked.

"Tanx." He turned and pulled Tanner in front of him. "Tell your girlfriend she's a fucking rock star."

Tanner stared at her like she was an apparition that would disintegrate at any moment. She reached her hand up to touch his cheek. To show him she was real. This was real.

She was Sami Jo, and she owned it, and the world still spun. Everyone was okay. And she was on a concert high she didn't want to come down from.

"I did it," Sam said, gripping the microphone and tuning out everything but the way Tanner looked at her. The way he smiled. The scent of him—musk and rock star and sweat and everything Tanner.

"I'm gonna kiss you," he said. "In front of all these people. You good with that?"

"Okay." She nodded.

He winked. Then he pressed his mouth to hers, took over the kiss before she ever even had a shot at an attempt for control.

That did it, snapped whatever thread of control the crowd had up to that moment.

Tanner seemed to sense the change, and he pulled her behind him, moving to the edge of the stage. Soon it was Hans, Tanner, and two bouncers pushing her into the kitchen area, out the door, and into a waiting car.

"I'm sorry," he said. "God, I'm sorry."

"You've apologized. Now, it's my turn. I'm sorry for hurting you."

"As long as you come back, you can always take time to think." He pressed a quick kiss to her mouth that ended up lingering longer.

"Where are we going?" she asked, holding his hand and loving every second.

"Home," he said. "I bought a Twister board for this exact moment."

"You saw this coming?"

"Well, not this exact moment. But for an exact moment I hoped would come. Turned out to be now." He shrugged. She chucked him on the biceps.

"Thought it might be fun to try naked Twister," he said, waggling his eyebrows.

"You're funny, you know that?" she asked.

"So I've been told." Tanner asked, totally serious because he'd get her out of there if that's what she wanted, "We're really in this, right?"

"I don't know about you, but I've been thinking about

rings. I want a big fat one that makes all your ex-girlfriends jealous."

He leaned in to kiss her. "That's my girl."

"Is that why you invited Catiana?" he asked.

She shook her head. "She tried to be a bully. Tried to tell me I don't have worth. I wanted her to see that I do."

They rode in silence before she finally said, "I love you, Tanx."

He squeezed her hand. "Same, Sammich. Same."

Epilogue
SAMANTHA

A year later

THERE WAS peace in the midst of the chaos of celebrity. A peace Sam never expected.

Dimefront was on tour again. And she was at the edge of the stage, every single night, watching them. Reveling in the energy of the masses.

That was after she performed first. Yes, she opened for Dimefront and she sang the damn mozzarella song every. Single. Show.

She waited in the wings tonight. Waited for her cue to get things moving. Tanner had his own pre-performance rituals. But hers was just being there. Closing her eyes and telling the little ten-year-old Sami Jo who wrote a song about cheese that they had made it.

Tanner moved where she stood. A year later, and the stylists still hadn't caught him.

He draped his arm over her shoulders, and pressed a kiss against her temple.

She looked up at him. At this man who sort of turned her world upside down. But once all the pieces settled, she'd realized there was no other way she'd have it.

"You feel like getting married?" he asked, as though he were seeing if she wanted to grab a milkshake with Courtney and Bax after the show.

This was so Tanner. What seemed like no big deal to him had the power to change their lives.

She grinned. Glanced up at him. "Are you proposing to me?"

His cheeks flushed only a little pink. That was odd. Generally these days his skin didn't turn red at all unless she leaned in and whispered something dirty she wanted him to do later. Or something she wanted to do.

Either way.

"I guess whether I am proposing depends on your answer," he mused.

Her stomach flipped. This was for real. He was doing this.

"I've gotta be out there in five minutes." Sam whisper hissed. "And you chose now to ask me?"

"Well, we've gotta beat Mach down the aisle," Tanner said with an eyeroll.

"He's not actually…" Sam glanced over to where Mach stood with the winner of his contest.

But that was a whole different story.

"Three minutes," Hans said from beside her. "So Tanner, please get to it, propose to your girlfriend before the band starts up."

"This is real. You are choosing now to do this?" Sam asked, her eyes unfocused because this was not at all like she'd expected.

Not that she'd had huge expectations or anything. She just figured if he asked, it wouldn't be on the fly in a hurry before she sang about cheese sticks.

"I had to choose now because otherwise the whole thing wouldn't work," Tanner said, his eyes glittering with mischief.

"What?" she asked. "What wouldn't work?"

"That." He nodded to the stage.

"You make no sense sometimes." She leaned into him.

He took her hand with a reverence that made her heart seem to skip a beat. Then, when she thought he was going to drop to one knee, he pulled her onto the stage instead.

Like right on the stage. In the middle of it where there was a spotlight and a stadium full of people and he just pulled her right there and pointed to the front row where...

Oh God.

Everything stilled. The whole stadium seemed to freeze, waiting to see what the hell was happening.

Babushka, Aunt Etta, Betty Jane... Mom. Dad. Even Dan stood there. And they all had handwritten poster board signs that spelled out SAY YES!

Betty Jane and Aunt Etta also held up the crochet puppet masterpieces of Sam and Tanner.

Holy goodness. This was planned.

Not a passing thought before she took the stage and prepped the crowd for his band. No. This was a thought-out moment, carefully crafted for her by the man she'd fallen in love with.

"You did this," she whispered.

This was a man she was going to murder because he could not pull a stunt like this right before she was supposed to be on. She sort of choked on the future. Hiccuped.

An audible gasp from the crowd brought her back to the present.

The Dimefront guys came on the stage. They started playing the first chords to her new song. The one she'd been working on with Tanner about playing hide and seek with the right person. The one they'd tapped out on the keyboard at his apartment the first night they... that.

Tanner fell on his knee, holding a fucking huge diamond ring. How was she warm and cold and numb and feeling everything all at the same time?

And why was she crying?

She snatched the ring from him, holding it up so she could get a better look.

"Holy… Tanner, this is…"

"Are you going to let me ask you?" he asked with a lopsided grin she would never say no to.

She nodded. Handing back the ring.

They were in a stadium with thousands of people, but it was only them. They were all that mattered.

The music played in the background. This moment was the stuff of viral TikTok and she was the center of attention.

"I have had a crush on Sami Jo since I was a teenager and you sang about cheese," he said, and somehow he was mic'd up.

The stadium went bonkers.

"And I have loved you since the first time I saw you playing Twister," Tanner continued.

The crowd stomped in unison, moving the entire stadium under everyone's feet.

This was what life with Tanner was—a sturdy floor that moved but never failed.

"Tonight, surrounded by our family and about twenty thousand friends, I'm hoping you will say yes when I ask you to spend the rest of your life with me. As my wife. As my permanent plus one. As the one person I want to eat cheese with."

She snorted a sound that was half teary. Then she nodded. "Yes. Yes. Always, yes."

Dimefront did their thing while Tanner kissed the hell out of Sam, because this was the stuff of happily ever after.

There's more Sam and Tanner!

**A special bonus scene Christina created
especially for newsletter subscribers!**

Claim the bonus scene at:
christinahovland.com/tapped-bonus

Acknowledgments

Thanks, as always, to my family: Steve and all four of our children. Mom, thanks for giving me a writing cave to escape into. Sereneti, thank you for always enjoying my stories and telling me so.

My dogs, Chloe and Lucy. My new kitten, Mayonnaise. He's just the best kitten in the world.

Thank you to Anna Gorman for brainstorming with me when I got stuck, and the book needed done. You are the best!

Thank you to my critique team and beta readers: Claire Marti, Serena Bell, A.Y. Chao, Dylann Crush, Patricia Dane, C.R. Grissom, Jody Holford, Deb Smolha, Renee Ann Miller, Courtney Lucas, and Becky Wesnidge.

Special thanks to my amazing readers who stepped up when I needed them most. They helped me by beta reading an early copy:

Beth Carbutt
Mel Dobner
Anna Lee Kint
Pamela Falke
Christy Garrelts
Wendy Metz
Kara Schilling
Melena Torretta

You are all amazing and I am so grateful to have you as readers, and now, friends.

Emily Sylvan Kim, agent extraordinare, thank you so much for all you do for me and my books.

Holly Ingraham, I just think you're amazing. Thank you for being my cheerleader.

Audrey Nelson, thank you for the awesome copy edits!

Shasta Schafer you are the bomb diggity when it comes to proofreading. Thank you, thank you!

Thank you to Autumn Gantz my publicist and manager. She's the one who keeps things moving with Team Christina.

Karie and Kiele—thank you for being my most excellent support team.

Denise Allen—my friend and supporter—thank you for loving my books and always being there for me.

And thank *you*, yes YOU, for making my dream of being an author a reality. This is a pretty great job I've got!

The Mile High Matched Series

Rock Hard Cowboy, Mile High Matched, Book .5
Going Down on One Knee, Mile High Matched, Book 1
Blow Me Away, Mile High Matched, Book 2
Take It Off the Menu, Mile High Matched, Book 3
Do Me a Favor, Mile High Matched, Book 4
Ball Sacked, Mile High Matched, Book 4.5

The Mile High Rocked Series

Played by the Rockstar, Mile High Rocked, Book 1
Knocked Up by the Rockstar, Mile High Rocked, Book 2
Married to the Rockstar, Mile High Rocked, Book 3
Tapped by the Rockstar, Mile High Rocked, Book 4
Reckless with the Rockstar, Mile High Rocked, Book 5

Standalone Novel(s)

The Honeymoon Trap

The Mommy Wars Series

Rachel, Out of Office
There's Something About Molly
April May Fall
Everything's Fine, Emmaline

Going Down on One Knee
Sample

**Turn the page for chapter one of
Going Down on One Knee!**

**He's a Rocker.
He's a Biker.
He's the wedding planner.**

Number-crunching Velma Johnson's perfectly planned life is right on course.

That's a lie. Sure, she's got the lucrative job. She's got the posh apartment. But her sister nabbed Velma's Mr. Right. There has to be a man out there for Velma. Hopefully, one who's hunky, wears pressed suits, and has a diversified financial portfolio. He'll be exactly like, well... her sister's new fiancé.

Badass biker Brek Montgomery blazes a trail across the country, managing Dimefront, one of the biggest rock bands of his generation. With the band on hiatus, Brek rolls into Denver to pay a quick visit to his family and friends. But when Brek's sister suddenly gets put on bed rest, she convinces Brek to take over her wedding planning business for the duration of her pregnancy.

Staying in Denver and dealing with bridezillas was not what Brek had in mind when he passed through town, but there is one particular maid-of-honor who might make his stay worthwhile.

Velma finds herself strangely attracted to the man planning her sister's wedding. Problem is, he ticks none of the boxes on her well-crafted list. Brek is rough around the edges, he cusses, and doesn't even have a 401(k). But trying something crazy might get her out of the rut of her dating life--so long as she lays down boundaries up front and sticks to her plan...

Chapter One
THE COUNTDOWN BEGINS

THREE WORDS. Three. Little. Words. Nothing important.

Okay, so the three words were important. Massive, really.

"Congratulations, you two," Velma Johnson rehearsed aloud to the vase of a dozen yellow roses gripped in her arms. With a reaffirming gulp of Denver's crisp spring air, she hustled through the open-air parking garage to the security door of her apartment building.

Her sister, Claire, had big news. To be exact, Claire and her boyfriend, Dean, had big news. Velma had a feeling she knew exactly what their news would be—they were moving in together. The next step in their relationship. Tension in Velma's neck strung tight at the thought.

A successful career and a posh apartment she could eventually rent out as an investment were steps one and two of Velma's elaborate five-year plan. She had ticked both those boxes. Dean, three kids, and moving to a two-story house just outside of Denver had been steps three through seven.

Not anymore. Now, her sister was moving in with the man Velma had crushed on for years. The one Velma measured all others against. The one she sang Prince and Madonna songs with at the office.

Yes, they were moving in together. That's why Claire had called yesterday and asked to take her to dinner. Velma had insisted they meet at her place instead. Her invitation had nothing to do with the fact she liked having Dean visit her apartment—even if he was with her sister. She'd offered because it made sense they'd want a private location for their big reveal. And when the announcement came that they'd be embracing that next relationship milestone…well, being on her home turf sounded pretty darn appealing.

Just as she reached the security door, the sound of a motorcycle that clearly had no muffler cut through her thoughts. She turned. The bike pulled up next to her car— into the parking spot meant for her guests. A super-muscled, badass-mother-trucker of a biker swung his leg over the side of the motorcycle and stood.

Her heart stopped with a *thunk*.

Vin-Diesel-biker-dude pulled off his helmet and—sweet mother of Mary, had the temperature jumped by ten degrees? She got the picture: he rode a motorcycle, hit the gym twice a day. The type she avoided because she did not do badass. She preferred the suspenders-and-slacks kind of man. Except, at that moment, she debated how important that preference really was to her.

Focus, Velma. Head held high, she approached him. "Excuse me? Sir? You can't park there."

He frowned at the number marking the spot.

Normally she wouldn't mind sharing the space, but with Claire, Dean, and his friend Brek coming to dinner, she needed both of her parking spaces.

This man was obviously not Dean's friend. Dean's friends were all buttoned-up, suit-wearing, Wednesday-afternoon golfers. She was nearly certain.

The black leather jacket and jeans ripped at this guy's knees looked horribly out of place next to her Prius. His longish, rock-'n'-roll blond hair was nicer than hers (although his could use a trim). She didn't even mind the dragon tattoo creeping around the side of his neck or the layer of mud coating his motorcycle boots. Everything about the man screamed masculine.

Velma shifted the heavy vase in her grip. *Fudge.* Which of her neighbors was letting their guests use her spot this time?

"No, see, that's the spot for my apartment." Oh, how she wanted to rub at the headache pulsing at her forehead. She didn't have time for this. Not today. "I'm sorry, it's just that my sister and her boyfriend and his friend are coming for dinner because my sister has big news. And while I have no idea what that news is, it's important to her. So that makes it important to me. Which is why I put on a pork roast, bought roses, and got out my crystal wine goblets. That's what you do when your sister has big news, you know? Never mind she's practically living my five-year plan without even trying, and I'm over here without even a boyfriend. *That* was not part of my plan. At this point, I should be at least six months into dating my future husband."

Oh God. She was rambling. And he was staring at her with a half grin that made her skin flush. Seriously, the way the man smiled should be outlawed.

She ducked her head. "Anyway, I have company coming and I kind of need my spot."

"Five-year plan?" he asked. As though that was the important part of what she'd just spit out.

This is how one makes an absolute idiot of oneself. "You know what? It's fine. You can stay right there. Don't worry about it." She shifted the flowers again and turned on her heel.

See? People said she was inflexible, but here she was, absolutely rolling with it. She smiled at her flexibility.

"One sec," Motorcycle Dude called. "This is the number they gave me."

She paused midstride and turned around.

He ticked his head to the side. "Velvet?"

Oh dear. She could easily be swayed by the gravelly way he said her name. Well, the nickname her family called her—despite her repeated cease-and-desist requests.

"Um, yes?" She gripped the glass vase harder with her clammy hands.

"Brek." He looked at her like she should know him and pointed to his chest. "Dean's friend."

Velma stared.

Oh.

This was Brek? She'd expected him to wear khaki pants and drive a Camry. He reached into one of his saddlebags and held up a six-pack of Coors and a four-pack of Bartles & Jaymes fuzzy-navel-flavored wine coolers. "Claire asked me to bring the beer and wine, since I'm crashing your party."

Wine coolers? She stared some more. *Be flexible,* she reminded herself. *Flexible. Flexible. Flexible.*

"Great. Fuzzy navel pairs perfectly with pork roast." Cheeks burning and arms full, she managed to open the security door.

"So, you're Claire's sister?" His lazy gaze trailed over her.

"The one and only."

His deep-blue eyes rivaled the color of the razzleberry lollipops she loved. The kind that made her mouth water just thinking about them and... *Focus, Velma.*

"Can I come up, Velvet?" His deep voice held a subtle hint of roughness.

"Velma," she corrected. "You're a little early. I'm so behind. Normally, I'm much more together."

"I can come back later." Brek's eyes softened, totally contrary to his outer badassery.

"No. I am officially the queen of flexibility. It's not a problem."

He did the darn grin thing again. She silently instructed her body to ignore it.

"Queen of flexibility. That ought to be interesting," he

mumbled mostly to himself but loud enough for her to hear. He stepped next to her, balanced the beer and "wine" against the impressive muscles of one arm, and slid the vase she carried into the crook of his other arm.

"Thanks." This time it was her turn to mumble.

Without looking back, she led him up the stairs to her apartment. Another glance his way, and she'd probably trip face-first into the wall or something equally embarrassing. To prevent herself from taking another peek, she focused on sticking the key in the keyhole of her apartment door as though it took every ounce of her concentration.

There. The door swung open. He stepped through the doorframe, close enough for her to catch the scent of leather and Irish Spring soap. Close enough for her to reach out and touch the stubble running over his jawline. Close enough for her to—she shook her head to dislodge the abrupt light-headedness.

"This place is huge." With a long whistle, he set everything down on her dining room table.

Vaulted ceilings, open concept, white walls and sofa, with pops of jewel tones in her carefully selected décor; it must all appear so unnecessary to a guy like him. But these were her things, proof of everything she had worked so hard to achieve.

Brek walked into the kitchen and glanced to the slow cooker on the counter. "This smells amazing, Velvet. You a chef?"

"Velma," she corrected him again, slipping on an apron with the words *Domestic Diva* embroidered on the front. "And no, I just like to cook."

Velma took in the dinner she'd spent the afternoon planning and preparing. Vegetables had been roasted in the oven, and a chocolate cream pie was setting in the fridge. Not the pudding kind, either. A real, honest-to-goodness, made-from-whipping-cream-and-two-kinds-of-chocolate pie. She hoped she could eat those leftovers while she binge-watched Rodgers and Hammerstein musicals later.

"Then what do you do, Vel*ma*?" His emphasis on the last syllable made her wish her name wasn't so frumpy.

"For employment?" she asked.

"Yeah…or pleasure."

The expression on his face and the way he drew out the word "pleasure" made her toes curl in her sandals.

Right, employment. He'd asked about her work.

"I'm a financial planner," she replied.

Brek rubbed his hands together. "Like Dean?"

"Yup." She and Dean had worked together for years. "Our offices are across the hall from each other. That's how Dean met Claire." Claire had come to visit Velma at work and had wandered into Dean's office by accident.

That was the day Velma's dream of becoming Mrs. Dean Stuart died—all because she had waited too long to make her move and lost her chance.

Mr. Right had met her sister and they'd ended up together, making kissy faces during Thanksgiving dinner.

Actually, they never made kissy faces. The two of them were much too classy for that.

Brek leaned his hip against her granite countertop and crossed his leather-covered arms. "No idea what Dean does at his job, either, but I'm sure you're both fantastic at it."

"We help people with their financial portfolios. Annuities, estate plans, investment management, things like that. What about you?"

"I'm in the music industry." He snagged one of the crystal wine goblets she'd put out earlier and swaggered toward her.

Her stomach did a loop the loop. The swagger affected her more than expected. "You play in a band?"

"Nah. I play guitar, but not professionally. I manage a band." He popped the top off a wine cooler and poured it all the way to the tippy top of the glass. Then he edged inside her personal-space bubble and handed her the glass.

"Thanks." Normally, she didn't drink much—especially on Sundays. Monday marked the start of the week, with new chances and opportunities. She preferred to start it at her best, not hung over with a headache.

Then again, tonight was the night of change. Big-news change. My-sister's-moving-in-with-my-dream-man change. So Velma would have a wine cooler—no use in wasting it when Brek had already poured it—and ignore her attraction to Dean. Steps to a new life filled with…finding a new man who was as perfect for her as Dean was. Baby steps and all that.

Brek slipped off his jacket and tossed it over one of the island barstools. Tattoos ran from the short sleeves of his black T-shirt to his wrists. They looked tribal, mostly wild, and super-hot. If one liked tattoos. Which, she reminded herself, she did not.

"Claire says you two are twins?" Brek asked.

"Uh-huh," she muttered around a gulp of carbonated peach drink.

"You and Claire don't look like twins," Brek said.

Velma pulled a stack of small, hand-painted dessert plates from her for-company-only dish cupboard. "We're not identical."

"No kidding," he replied, serious. "It's the eyes."

Ha. Hardly just the eyes. Velma's eyes were muted gray, like a painter had finished painting for the day and just didn't feel like adding more cyan to the palette. Claire's were a rich brown. More than that, Claire was thin and Velma, well…she was Velma. All curves, like her mother. No matter how many calories she counted or steps the app on her phone registered, the curves stayed put. Velma's hair was dirty blonde. Not the attractive kind, either. In-desperate-need-of-highlights blonde was more like it. Claire's hair was a beautiful deep-chestnut color.

"Why does Claire call you Velvet?" Brek asked.

She sighed and paused, plate in hand. "Family nickname. No matter how many times I ask them to stop."

"Velma." He seemed to be testing the name, letting it melt on his tongue like warm chocolate on a vanilla sundae.

"Not a name I'd lie about." She set out the last of the plates on the table.

"I like it. It's original." The low, rumbly words made her lungs constrict in a warm way she refused to acknowledge.

"Unfortunately, it's not even original." She pulled a cutting board from the pantry. "Claire was born first, so she got the cool name. I was born three minutes later and got Velma."

"It's an interesting name."

"Velma was my grandmother's name. But there couldn't be two of us in the same family, so they all call me Velvet."

"I like Velvet," he said.

She scrunched up her nose. "I don't."

When she was a child, everyone bought her clothes with cheap velvet fabric. They itched. She hated them. As far as she was concerned, velvet was scratchy and uncomfortable.

"This news. Any idea what it is?" Velma asked.

"You don't know?" Brek replied.

"No idea." Except she was absolutely certain they were taking the next step in their relationship by moving in together, and maybe getting a puppy.

Brek popped the top on a Coors. "I figured you and Claire shared everything."

"Nope." Not this time. "Claire just said she has big news."

"Maybe she's knocked up," Brek suggested.

Velma's heart skipped five beats. She grabbed a knife and sliced into an onion with renewed energy. "No way."

"I don't know." He ran a palm over the back of his neck. "Seems reasonable to me."

"Then you don't know Claire. She's way too involved in her career to get pregnant right now." Velma set the onions aside and went to work on chopping carrots to top the salad.

Brek motioned to the cutting board. "Can I help you with anything?"

"Do you know how to julienne carrots?" Velma replied.

"Nope." He shrugged. "But I know how to cook a steak."

She laughed. "Well, tonight it's pork roast, so I'll have to take a rain check on your culinary skills."

"Absolutely. Next time I'm in town, I'll grill you up a steak." He raised his beer to her.

She stared at him. He couldn't actually be serious.

He was serious.

"Maybe they called us here because Dean needs a kidney?" he asked.

"He doesn't need a kidney." Although, Velma would probably give him one if needed. She had a remarkably hard time telling him no. "They're probably just…" *Say it out loud, Velma.* She sighed. "Just moving in together."

"Nah. They wouldn't have dragged me here for that. Maybe their big news is they're gonna try to hook us up."

"You and me?" Velma pointed the knife at Brek, then back to herself.

Of all the options, that one was the most reasonable. And, yet, totally unreasonable. No way would Claire pair the two of them together.

"You said you don't have a guy." Brek's tone turned serious.

Her body irrationally responded to his apparent interest with tingles.

"No." Of course she didn't have a guy.

She'd had lots of first dates lately.

"I get the feeling you need some help loosening up. Enjoy

some time away from your five-year-husband-seeking plan. There's a club downtown with a great band playing later. We should go." Brek's gaze raked over her.

His pointed interest was actually…nice. Still, there was no way she would go clubbing later. Brek wasn't her type. Not only because of the tattoos or the extreme need for a licensed barber or his ripped jeans. No, it was more the general sense of unease he stirred within her. Also, it was Sunday. What kind of a club was open on a Sunday night? Definitely not one she should visit.

"You stressed about the dinner?" he asked.

"No," she lied through her teeth.

"You're stressed about the dinner," he declared. "I get that, but there's nothing to worry about."

For a half second, she believed there was nothing to worry about. Truth was, there was always something to worry about. Starting with her clothes. She needed to change into something that wasn't yoga pants before her sister arrived in what would undoubtedly be a perfect sundress.

"I'm only in town for a few days anyway," he continued. "We'll get through the part where Claire and Dean do the awkward   you-two-should-get-to-know-each-other   schtick. We'll eat and then we'll send them on their way. You don't want to go to a club? That's fine. I'll stick around. What do you say, Velma?"

The way he said her name felt like silk against her skin. Silk was so much nicer than velvet.

She tried to tug off her apron, but her hair was stuck in the tie at the back of her neck. Crud. Another tug. Her hair was really stuck. "You want to go clubbing on a Sunday night?"

"Absolutely." He nodded to where her hair was caught. "Need some help?"

"Yes, please." She pressed her eyes closed.

He looped a finger under the little bow tying the apron at

the back of her neck. His calloused fingertip traced the ribbon along her shoulder to the collar of her sweater, unraveling the knot of hair and sending little shivers along his path of exploration.

Maybe she could get away to the club for a little while. It wasn't like she had better things to do. "Where is this cl—"

"Hey, Velvet." Her sister, Claire, shoved open the front door. "Hi, Brek. You made it. Dean's so excited you're here."

"Did you lose him?" Brek squeezed Velma's shoulder.

A hit of sizzle deep in her belly echoed the motion of his touch.

"He's parking the car." Claire closed the door and sauntered to the kitchen with her svelte build and Audrey Hepburn grace. "Okay, I know I've made you wait. But..." Claire bit at the light-pink lipstick on her bottom lip. "Surprise!" She held out her fingers with a little jazz hand motion.

An *engagement* ring perched on the fourth finger of Claire's left hand.

Velma's heart skidded to her toes. She blinked hard. No, it couldn't be.

A ring.

A wedding.

Satin and lace, champagne toasts and flower girls.

This wasn't a puppy. And it was so much more than an apartment.

Velma reached for Claire's hand, her throat constricting. "Oh my gosh."

"I know, right?" Claire squeezed Velma's fingers. "I had to tell you in person."

"Oh. My. Gosh." Velma said again, this time more slowly. She looked straight into Claire's eyes and saw it—excitement and love for Dean. Happiness. Velma glued a grin onto her face. Her sister was happy. That was all that mattered. "Claire. It's perfect."

"I'm gonna go find Dean." Brek caught Velma's gaze and winked. "Now that the cat's out of the bag."

"Wait, you knew about this?" Velma asked.

"Hell yeah, I knew." Brek opened the door. "Didn't want to ruin Claire's surprise, though."

"So you asked me out instead?" Velma asked.

Claire scrunched up her forehead. "Brek asked you out? Like on a date?"

"Oh look, it's Dean." Brek feigned innocence as he held the door wide. "I'm officially saved by the groom."

"She finally told her?" Dean strode inside and glanced to where Velma stood in a swirling vortex of time.

"Uh-huh." Claire nodded, her eyes misted over.

A suit. Dean wore a tailored suit complete with shined cap-toed shoes and gold cuff links. Each black hair on his head lay precisely where it should. He was absolute perfection.

Velma swallowed the heaviness in her throat and tried to pretend it was from excitement for her sister.

"Well, then—hey, sis." Dean strutted toward Velma and wrapped her in a hug. "Claire made me keep my mouth shut for a whole week."

Velma's insides did a little flutter that was totally unacceptable. Time moved at the speed of a sloth. Like watching a car accident happen in real time, when everything went slow and then fast again all at once. "You've been engaged for a week and didn't say anything?"

They'd sat through a load of sales meetings. Two client lunches where he'd driven them both to the restaurant. He'd never given any indication he'd freaking proposed to her sister. They'd discussed retirement plans and supplemental income sources. He hadn't mentioned anything that would've even whispered of proposal news.

"Believe me, it was hard keeping my mouth shut. Can you

believe you're going to be my little sister?" His breath brushed against the top of her head.

"Uh…nope," Velma said through gritted teeth.

"It's great, isn't it?" Dean leaned back and scanned her face.

Her knees went weak, like a cheesy movie heroine.

"It is great. Totally. Great. I'm so excited." Velma stepped away from him, refusing to show anything but happiness for her sister's sake. Any feelings from now on would be purely of the appropriate sisterly kind.

Claire and Dean were engaged.

Yup, Velma's Mr. Right was going to marry her sister.

Enjoyed the sample?

Grab your copy today!